MISTRESS OF THE STREETS

There was an atmosphere in London of calm
before a storm. Nell could feel it . . . tense and
hidden but still there, lurking in the background.
She came from the gutters of the city and
she could feel that the mood of the city had
changed. Would the King return or would there
be another civil war? Would General Monk
rule as another arrogant dictator, like to the
one buried a twelvemonth before?
Just below the window an apprentice ran by,
whistling, and then she heard his shrill voice
shouting,

> 'Ding a dong ding, I heard a bird sing,
> The Parliament soldiers are gone to the
>   King.'

So that was it! The King was going to return;
Nell was as sure as if she had been told.
Everything fell into place, Mr Pepys' allusions
included. She leant forward on the windowsill,
her eyes bright as she looked out over London.
St Paul's spire shone out in the mist over the
city at her. Life was going to begin again –
there was hope. And she – she would be part
of it.

ISBN 0 340

Mistress of the Streets

The early adventures of Nell Gwynne

Richard Sumner

First employment was with open throat
To cry fresh herrings even ten a groat,
Then was by Madame Ross exposed to town,
I mean to those who will give half a crown.

Satire of my Lord of Rochester

CORONET BOOKS
Hodder and Stoughton

To my mother

Copyright © 1974 Richard Sumner

First published in Great Britain in 1974 by
Milton House Books, The Dolphin Publishing
Company Limited

Coronet edition 1976

Printed and bound in Great Britain for
Coronet Books, Hodder and Stoughton, London.
By Hunt Barnard Printing Ltd,
Aylesbury, Bucks.

ISBN 0 340 20003 0

CONTENTS

PART I

LONDON 1660

CHAPTER I

Ding a dong Ding
I heard a bird sing
The Parliament soldiers
Are gone for the King.
Anon

Mr Samuel Pepys sat up in bed with the blankets tucked securely round him. The bedchamber was dark and musty; the only warmth came, ineffectually, from a fire of banked coals, which gave an eerie glow to the room as the flames cast weird reflections on the walls. Mr Pepys settled his night-cap securely on his head against the draughts and lit a candle, striking a spark from the tinder box by his head.

He looked down at his wife, long asleep next to him, breathing heavily; then he pulled from underneath his bed a heavy and dusty volume, and settled it on his knees. Mr Pepys was writing his diary.

Taking up his quill, he stopped for a moment to collect his thoughts before he inscribed the date at the top of the page. The writing was tall and sloped gently in the golden candle-light. Mr Pepys gazed into the darkness, reviewing the day's events, his eyes half closed as he relived the past twenty-four hours. He dipped the pen into the inkwell by the bed and wrote swiftly: 'March 3rd 1660. This day I did meet with Tom Harper, who took me into a place in Drury Lane, where we drank a great deal of strong water, more than ever I did in my life at one time before.' The pen faltered and stopped with a splutter of ink. Mr Pepys leant back against the pillows and stared deep into the dying fire with content. The afternoon had been one to remember, though he had such low hopes of it. Tom Harper had never been a great friend; indeed Mr Pepys disliked him with his shifting eyes, whining voice and watery nose. But the afternoon – ah! that was different.

It was ages since he had supped wine like that, French it was

9

he was sure. His tongue ran round his mouth in fond remembrance. There was little good wine to be had nowadays, he ruminated sadly, only the watery ale sanctioned by Parliament in such alehouses as still kept open – and there were not many of them. Now the theatres were closed and the Puritans wouldn't even let a man whistle because it was levity. The Spring Gardens at Vauxhall had been closed, and dancing forbidden, to propitiate a wrathful God. Life was hardly worth living.

Cromwell's wars with half Europe might have been glorious for him but they had ruined his countrymen. Taxed to the utmost, living under the shadow of the informer – even copulation was condemned as sinful. Mr Pepys' chubby face looked aggrieved in the candlelight. Then he thought again of the afternoon.

The tavern had been renamed by the rule of the Parliament the Well of Samaria instead of the Rose and Crown as it had been in happier days. But the new title did not change its customs. Mr Pepys grinned. The girls he had seen, and such dresses! Why, he could never remember seeing them so low cut! They might as well have been naked! It was disgusting . . . well, was it? Mr Pepys' mouth took on an uncommonly mutinous look. No, he decided, he had enjoyed it; every second. More than he could remember having done for years past. Mr Pepys, though he hated to admit it, had always liked a good time.

'There's more to life than preaching and prosing,' he murmured to himself in the silent bedchamber. His face looked suddenly serious as he gazed into the fire now, for he had heard news that day – news as he had scarcely dared to hope for, news he must not breathe to a soul. Excitement showed in his face as he sat in the dark.

His cousin, the great Edward Montagu, General-at-Sea of the English Fleet, had today informed him privately in his Office at the Admiralty, with the door closed, that the King, Charles the Second of infamous memory, would return. Mr Pepys' eyes sparkled at the recollection. His Majesty the King would come into his own again. Men had dreamed of it, prayed for it for years. Of course, everyone had been saying the King should come back for three months or more, and secret healths to his name were drunk in many a tavern when drink overcame discretion. There had been rumours and counter-rumours ever since General Monk had ridden into London with his whole army from Scotland but five weeks before, and sworn to call a free Parliament – the first for nearly twenty years.

But he had been very cautious. Everything was moving secretly behind the scenes; in the places of power things were shifting. But there had only ever been whispers, never proof until now! He remembered how earnestly he had sworn on oath to keep silent as Sir Edward Montagu had bade him take a seat, and then poured forth such a tale of secrecy and plotting as he had never heard. Apparently, Sir Edward had been in contact with the King for the past eight months. General Monk not only knew of it but approved! Sir Edward had crisply informed Mr Pepys of the outcome of such correspondence. His Majesty had promised to respect the liberties of his subjects and not seek revenge for the late wars that had brought such misery to his family. He promised religious toleration and a rule under the benign Parliament chosen by the people. Mr Pepys had been shocked nevertheless and said so. Sir Edward had always been such a staunch Parliament man, and this indeed had been the main reason for Sam's own Roundhead principles.

The Admiral had looked at him, Mr Pepys remembered, with eyes dark from weariness and defeat, and sighed: 'The country is all to pieces, Mr Pepys. There is no order left. I have always believed the people to be sovereign, unlike those lickspittles like Hazelrig whose views change as the wind blows. The people want peace again, they want freedom, they want the old days back. They want the King. I support their decision, Mr Pepys. They shall have him.'

Mr Pepys hugged his knees in the fire-light as he sat up in bed. Arrangements had been made for England's Fleet to set to sea. Within six months His sacred Majesty would return and he, Sam Pepys, cousin to Sir Edward Montagu, would be on the boat sent to fetch him home. It all seemed too good to be true.

Sam's wife stirred in her sleep and sighed gently, recalling Mr Pepys from his dreams. He looked down at his diary regretfully. Would that he could inscribe the joyful news in there. He picked up the pen but stopped. 'It's too dangerous,' he murmured. 'As yet it can't be done. But one day, one day it shall be done, when the time is ripe.' He finished the day's account with a flourish, waited for it to dry and then softly shut the book, pushing it carefully under the bed again.

The watchman passed outside, shouting loudly. 'One o'clock, a fine frosty morning and all's well.' His bell gave a muffled dong.

Mr Pepys kissed his sleeping wife on the nose. 'Goodnight, my Lizbet,' he said softly, and blew out the candle.

The wind whistled outside the house. Mr Pepys heard it as he lay under the blankets and dreamily recalled his afternoon's pleasures. His wife had been cross when he had returned home drunk, he remembered with amusement. Nevertheless he would go again. It would help him to keep silent and bide patiently the King's coming. Yes, he decided, as he rolled over to sleep. He would go again tomorrow.

At the same time as Mr Pepys was settling comfortably down to sleep, a small figure swathed in an over-large blanket was making its muddy way down the pitch-black, winding path of Coke Alley. The night was dark and cold. The figure hunched against the wind that took the flapping blanket and tore at it so that it threatened to come off at times. Bravely, with one hand out to feel the way, the child trudged slowly on in the teeth of the gale.

The solitary lamp hanging out over the street at the corner was caught by the wind and guttered all at once. The young girl was in total darkness. Down in the gloom of the timbered houses, she made out the corner vaguely at the end of the street and, feeling her way, slowly faltered towards it. The night air was rent with a shrill curse and splash as she accidentally trod in the pool of filth that ran down the central open gutter in the alley, but she travelled on – a small defenceless figure in the night.

Suddenly there was a voice from the shadows. 'Psst!' A hissed whisper cut through the night air.

The young girl cowered back and melted into the shadows in fright, with her back against the wall of an overhanging house. Was it the Watch? God forbid! To be out at such a time required explanation. They might not believe her. She might have to spend the rest of the night in the lock-up or even, say, Newgate. Her eyes gleamed with fear. But as a bent figure hobbled into view, she relaxed.

'Oh, it's you, Hobey,' she sighed in relief. The figure came out into the open, carrying a small lantern high to see the way. It was an old beggar, unkempt, dressed in little better than rags, his wispy beard and long straggling grey hair partially covered with a threadbare cloak and hood. He had only one leg and used a crutch to hop along slowly as he approached the girl, the light from his lantern throwing up frightening shadows and heightening the pallor of a face already thinned by hunger and neglect. The girl seemed glad to see him.

'What be you out at this hour for, child?' The beggar's voice was concerned. The girl shrugged. 'We don't close till the gentlm'n leave. You know that, Hobey. And old Ma Ross runs a good night's business these days. I just left now.'

The beggar turned and hobbled along beside Nell, wheezing as he walked. The sound was reassuring to her. She had heard it so many times before.

'It's wicked, wicked,' he muttered under his breath, over and over again, in time to the beat of the crutch on the cobbles. The two walked slowly along Coke Alley and turned right into Drury Lane in companionable silence.

'It's a night, this is, ain't it?' said the beggar conversationally, looking up at the wintry sky. 'Feels crisp, don't it? Snow soon, I shouldn't wonder. Real soldier's weather.

Reminds me of the night before the company sailed, Nell. Same sort of night, that was.' The beggar rambled on in reminiscence of his favourite old story.

Nell had heard it all before, but she didn't stop him. She was too weary for unnecessary words and the voice filled the silence. The old man liked to talk. He was an old soldier, she knew, but his last campaign had been years ago, at La Rochelle in '25. Hobey had had his left leg carried off by a cannon ball from a French man-of-war, yet now he was left to beg on the streets as best he could. With no family of his own, he was pathetically grateful for any attention the small Nell showed him, and cared for her with rough kindness. His Christian name, Obadiah, she had quickly shortened to Hobey. She never called him anything else now. Hobey's story rolled on to its close. But the old man was preoccupied.

He coughed and then spoke slowly. 'I bin thinking,' he said. 'You shouldn't have that job, Nell. It's no job for a girl, isn't that. You were better off with me and the herring-stall, I warrant you. You didn't ought to 'ave gone into Madam Ross's at all. I told Rose, I warned her.'

'You got to work to live,' said Nell wearily, the acceptance of the sentiment jarring oddly with the shrillness of the childish voice.

The beggar shook his head sadly. 'I still think it's wrong, child. You didn't ought –.'

But the child rounded on him with a curse.

'For Gawd's sake be quiet, Hobey!' she cried hotly. 'Of course it's wrong. Just as wrong as it is for you to end up in the gutter just 'cos your leg got blown off by a bleeding cannon ball. It's all wrong, but you got to live with it. I got to earn my living 'cos Ma's a drunken sot and Rose cares for naught but herself, and I've got to live with it. I'm lucky I ain't got to 'ave me petticoats round me waist in Fleet Alley. There ain't nothing you can do. That's the way it is.'

The beggar looked stricken at the girl's anger and said nothing, sucking in his cheeks and staring at the ground. The child's voice dropped and she patted his arm gently.

'Lor', I'm sorry Hobey. I know you mean it for the best and you stayed behind to meet me an' all. But it's no good, is it? You know we couldn't both live off of that 'erring-stall, no more than we could before. Anyway, mayhap things will look up. Don't you fret about it; I'm all right so long as I've energy to kick 'em away with.'

Hobey did not reply, but his lips were tightly pursed as he followed the small figure into Turnagain Lane. He stayed a step or two behind as Nell stumbled on, eager for home and bed. His eyes were blank and tired as he looked at her; dark with defeat and watery with age. He was old, old and useless – and he could do nothing, he thought.

Nell called shrilly for more light from the lamp. ' 'Ell, this cold, ain't it?' she said flatly and continued walking on. He glanced at her familiar curly head with its snub nose, peppered with freckles, and its aggressive chin. He had known her ever since she was tiny, right from when she'd been a snotty five-years-old brat, running down the alleys of St Giles, screaming and brawling with the other urchins. Hobey loved children. It was he who had taught the child and her sister their letters, squatting at his knee outside the 'Leathern Bottle', though neither was exactly of a studious nature. He knew her family well; Nell's mother used to get stewed in all the taverns Hobey frequented with his begging bowl. Sometimes she was so drunk she gave him a groat. Nell's father he never knew – and of course people said there never had been one, leastways not so as Madame Gwynne could pin down.

But Hobey had heard the tale from Rose. The father had disappeared one night close on a year after Nell had been born – so Rose had told him, her voice tight with hate; gone out one night for a drink and never came back. He might have been murdered, or just gone, Rose didn't know and cared less. Ah, she was a right one, Hobey smiled to himself wryly, as pretty as a picture but with a heart as close as a Puritan's purse. Life had treated her badly and she wanted her own back. She'd wrung quite a lot back already, thought the beggar, remembering the strings of jewels and numerous gowns Rose's many admirers, usually military, left her when they returned at the end of their leave to their regiments. She was generous with her charms, that one.

Nell saw little of it, though. Rose's life revolved around Rose and that was that. The kid might have starved when Hobey had first seen her – dirty, thin, lice-ridden, and clothed in naught but rags. Hobey had spent all his savings on setting up a herring-stall and kept Nell to run his errands round the courts and alleys nearby. At least it meant she got a few groats for food and kept her from actually starving. She'd done well for a few years, he thought with satisfaction, but times were hard. The stall couldn't really keep both of them and then one day, about six months ago, Nell had made that fateful delivery to old Madam Ross's establishment.

That evil old hag; Hobey spat savagely on the ground. For years – even through Cromwell's dreary rule – she had kept going her establishment of whoring and drinking, in Lew-kenor's Lane. Even Holy Noll's soldiers needed to slake their thirst and satisfy their lust. Behind the dingy shutters of Madam Ross's, many a night's entertainment could be found. Fat and tawdry, she kept an ever-open eye for new girls, young damsels to replace the jaded females who plied their trade for her. She'd liked the look of Nell and she was short of girls, at least of girls as young as Nell. Besides, she needed a maid of all work for now, and in a few years she might tumble with the best of them.

Madam Ross knew Rose well by sight, and by reputation, and the rest took no time at all. Hobey had weakly protested; he had even gone to see Rose, but the girl tossed her head and told him to mind his own business. They all had to live, she had informed him, and the kid was too young to come to much harm. A week later Nell went as skivvy to Madam Ross at Lewkenor's Lane.

All of a sudden a window far above them opened, and out of the darkness down came a stream of slops and filth with the usual cry of 'Gardy Loo!' Hobey saw it coming and pressed back against the wall under the overhanging beams, but Nell was completely drenched in cold, filthy water. Her blanket slipped off and she screamed in terror and anger. Curses followed in swift succession as Nell shouted at the blank window: 'Cow! Stupid, lep'rous bitch! Why can't you look where you're flinging your dirt – pot-bellied whore? Rot your guts, you whey-faced slut!'

Anger faded; the adult curses were followed by the child's howls, which rent the night air. She stood huddled in the street, a small figure shaken by sobs. Hobey caught her in his arms and pressed her to him, burying her face in his shoulder. Tears streamed silently down as Nell lifted her face and looked at Hobey, her lip trembling and her eyes brimming with water. Her expression was stricken.

'We don't have much of a time of it, do we, Hobey?' she sniffed. 'You and me...we haven't got much of a *life*, 'ave we?'

'Nell–.'

The girl wiped the water from her eyes with her fingers and stopped him. 'Hobey it's late. You'd better go now. I can find me own way home now; it's only down the alleyway.'

She turned and picked up the blanket, now sodden and smelling vile. She draped it round her.

' 'Night, Hobey. Pox on this filthy blanket!'

' 'Night, Nell.'

Hobey held the lamp high and watched as she shuffled wetly out of sight down the alley, until she was swallowed up in the dark.

'A pox on you, filthy slut! At your tricks again, eh?' A large brawny arm shot out and a small body shot across the low-raftered room of the tavern, knocking tables as it flew, to land in a corner amidst a tumble of chairs and spilling pewter mugs. Ale dripped on to a curly reddish head above a face suffused with anger. Bruised and panting, the child's skinny arms clawed at the pile of furniture to rise shakily to her feet. A Cockney voice split the air, liberal with its abuse.

'You son of a whore, sperm of a toad,' she shrieked, waving an accusing finger across the width of a chamber at an enormous coal-heaver who sat unconcernedly downing his small beer. 'May God curse you, may He gripe your bowels, may He rot your bones with palsy, may He –.'

'May He look to you, little worm, if I see your paws in my pouch again,' tossed the coal-heaver over his shoulder at the screaming termagant in the corner. The wrath redoubled.

'Two tankards today, two yesterday, and for what? Your pouch is as empty as a beggar's belly, you hulking cheesecurd. Go and drink from your chamber-pot if you can't pay! Three groats and not a farthing less you owe.' She came nearer as she spoke, her eyes bright with anger. 'I have a mind to –.'

'What?' muttered the workman good-humouredly with his back to the tirade.

'This!' screamed Nell, bringing down a stool with all her force upon the man's head. But it was too heavy for her small arms, and the blow was ineffectual, missing his head and sending the mug of ale spinning to the floor. The table collapsed gently to the ground.

The coal-heaver turned and stood up, swinging a chair in his huge ham-like hands.

'Enough,' he said softly, then flung the chair from him with a crash. The tavern emptied in five seconds.

Nell felt her neck clasped by a grip of steel. A pair of smouldering eyes under black brows bored into hers.

'Little swine,' hissed the voice softly. 'Brain me, would you? I'll screw your neck off like a chicken, you gutter-bred she-devil.'

Nell felt as though her eyes were bursting from their sockets. Her hands beat feebly against the coal-heaver's huge chest, her feet, barely touching the floor, kicked wildly. But her struggles became weaker, and a red, dizzy blur was passing before her eyes as there came an explosive crack and she found herself beneath the prostrate workman on the floor of the dingy tavern.

Dazedly she scrambled free of the unconscious form, and massaged her neck painfully. She became aware of a pair of brown eyes regarding her with amusement. A red-faced, portly gentleman, with a good-humoured smile creasing his cheeks, stood with a stout three-legged stool in his right hand, his hat and cane in the other.

A chubby hand aided Mistress Nelly Gwynne to her diminutive stature of a child of nearly eleven. She beamed up at the gentleman and saw with surprise that he had a companion with him, who looked obviously ill at ease. The first gentleman seemed supremely to be enjoying the situation. As he looked around the tavern, Nell looked at him.

His dress was certainly daring for one in an England still ruled under the Rump Parliament. Though Cromwell had passed on a year before to the God he had so neurotically feared in life, England was still the domain of the Puritans; the Army ruled, through the Parliament which did its military will, and observed its joyless strictures.

This gentleman obviously scorned such dreary souls. His hair, though not curled in Cavalier lovelocks, was *long*, much longer than Authority could approve, while his suit, not the sombre black that was *de rigeur*, but a dull maroon velvet edged with Italian lace at the cuffs and collar, was of flamboyant cut, with great skirts. Ribbons of black gartered the knee but were anchored by tassels that could not fail to draw down disapprobation for frivolity.

Behind him, his companion shuffled from foot to foot unhappily. He, on the contrary, was dressed regulation-fashion in an ill-fitting suit of black fustian, with a grubby collar encircling an equally grubby neck. Beneath his tall Puritan hat, a pair of watery eyes stared with obvious embarrassment at the diminutive Nell. 'A regular sobersides!' she summed him up at once.

The urbane gentleman introduced himself. 'My name, young woman, is Mr Samuel Pepys. May I introduce my friend, Thomas Harper.'

Nell curtseyed in round awe. 'And I am Mrs Eleanor Gwynne, sir, delighted to make your ac ... quaintanceship, I am sure.' She made vague attempts to hitch up her bodice, spotted with ale and rucked under the armpits.

His eyes twinkled. 'Delighted, Madam. Mr Harper and I had come here today, as is our wont, to partake of Madam Ross's strong waters, but we seem to have interrupted an altercation.'

Nell crimsoned. 'He refused to pay his ale and he hasn't paid this sennight. Mrs Ross said he wasn't to have more till he paid his shot. I was just asking for the money.'

Mr Pepys coughed gently. 'Does this always happen when a bill is paid?'

'Oh *no*,' Nell reassured him. '*That* only happened when I threw the stool at his head.'

'Oh –,' replied Mr Pepys, looking around him.

She remembered, and clutched his hand with a desperate grip. 'Thank you, sir, thank you. Truly, you arrived only just in time. I was close fainting. . . . '

Mr Pepys disclaimed any such eulogy with a wave of his hand. 'A pleasure Mistress Gwynne, I assure,' he murmured, though Nell noticed he cast a nervous glance at the unconscious bulk of the work. 'But won't Madam Ross be a little perturbed at the disorder produced by your no doubt righteous indignation?'

'What, sir?' asked Nell.

'The mess,' explained Mr Pepys kindly.

For the first time, Nell looked around in horrified awe. All across the long, low, chamber, furniture lay in crazy piles. The light which filtered through the clouded-yellow, leaded, window panes, showed a floor bestrewn with pools of ale, and forlorn pewter mugs nestling in the corners of the dingy tavern. Broken chairs and the remains of three-legged stools were piled up against the counter, while pieces of smashed furniture littered a wide area. A fetid air of stale drink hung over all. There was a large crack across the face of a shabby gilt mirror, which hung at a crazy angle on the wall.

'Lor', she'll kill me,' she breathed.

'Let's away Sam, we'll find no entertainment here,' mumbled Mr Harper, plucking his friend's sleeve.

'A moment, Tom,' said Mr Pepys without moving. To Nell

he added, 'When will old Mother Ross return, child?'

Nell cast a nervous glance at the door. 'In a half-hour or less, I suppose. She's out on business, the *usual* business.' The child's mouth shut in a tight line as she nodded her head in the manner of one possessing secret knowledge.

Mr Pepys looked blank.

'Whores,' said Nell simply, as if explaining to an innocent child.

'Well, might I suggest that you lose yourself for a few hours until Mrs Ross's anger has deflated somewhat, or else I foresee a rather nasty time ahead when. . . .'

'I daren't leave, sir. Gawd knows what would happen if the place were left. You know what it's like round here; I swear 'tis not safe to leave a kerchief for five minutes.'

'I can guess, I can guess,' said Mr Pepys impatiently. 'But that's Madam Ross's pigeon. Anyway,' looking around, 'there's not much left worth pinching, is there?'

Nell giggled irrepressibly. 'Gawd, no!' she said with an air of triumph.

Mr Harper looked even more impatient, and cast horrified looks at the door as though expecting the redoubtable Mrs Ross to bear down on him at any minute. Mr Pepys gave him a scornful look and then offered Nell his arm.

'Home, Mistress Gwynne?' questioned Mr Pepys.

'Lor', no!' gasped Nell in horror.

'Then you must come with me,' he said firmly.

'Thank you, sir,' breathed Nell gratefully.

Preceded by the now almost gibbering Mr Harper, Nell and Mr Pepys left the tavern; Nell squeezing the arm of her benefactor, who gave a pewter mug a magnificent parting swipe with his cane as they stepped out into Lewkenor's Lane and the narrow alleys that made up the district of St Giles, in the underworld of London.

Halfway along the street, Mr Harper begged leave to depart. Muttering something about appointments and colique, he shuffled off in the opposite direction, ramming his greasy hat upon his equally greasy hair. Nell looked after his retreat with a sniff.

'What a cow's bastard!' she said, summing him up in a word.

Mr Pepys schooled his expression to one of severity. 'Mistress Gwynne,' he said coldly, 'please refrain from giving tongue to your homely expressions in connexion with one I count a friend.'

'What sir?' asked Nell in awe.

'Don't be rude!' said Mr Pepys.

'Sorry, sir,' said Nell. There was a pause. 'But he *was* a cow's bastard if ever I saw one....' She shook her head sadly.

Mr Pepys strode on, his lips twitching.

CHAPTER II

Everybody now drinks the King's health without
any fear, whereas before it was very private that
a man dare do it.

The Diary of Samuel Pepys

As they came to the end of Lewkenor's Lane the air grew
lighter and the smells less unbearable. Half running to keep up
with Mr Pepys' brisk stride, Nell found herself leaving behind
the narrow and dimly-lit passages of her own district, and all
of a sudden in the midst of the bustle and life of London. To a
child who seldom strayed beyond the stinking alleys of St
Giles from whence she sprang, the sights revealed were awe-
inspiring. It was like entering another world. Her sister Rose,
now a mature young beauty of eighteen, had of course told her
of the sights to be seen in the City but her stories consisted
mainly of *affaires*, of long evenings lit with candles and above
all of the meticulous description of male admirers, on whom
she dwelt at length until they were tossed aside a week later
in favour of another.

Houses loomed above Nell, higher than her eye could see.
These were proper houses too, not the plaster and daub
hovels which Nell had been used to see, but tall, timbered
constructions with huge, winking windows of diamond-leaded
panes and carved and brightly-painted beams, leaning towards
each other as if to shut in the life of the city. From alleys and
taverns came the smells of ale and human sweat, mixed with
the dung of the horses and the filth in the gutters that ran down
the centre of the crowded streets. High above the jostling
crowds swung gilded signs; creaking in the wind were the
arms of the guilds, inn signs of all descriptions and boards
proclaiming the skills of the craftsmen that lived below. A
grinning Indian woman, crudely painted, beckoned citizens
into the drapers; long poles indicated the shop of the barber
and tooth-drawer, both occupations being performed by the

same individual. From within a low doorway came the familiar musty smell of the apothecaries, offering health-giving tobacco to ward off the plague, powdered unicorn's horn, or the new turpentine pills that were fast becoming so fashionable. A world of smells, of colour, and above all of movement, of life.

The noise defied description. Coaches rumbled down the narrow paths between wooden posts set up to protect the passers-by, horses cantered along, their hooves drumming on the uneven cobbles. Apprentices bawled their masters' wares. Through the crush staggered chairmen, bearing forth a gentleman to his business, loudly complaining of the lateness of the hour.

Across the street two apprentices stuck out their backsides at two startled ladies. 'Kiss my Parliament,' they shouted with villainous glee, referring to the unhappy Rump Parliament still sitting, and then ran off down an alley shrieking with laughter. Parliament had certainly sunk in the people's estimation, or so it seemed.

Mr Pepys strode on briskly, clutching his cane. Nell stumbled after the urbane figure, who presently waved his cane languidly to call a hackney coach. A plain carriage drew up before them and Mr Pepys opened the door and looked at Nell.

'After you, Mistress Gwynne.'

Nell looked at him searchingly.

'Why?' she asked suspiciously. 'I'd have you know, sir, I'm a respectable girl. Rose told me not to go with gen'lm'n what offer rides in coaches.' The snub nose wrinkled in caution and the long-lashed eyes narrowed. '*That*'s what happened to Rebecca Bates and all St Giles knows what followed – for all he was a praying Presbyter. Not a penny groat did she get. She's in Bridewell now. . . .'

Mr Pepys clutched the coach door, while Nell peered at him to see what was wrong. As he straightened up, she saw tears of mirth roll down his face. She stiffened in resentment. Mr Pepys mopped his face with a lace handkerchief and apologized profusely.

24

'Indeed Mistress Gwynne, I heartily agree with your friend Rose's advice. . . . '

'My *sister* . . .,' corrected Nell coldly.

'Er . . . yes . . . your sister, to be sure. But, s'death, sweetheart, I assure you, you have nothing to fear. You seem remarkably knowledgeable for one so young.'

'You have to be, where I come from,' rapped back the diminutive sprite standing before him.

'Yes, yes,' agreed Mr Pepys hastily. 'But what if I told you I have been married for close on five years and have no intention of finding myself a mistress ?'

'Then,' said Nell, 'I would believe you. Not because of what you say – for Gawd knows married men are the worst. But 'cos you helped me back there,' jerking her head behind her. 'And I've taken a fancy to you . . .,' she added, in the manner of one granting a favour. 'Mind you, there's tales I bin told by Rose that –.'

Mr Pepys coughed.

'The coach awaits, Mistress Gwynne.'

'Lor'! Sorry sir,' said Nell humbly, climbing in.

They took seats opposite each other in the coach, and when the door closed man and child gazed interestedly at each other.

Mr Pepys found Nell a profound shock. From outside she appeared a child of eleven or twelve; a small, thin, and not too clean one, either. One saw such urchins running about the alleyways of London, and down by the waterfront – usually undersized, ragged and grubby.

In age she was of a muchness with Jemima, Montagu's daughter, whom Sam played with. They were very fond of one another. Age linked 'Jem' with this gutter-bred child. Yet there the resemblance ended. How ?

Mr Pepys leant forward, the better to survey his passenger. Small and childlike she might be, he mused, but – with an experienced eye in such matters – she was not bad looking. Of course, she had no figure as yet, but that would come; and in her countenance something caught his attention. He looked at her face, and in that instant Nell caught his eye upon her

25

and smiled – though she shyly looked at once out of the coach window.

Mr Pepys was quite stunned.

That was it, of course, he realized. She wasn't a child at all. No one could be who came from where she had come from. Childhood was as short as innocence, and killed by the swift poison of London. She sat like a woman; her very pose was artlessly seductive. Her smile, though naive, was already that of the courtesan. There was nothing childlike about the way she had looked up at Mr Pepys from under long dark eyelashes – and beneath the grime her skin was smooth and fine. Yet this was the curiosity, for, as he glanced at her again, he saw that in truth she was physically rooted in childhood and would be for some time.

The blend of innocence and knowledge Mr Pepys found amusing, and her tart little rebukes and recriminations he found whimsically alluring. Such cynical maturity from a child was vaguely disturbing. She would break hearts, he decided knowledgeably, when childhood finally let her go.

Nell was unconscious of such interest in her appearance. She leant forward eagerly, her mouth a little open, to see better the sights of London passing the coach window. Sweeping around the corner of Drury Lane, the hackney was caught in the flow of traffic that lurched its way down the thoroughfare of the Strand, towards Whitehall. The coach was passing along the wide street which was the show-place of London, and home of the wealthy. From the left coach window Nell was amazed at the mansions that now came into view, homes of nobility dead or gone. Set back from the road of the people lay the strongholds of privilege – the great houses of the aristocracy from the time of the Plantagenets. Behind high walls, screening them from the views of the vulgar, lay the Tudor magnificence of gabling, crenellation and ornamented chimney-pots, and the gracious stateliness of the palaces of her own century. Windows, row upon row, set in walls of huge dimension, gazed down austerely at mere mortality which crawled by beneath. The coach rumbled past the monuments of the great names of England – Howard, Seymour and Devereux – and left Nell oblivious but awed. From beyond the lawns which stretched down to the river, she could see the muddy Thames, stinking and grey, lapping against its banks; she heard the oaths of the Wapping watermen as they plied their trade and threatened all and sundry. Small wherries and ponderous barges could be seen making their way up and down the water highway of the river.

Apprentices ran alongside the slow-moving coach, caught in the traffic, and, though Mr Pepys stared calmly ahead ignoring them, everything from ornamented combs to bolts of cloth was proffered for their inspection. Never had Nell seen such shops, and wealth in such quantity. Behind the posts set for their protection, strolled London's prosperous citizens, dressed in low-hued, rich clothes, inspecting the wares before them. And all the crowd seemed drawn to the magnificent building of the New Exchange, jostling for attention from the stallholders, and attended by servants who flowed out on to the street around the lines of chairs waiting outside for their masters and mistresses. Hackneys fought in queues for customers, their drivers going so far as to hustle likely looking ladies into coaches before they had time to protest. Such sights bore little resemblance to the London Nell had known.

Mr Pepys' ears were suddenly assailed by a loud voice that he thought familiar. 'Samooel, Samooel! *Attends mon cher!*'

He pulled down the coach window and stuck his head out. Sharply he called to the driver to stop the coach, and then, opening the door, bent to hand in a lady dressed in the height of fashion. She was to Nell a vision; a picture of ultimate femininity.

Her dress was characterized by the absurd. She wore three pairs of gloves at once, each edged with a lace of a different hue, so her fragile wrists were frothed with frills. Her dress was high-waisted and of stiff silk of a glimmering turquoise shade, dotted with beads, with a solitary pearl at the top of a low-cut bodice. From an extravagantly curled hat with drooping feathers, a veil of fine lace came down, covering her visage.

With a twirl she now tossed it back disclosing a face which, while not being pretty, was small and alert with life and framed in curls of dark chestnut. Almost like an imp, Nell thought to herself.

She settled herself with a rustling of skirts and pulled off her gloves one by one, as she laughed to herself and wagged a finger at Mr Pepys, murmuring in a way which Nell could not understand: '*Méchant, méchant, mon petit!* Samooel, *ou étais-tu-allé? Non, ne repond pas. Je connais vos mensonges.* Oh! la, la. . . .' She tutted briskly as she divested herself of her gloves.

Then she saw Nell, huddling in one corner of the coach, gazing at her with eyes wide open in surprise. Her brows lifted significantly. She looked at Mr Pepys and began to speak in English, with a noticeable foreign accent. 'Samooel, 'oo is that, please?' Mr Pepys blushed, but struggled manfully to appear unconcerned. 'That is Mistress Nelly Gwynne, my dear. I have just rescued her from an unfortunate fracas at a tavern where she was being assailed by a large workman of great strength and . . . er . . . little mercy.'

The lady's eyes glinted.

'A tavairn wench! *Eh bien,* you 'ave become the *chevalier,* Samooel, rescuing *les demoiselles en distrait* now?'

Her voice was soft, but her face grew hard, and there was a dangerous undercurrent of sarcasm in her tone.

Mr Pepys coughed.

'Now, now, Lizbet! I swear there is no harm. 'Tis only a child, look you – I merely extricated her from trouble and. . . .'

'And now you wish to keep on this . . . extricating. You are right, I see very well. Where is this, this tavairn?' She flicked her fingers impatiently as a gesture to the maddening vagaries of the English tongue.

'At Lewkenor's Lane,' mumbled Mr Pepys.

'Aha, now I see even more. You procure both wine and women do you not? Yesterday you went there . . . I know it.' She pointed an accusing finger at him. 'And you come home *de trop,* with the stains of it running all down your coat.' The

28

lady's eyes had become very bright and there was the hint of a tear on her cheek. 'Me, I do not think you go to this tavairn to rescue these *belles filles*. I think, *peut-être*, you 'ave other ideas in your mind at the time, *bien sûr*. . . . '

Nell watched the two as the argument grew high in the confines of the lurching hackney. She decided to leave, seeing the signs she knew so well, that always ended in trouble and usually painful consequences for herself. Interrupting the lady she drew her grubby skirts primly about her and spoke.

'What Mr Pepys has said is quite true, Ma'am. I know not who you are, but I'm a respectable girl and you can take my word for it there's been no dalliance in *this* coach.' The girl's eyes sparkled with fire.

The lady looked amused.

'Why 'ow is this, a veritable termagant, Samooel.' She gazed at Nell interestedly, her head on one side and her dark eyes glowing. 'Where are you from, child?'

'I come from the Coal Yard, Ma'am, and I make no doubt but that you'll never have heard of it. So if you please, stop the coach and I'll go back there. . . . '

'Softly, softly, *ma chérie, tais-toi alors*. Sit down again and tell me of this unfortunate happening in which my husband seems to have taken so *virile* a part.'

Mr Pepys looked uncomfortable and stared out of the coach window.

'Your husband?' faltered Nell.

'But yes, *ma petite*,' tinkled the lady. 'I am – 'ow you say in English – Mistress Pepys. So tell me. . . . '

Nell began stumblingly to recount the afternoon's happenings, but soon warmed to her theme and described with great gusto the fight in the tavern. When she arrived at the point where Mr Pepys had felled the coal-heaver, Mistress Pepys clapped her hands in amusement and burst out laughing.

'My Samooel . . . with a tavern stool? Oh, I swear 'tis too much. This part of him I 'ave nevair seen. He becomes the knight in armour, *bien sur*. Is it not so?'

Nell warmed to this lady with the delightful dress and

29

delicious laugh. She could see how the two people were man and wife. Both, it seemed, enjoyed a good time. She loved everything about Mistress Pepys; her clothes, her expressions, and the way her hands moved exquisitely as she talked to demonstrate a point. She was very French, very petite and very feminine. Nell was enchanted. She finished her account of the happenings until the point where she and Mr Pepys had arrived in the coach, but the lady still seemed intrigued.

'Tell me again how Samooel knocked down this huge-proportioned *ouvrier*. . . . '

Mr Pepys broke in in embarrassment: 'Damn it, Lizbet, will you be quiet? Now you know, be silent, can't you?'

Mistress Pepys leant forward to Nell sitting opposite.

'My 'usband,' she hissed in a deliberately audible whisper, ' 'e is *embarrassé, n'est ce pas*? It is so silly, I think, but he is English and all the English are, 'ow you say, eccentric. *Vraiment*, my Samooel 'e is *Anglais de tête à pied*.' She looked round at Mr Pepys wickedly. '*Alors*, my 'usband,' she said softly, 'be calm again, I will ask no more. . . . '

She straightened her hat and let down her veil again, then turned to her husband.

'I cannot come with you further, Samooel. I am promised to Lady Montagu at Westminster Stairs. We go shopping this afternoon to buy clothes *pour les enfants*; it is most *fatiguant*. My lady, she wishes to become as modish as her husband's sister, the so-fine Lady Pickering. We shall spend all afternoon in Paternoster Row, I know. It is most wearing for she 'as no taste . . . no taste at all.' She spread out her hands in an expressive gesture of resignation.

An elegant glove rapped on the coach ceiling and it stopped halfway down the Strand. Nodding good-bye to Nell, she leapt down in a twirl of petticoats, then closed the door and turned to Samuel.

'*Et maintenant, mon mari, je vous laisse à votre amour*.' She chuckled naughtily and waved as the coach drew off down the Strand. Mr Pepys said nothing for a long while, but Nell noticed a fond smile light his face as he gazed out of the coach window. He appeared to bear his provoking lady no ill will.

The hackney rumbled on until it had nearly finished its sixpenny ride of half a mile. Nell was lost in dreaming of the elegant dress of Mr Pepys' vivacious spouse, when the hackney driver called down to Mr Pepys: ' 'Ow much further, your honour? Was it a shilling go you was wanting?'

Mr Pepys leant out of the coach window and shouted to the driver. Abruptly the coach drew over to the right, ignoring the curses of the coach drivers behind, and pulled up by a respectable-looking hostelry which sported a large sign portraying a golden bell tolling, against a weathered white background.

They both entered the tavern and Sam led Nell up the staircase into a small but comfortable private chamber, looking down over the busy street.

Nell sat down gingerly on the edge of a chair and eyed Mr Pepys guardedly. He spoke swiftly to the fat innkeeper and then leant back with a sigh.

'Luncheon is bespoken, Mistress Gwynne,' he said, and rubbed his hands in anticipation. The girl gazed round the quiet chamber in surprise. This was nothing like the sort of thing Ma Ross supplied. Her ale-house was never quiet, nor as clean as this. Downstairs at Lewkenor's Lane was just a damp room with a few chairs and tables and a smell of sour ale, while upstairs was a line of chambers lit by tawdry lights and adorned with cheap decorations – and equally cheap women plastered in thick make-up to disguise advancing years. Nell was impressed.

'I've never seen nothing like this before, sir. You know 'tis dark where I come from – that's the first thing I noticed – you don't get no sun creeping in round about where I live. I've only just realized. 'Tis odd.'

Mr Pepys straddled a chair, and gnawed at his thumb as he listened to her.

'Here's me serving old Ma Ross and getting near laid every night, when they've had a few – it's not the same, is it?'

Mr Pepys was shocked. 'But you told my wife you don't. . . .'

Nell smiled mischievously. 'Lor' no, sir, I don't. I do the

skivvying. I don't go upstairs. Leastways, not yet I don't.'

'Upstairs?' said Mr Pepys blankly. 'Oh I see.'

The door creaked open and there was a clatter of plates. Luncheon was served.

Mr Pepys took a long pull at his tankard and looked over the rim at his guest, who had just eaten a very full meal. Never had Nell seen such delicacies. Joints of roast pullet piled in a dish, with neat's tongue, Colchester oyster and a huge dish of botargo, garnished with aspic, of which Mr Samuel Pepys was inordinately fond. She had eaten till she could eat no more and was content. Dreamily she smiled back at him and blinked her eyelashes slowly.

'Thank you, sir.'

Again that effect. Mr Pepys coughed nervously, and, pulling at his cravat, rose and strode over to the window. He opened the casement and stood breathing in deeply. Sounds of the thoroughfare below wafted up noisily. He called to Nell: 'Come over here, child.'

Obediently she went to stand by his side. The window looked out over the city, which spread before them. Down the Strand ran the lines of traffic and the rows of shops and houses, spreading out and out into the mass of buildings in the streets, courts and winding alleys that made up London.

Way off in the misty distance could be seen the bright ribbon of the Thames, zig-zagging down to Whitehall Palace, which was glimpsed vaguely beyond the chimney pots.

'London,' said Mr Pepys dreamily. 'Do you like her, Nelly?'

'I – don't rightly know, sir.' Nell thought of the alleys where she lived, and her nose wrinkled in distaste. Then she thought of all that she had seen and experienced that afternoon. She wanted it. She knew that now – all those things she had seen, that she knew she could not live without . . . gowns, jewels, coaches, perfume. Yes, she wanted them, and, she thought rebelliously, one day she would have them.

'Life is what you make of it, sir, I reckons, wherever you 'appens to be. In London same as any place.'

But Mr Pepys wasn't listening. He looked out across the city.

'When will you wake again?' he murmured. 'Will it be soon, I wonder?'

Away down the river the barges were taking their passengers into the mist. Mr Pepys stood looking through the window, with his hands laced behind his back. He began to speak: 'Eleven years ago I went to an execution –.' He paused and Nell stared up at his face, now taut, his eyes looking into the distance unseeing. ' 'Tis eleven years ago I watched the King, His late Majesty, die. I wanted to see it. I flocked with all the others to see the execution of one whom I thought a man of blood, a malignant, an oppressor. But when his head fell, no one cheered, not a soul. There was silence . . . and then a groan from all the crowd rose up, drowning the voice of the headsman showing the head to the people. He died in one moment that cold morning, and we all thought a new world had come into being, a new, perfect world. Just because he was dead.' Mr Pepys sighed. 'It hasn't, of course. They never do. We never can know the future. Perhaps it's best we don't.'

He turned and looked down at the small figure beside him, as if he had only just recalled her presence. A smile crinkled his lips.

'What does life hold for us, Mistress Gwynne?' he asked. 'What does it hold for me or for you?' He flicked her chin with his finger. 'Who knows,' he said with a laugh. 'Perhaps one day you might be a rich, beautiful lady with – even a coach and four!'

Nell looked back at him in bewilderment, but she answered firmly. 'That may never be, sir. I don't know what life holds. I haven't got the gift. But one thing's certain –.' Her eyes met Mr Pepys' and held them. 'I'm getting out of Ma Ross's as soon as ever I can. I'd rather die than stay in that 'ole. I'll claw, bite or kick – but I'll get out somehow, by God!'

Mr Pepys was shocked at the force and the intensity of her voice. He gazed at her searchingly.

'You're a curious child, Nell.'

3

The door of the chamber opened suddenly. A young man, dressed quietly as a secretary or clerk, hurried in a harassed manner into the room. His brow cleared as he saw Mr Pepys, who seemed to recognize him.

'Jeremy –.'

'I come hot-foot from Sir Edward, sir. Your presence is required immediately at the Admiralty. Thank heaven I found your direction from Mr Harper.' The man stopped and looked questioningly at the small girl staring open-mouthed at him. Then Mr Pepys took him into a corner, talking urgently in a lowered voice. Nell heard snatches of conversation.

'The fleet . . . out to sea . . . arrangements . . . the King's declaration,' from the secretary and then, quite distinctly, from Mr Pepys: 'Then 'tis certain that he will return!' His face lit up.

Nell looked blankly at Sam who was now shrugging on his coat. He glanced at Nell.

'Can you find your way home, child?' he asked, but before she could answer pressed a coin into her hand. 'Here, you'd better take a chair.' Nell looked down and saw a guinea. She ran and flung her arms around Mr Pepys and kissed him on the cheek with a child's warmth.

'Thank you, sir. Thank you . . . oh, for everything.'

Mr Pepys smiled. 'Don't lose your way, Mistress Gwynne – and for me, keep kicking till you're out of that . . . that 'ole.' He winked and in a second was gone. Nell could hear him still talking earnestly as he clattered down the stairs and watched from the window as both of them lurched off in the direction of Whitehall in the waiting hackney.

She clutched her guinea tightly in her hand and thought of the conversation she had just heard. What was it they had been talking of . . . ? The King was mentioned, she knew. Would he ever return? Were any of the rumours true?

The drab London which Nell had always known was brightening. It was as though a shutter had been drawn back, letting in light and fresh air to an atmosphere long polluted and dark. What was happening? The world as she knew it was changing, changing. Everything seemed to be breaking up. Nell could see the clouds had moved in the world around her; people were not so cowed, they were lifting their heads and waking up. It was as if a shadow was moving from off the face of England. The iron grip of the military government was weakening, people were openly scoffing at it and deriding the repellent Puritan morality in a manner they would never have dared before. What was more, nobody stopped them or even seemed interested. Apprentices like the ones Nell had seen that day poured contempt on Parliament, and the only people offended were the middle-aged ladies they insulted. No recriminations ensued. It was like kicking at a corpse already long dead. And if dead, what did the future hold?

There was an atmosphere in London of calm before a storm. Nell could feel it . . . tense and hidden but still there, lurking in the background. She came from the gutters of the city and she could feel that the mood of the city had changed. Would the King return or would there be another civil war? Would General Monk rule as another arrogant dictator, like to the one buried a twelvemonth before?

Just below the window an apprentice ran by, whistling, and then she heard his shrill voice shouting,

'Ding a dong ding, I heard a bird sing,
The Parliament soldiers are gone to the King.'

So that was it! The King was going to return; Nell was as sure as if she had been told. Everything fell into place, Mr Pepys' allusions included. She leant forward on the windowsill, her eyes bright as she looked out over London. St Paul's spire shone out in the mist over the city at her. Life was going to begin again – there was hope. And she – she would be part of it.

CHAPTER III

Else never rejoice till I hear the voice
That the King enjoys his own again.
Anon

In solemn state, Charles the Second, by the grace of God King of England, France, Scotland, and Ireland, rode back into his capital – the city he had not seen since the age of twelve, eighteen years ago, when he had left it to join his father to fight rebellious subjects. And now these same subjects lined the route of his progress, hung out of windows throwing flowers, and dropped to their knees before him in joy. The King waved graciously but his eyes were sardonic as he viewed the hysteria all around him.

The day was symbolically clear, as clear as the faces of the citizens now thronging his path, kneeling before his horse and promising eternal loyalty to him and his House. Thankful that drabness and repression were past, they wept to see return their sovereign, whom they had once dubbed 'that traitor Charles Stuart', and harried out of his kingdom after the bloody escape from Worcester. Charles Stuart had returned to reclaim the home of his fathers – Whitehall Palace, death-scene of Charles the Martyr. As the day had dawned, they had known that no new chaos had erupted, that they were delivered from the iron glove of the Army in whose merciless grip they had languished so long. In the King they saw their deliverer returning to them, a powerful representative of sovereignty by the Divine Right they had once condemned as oppression.

Through the narrow streets of London poured more than twenty thousand men on horses and foot, carrying before them the arms of Stuart, now restored to power and seen everywhere: gilded on tavern signs, and displayed on house fronts and even women's dresses. And the city opened wide its arms to receive them.

Ladies hung out of windows, strewing flowers on the heads

36

of the Cavaliers now returning; the streets were decked in ribbons and bunting. The bells of the churches rang joyously as the conduits ran with wine. After eighteen years of war, privation, and fear, London awoke, hysterically, madly, abandoning any restraint. Revelling in her debauchery now let loose with such relief, London came back to life.

For hours and hours, on flowed the gilded procession, winking jewels and cloth of gold as it went. At the head rode the Lord Mayor of London, followed by the aldermen, all in their deep rich robes, and behind them the city's companies of the guilds, carrying their banners and arrayed in their liveries. They were followed on horse by the glittering concourse of the nobles: returning Cavaliers, dressed in borrowed finery and still with little money, but filled now with buoyant hopes for new fortune – and revenge. Cloth of silver, cloth of gold, satins, velvets, feathered hats, sashes, and jewelled sword hilts passed before the awed gaze of the citizens. And as they passed, the ladies threw down their love-knots and blew kisses as unashamedly as if Oliver Cromwell had never lived.

The slow progress through the stuffy streets was wildly received. Trumpets blew incessantly but were drowned by the cheers of the crowd – myriads of people who pressed round, not only Londoners but people from the country, as far away as Rochester, who had tramped in to see their King return. The cannon boomed dully in the distance and the procession proceeded on from London Bridge through the streets towards Whitehall. But the eyes of the people scanned the procession past the Mayor and his minions, past the banners and musicians, along the moustached faces of the gay nobles until, in the midst of all the magnificence, they saw what they had come to see – their King.

Riding easily along, one hand on his hip, came Charles the Second, occasionally waving to the crowd that nearly swooned with hysteria at sight of him. Over six feet tall, he looked powerful and every inch a king born of his French mother, descended of the line of Henri of Navarre. His face was swarthy and dark. Harsh lines lit up the visage of the man whom they had called the Black Boy, when they had prayed secretly for his return and toasted in fear. Any naïvety had been knocked out of Charles by ten years, ten long years, of poverty and humiliation abroad. Rejected by his subjects, scorned by foreign courts whose asylum he sought, Charles had learnt to expect little of people and not value deeply their protestations either of love or loyalty. But he was not a sombre man. His Chancellor, Edward Hyde, Earl of Clarendon, had often wished he were more so, and told the King as much. But Charles just laughed at his gloomy minister and continued a life in search of the ladies, whose seduction was his main amusement.

Charles enjoyed life and he was resolved to go on doing so. There was amusement and kindness, as well as cynicism, in his dark eyes as he surveyed the acclamations of his errant people. Let them enjoy life too, he thought. He was willing that they, too, might know happiness again. While they were happy his throne was safe, and Charles was resolved not to go on his travels again.

He spoke to his brother on his right in the noisy row around them.

' 'Odsfish, James! I wonder I have stayed away so long – they seem glad to see me! Since we landed, everyone I have met assures me he has done nothing but pray for my return.'

James, Duke of York, smiled tightly, with lips compressed, but said nothing.

'But love me or love me not,' continued the King, eyeing their present transports, 'they've got me back for good. I am not so much our father's son.'

James said nothing, but gazed around him with faint disgust. Charles sighed. Really, James was so tactless! Could he not at least try to look happy? He even looked miserable when he *was* happy, thought his brother wryly, which hardly endeared him to people. His dislike for dissembling would, Charles shrewdly guessed, lead him one day into serious trouble.

James was a true Stuart; blond and blue-eyed he resembled his father, perhaps more than any of Charles the First's children, and he possessed his father's stubbornness. He had his brother's looks, and his vices, as a full sensuous mouth betrayed, but none of the humour or kindness which made Charles forgiven and loved by so many. Perhaps that was why he had more than any other the melancholy eyes of the House of Stuart. Now, as his royal brother acknowledged the cheers of the crowd, his mind was still full of the past and its privations, and his brow was dark and his expression petulant as he looked without feeling at his countrymen. A cloud of rose petals dropped around them, settling pink in the King's dark, curling hair as the vast procession moved along Fleet Street.

The King's horse stumbled, and Charles was wrenched back to reality. His eyes were tired, and there were lines of weariness reaching down from his nose and pinching his nostrils. The procession had been going for five hours now, and back – back for four days since he had landed at Dover. He had found little time for rest. The incessant demands to smile and say the right things, to kiss the numerous Bibles presented to him and vow an Anglican piety he did not feel, to kiss Mrs Monk and call General Monk 'father', to shake hands and bow to crowds he had never seen before and did not wish to see again! They had been days of living in public like a bird in a cage, as he had described to his sister Minette, still in France.

All of a sudden people wanted him and courted him, promising a love he knew was false but yet had to pretend to accept. A sea of faces whirling before him smiled vacuously and he wished to be rid of them even as he raised his hand in greeting. He wished that it were all over so that he could rest alone in his bedchamber away from all the prying eyes and chattering questions. No, not quite alone. Charles remembered the creamy white arms of Barbara Palmer, his mistress, and his pulse quickened. He could see her even now in his mind's eye: her red, pouting lips and luminous, imperious eyes, set in a stormy face of exquisite beauty, framed by masses of tumbling auburn hair. Tonight he would forget all these people, in enjoying the sensuous, voluptuous body of

Barbara Palmer, who clung to him with the possession and passion of an animal, which satisfied his soul.

All at once he saw before his horse, standing in the street in his path, a small girl whose hair was bound up roughly in a bright scarf and who smiled up at him shyly as she held out a lavender love-knot. She curtseyed demurely.

'For you, Sire.'

Charles reined in his horse and stared down at Nell Gwynne. For a second their eyes held, Nell's shining in awe at the splendid figure before her, Charles looking down in amusement. To be thinking of Barbara Palmer in all her beauty and then to be confronted with this small girl from the backstreets was quite absurd. He leant over towards her and took the love-knot, tucking it in his buttonhole.

'Thank you, child,' he whispered softly and kissed her full on the lips. For an instant Nell felt a hard mouth on hers and the narrow black moustache brushed her cheek. Dark eyes laughed at her. Then in an instant he was gone, the procession moved on, the horses which had stopped while the King kissed her now sweeping by, haughty faces looking down at her in disdain as they passed.

But Nell was oblivious. She was looking after the figure in the distance, now laughing loudly with his royal brother, and her fingers gingerly touched her mouth. She had been kissed by the King and she knew something had happened to her that she would never forget.

'You backsliding jade!' A voice of mock severity sounded just behind Nell. She whirled round to see a tall, dark girl, with a full, laughing red mouth and a cloud of deep black curls, standing, arms akimbo, behind her.

'Rose . . .,' muttered Nell in confusion. 'I was just. . . . '

'I know, just about to return home, weren't you? Where've you been all morning? Ma's swearing fit to bust 'er guts.'

'I came early to see the procession.'

Rose looked impatient.

'Well, you'd better get back quick or there'll be trouble. Old

Ma Ross'll want you round at the Lane soon and you'd better not get on her wrong side. Not after the last nasty business.'

Memories of the broken mirror and Ma Ross's heavy hand came uncomfortably into Nell's mind. Her eyes widened in horror.

'Lor', no!' she said in revulsion.

Nell's eyes travelled over Rose, dressed as usual in the height of fashion, in a scarlet cloak and hood edged with miniver. Rose always looked after Rose, thought her sister wryly. Then her glance was taken by Rose's tall companion. From a very great height a stranger looked down at Nell, his eyes alight with humour.

Rose glanced at him through slanting eyes under dark, arched brows, and drooped her eyelashes seductively.

'My sister, Jon.'

The gentleman bowed low.

'I' faith, I think we have met, have we not, er . . . Nell, isn't it?'

The girl crimsoned. She had seen the gentleman before, since he was often to be found in Ma Ross's chambers. Not that he was the usual sort of person to be found within the confines of that establishment. He was tall and aquiline-featured, with long tapering white fingers and an unmistakable air of elegance at variance with the company he kept. His name, Nell knew, was White Jonathan, in ironic reference to his dress, which was always of black from top to toe, with even – of all affectations – a black silk neck-cloth. This sobriety was unrelieved except for one diamond pin which sparkled from its sombre folds. Yet the effect was not Puritanical. The gentleman, for such he undoubtedly was, wore a fashionable attire – his ankle-length cloak was edged with sable, his high riding-boots were of impeccable, glossy leather unsmirched by mud, and his suit was intricately embroidered with black beads of jet; and – further eccentricity – black lace frothed at his white wrists.

Mit, the little kitchen-maid at Ma Ross's, said he was a high-wayman, but if he was, Nell privately thought, he was of a different kind from the usual footpads, bridle-culls and nabbing cheats who inhabited St Giles and the district of Alsatia, London's sanctuary for criminals.

For all the speculation about the black figure, his past or his occupation remained a mystery. For White Jonathan never vouchsafed an answer. He would come and sit in a corner all evening at Ma Ross's, saying not a word to anyone, and his air of finesse and calculated aloofness tended to make those around him feel uncomfortable – until they forgot his presence. But Jonathan never suffered from insults, jibes, or rudeness. The wicked, slender sword hanging in its plain sheath at his side warned off any foolhardy man, even those replete with small beer, from picking a quarrel with the stranger. Behind the pair of lazy blue eyes there was a warning glint and a touch of hauteur which precluded impertinent curiosity even amidst the bawdiness of Lewkenor's Lane.

Nell looked up at a face now edged with fatigue, thin and distant. The expression was odd and forbidding, and yet, as he smiled, Nell found herself shyly smiling back, sure all at once of a warmth behind the icy barrier of the exterior. . . .

She curtseyed.

'I believe I have seen you before, sir, at Madam Ross's, of an evening.'

The gentleman looked down a high, straight nose at Nell, but his voice was surprisingly kind.

'I regret to say you are right. What are you doing in such a place, sweetheart?'

Rose looked embarrassed. She laughed nervously.

'Lord, what should she do at her age? I vow and swear she'd learn all about the sins of life just as soon, wherever she was in the city. And now the King's back, I doubt not but we'll see more sport.'

Jonathan glanced at her and his lip curled slightly, but he said nothing.

Nell decided that she liked the stranger.

'Are you Rose's latest goat, then?' she inquired easily, to his evident surprise. Her sister's eyes shot daggers but the gentleman chuckled, his cold eyes crinkling with a strangely warm amusement.

'Yes,' he admitted, 'I suppose I am.'

Nell was enraptured. 'I thought so,' she confided. 'And I don't believe half the tales they tell about you, and so I promise you.'

Jonathan bowed. 'I am gratified,' he said gravely, though his eyes twinkled. 'I imagine I am put down as a sadly unsociable fellow. What do they say of me, then?'

'Why, all manner of tales. Some were used to say you were a Royalist spy, but that's a dead tale now the King's back. Someone once said you were the Duke of Buckingham in disguise. 'Twas known he came to London at times, or so rumour had it.'

Jonathan laughed. 'I fear someone had a too vivid imagination, though I know some of the King's friends never did have much idea of security. I swear all London knew more of their plots than the King himself. What else did they say?'

Rose smiled nervously, but the glance she threw at Nell was frosty.

'Oh, well.' Nell looked uncomfortable. 'They didn't exactly *say* . . . they just hinted, if you know what I mean. But I *knew* they couldn't be true, sir. Mit – she's the kitchen-girl – said you were a thrice-turned stocking, and some made out you were hiding from the Constable and haunted Alsatia. But I *knew* it couldn't be true. I told her you might look a hawk, especially with *that* nose, and of course anyone could tell you fancied yourself, but I wasn't deceived. No one could be that bad, I told her, not with *those* eyes.'

Rose looked around wildly, as if expecting some kind of hand of Fate to come down from the heavens and remove her small grubby sister.

Jonathan coughed shakily into his handkerchief. Rose tittered in a brittle fashion.

'I vow the girl does run on like a preacher, sir!' She turned to Nell. 'Be off with you, child, and take your gossip with you. You'd better go home if you're not due at work yet. Go and

43

help Ma. Be sure she could do with it. She was rollicking merry when I left her and the house is in a filthy state, no better than the Fleet prison, I declare.'

Nell hesitated, and looked up at Jonathan as though expecting him to say something, but he just looked at Rose in a way Nell had come to recognize. The procession was still passing but the glitter had gone. It was just the sober lines of the city tradesmen that trudged by now, followed by the all too familiar tramp of pikemen, and foot-soldiery. Many people were dispersing, either homewards or on to the Strand to catch a second glimpse of the King as he entered his Royal Palace of Whitehall. Stepping through the fallen rose petals, Nell left her sister laughing in the arms of her lover. She knew she was totally forgotten.

Mrs Gwynne looked up wearily. She was slumped over a table in the centre of the chamber which served as kitchen, parlour, and bedroom, as her daughter entered and flung her cloak down on a chair. She lifted a tin mug and drank deeply, and then straightened. Her voice was slurred and slow.

'And where've you been, you – mucky – hussy?' The words were separated, yet indistinct.

'Lord, Mam, I went to see the procession, of course. Where else could I go today?'

Her mother seemed uninterested and didn't answer, but took another swig and sat moodily staring ahead of her. Nell looked at the lodgings, which were in an incredible state. Through the dim windows, which were of oiled canvas, since glass was unheard of in the district, light filtered through in a sickly, yellow fashion. The sun had never entered the Coal Yard since it had been built, and few houses had been touched, but left to decay. They leant up against each other in a crooked fashion around a muddy quadrangle of uneven, cracked flagstones. The Londoners, as all foreigners noticed, were not a particularly clean race – indeed their dirty ways were legendary with the Dutch over the water. Not that the Londoners cared; they hated the Dutch anyway, and no one was too nice over a bit of grime here and there, certainly not in areas like the Coal Yard where life was too short and was concerned with greater things – like the next meal and the next woman – to worry about some rubbish in the gutter that had lain there as long as they could remember. All too often, nearly every time the summer came to the city, the symbolic bale of straw would hang on a pole outside the house in the Coal Yard, or in Coke Alley, a sign that the pestilence was ravaging within, and the people shut inside till it should have finished doing its worst. The air in the Coal Yard was dead and heavy. It hung on people's lungs in a stale, vile way and dragged all too many to an early grave. All the houses – built in the long past days of the first Elizabeth – were rotten and keeling over with age. But their damp interiors were worse.

The furniture Nell could see was scanty and shabby. In the centre of the room stood a rickety table surrounded by three chairs, much the worse for wear, one with a leg missing. There was little else to furnish the room. In the corner stood a dresser littered with five or six tin mugs and an unwashed pile of earthenware plates. The hearth was graced with no fire; an iron pot hung cold from the trivet with a forlorn pair of charred faggots lying beneath. An air of neglect pervaded the entire room, mixed with that subtle odour that spoke of poverty and dirt.

Nell's mother slouched at the table, a pathetic, gross wreck of a woman, fatly encumbered in a cotton print gown bulging at the bodice and stained under the armpits. There was little trace of any of her former beauty. Her whole person reeked of spirits and sweat, and upon her face could be seen the ravages of the drink which had formed the major part of her existence for the past ten years. Through bloodshot eyes she muzzily glanced at her daughter and then tipped the dregs of the spirit down her throat, trickles running down fat jowls and spotting her dress. She wiped her mouth with a massive forearm and sat motionless, staring at the door.

Nell was used to seeing her mother like this. She had had bouts of drinking as long as the girl could remember. Any affection or upbringing had always depended on the careless ministrations of Rose, who was usually otherwise occupied. There were hundreds of women like Mrs Gwynne in the slums and alleys of London; married at fifteen and finished at twenty-five. Childhood was short, violently and quickly destroyed by St Giles'. Life was shorter. By the time they were thirty most of them looked gross and ancient, after spawning eight or nine unwanted children most of whom died in infancy.

Nell sighed and began to attempt to clear up the mess. Grabbing a twig-broom she started to sweep the hardened earth floor clear of the remains of food and dirty straw that littered it, talking as she did so to break the brooding silence.

'Strike me, Mam! You should have seen the procession! I never saw nothing like it. Talk about fine! And here, guess what, mam? I saw the King himself ride by. Lord, he did look grand, dressed in naught but silks and satins, and waving like he was glad to be back.'

Nell said nothing about the King's kiss, wishing to keep it to herself. No one should know, only she. And she would never forget.

Nell's mother answered wearily.

'I should hope he is glad to be back. At least he'll have some money in his pocket now, poor lad. So the Stuart star has risen. Mayhap life can begin again. Not that it signifies. It's too late for me now.'

Nell looked up from her sweeping and opened her mouth; then she stared at her mother, closed it again, and went on with her work.

Mrs Gwynne's eyes grew misty.

'I can remember the good days, before we 'ad those prating Puritans – you wouldn't know, Nell. A wench could stand by a pillar in St Paul's and pick up a gallant any day of the year. It wasn't just notices of servants for hire they posted up, you know. Oh dear me, no! The gentlemen'd come and walk up and down, showing off their fine clothes and laughing and eyeing any girl nearly, to see 'er blush. Oh, those were the days. I was young then. . . . '

46

Nell moved over to the pots and pans, making a great clatter so as to break the awkward silence which had fallen. She peered in the pot, then drew back waving her hands in front of her face.

'What the hell have you got in there. Cromwell's body or something?' She turned to face her mother and looked at her in exasperation. The whole room was crawling. Nell wasn't fastidious; you couldn't be, she thought with ironic amusement, in the Coal Yard. Still, it was obvious the old woman hadn't lifted a finger for days.

You couldn't do anything with her when she got these moods. She just sat and you might as well talk to the moon for all the sense you got out of her. Nell glanced at the rumpled, fat figure with disfavour and spoke briskly.

'Here, come and give us a hand to get this pot off the hook. It stinks like a sewage cart. I don't doubt we'll all be down with Plague in the week. It needs a scrub out.' She tugged at the offending ironmongery.

There was no answer.

Nell's voice became shrill. 'Look here, Mam, come here and help just a bit, can't you? You always just bleeding sit like a dollop of pudding. Like a corpse you are, except you need feeding; you'll find yourself fixed to that chair one day. Come on, you fat old cow!'

There was little respect in Nell's voice. Her mouth tightened as she looked at her unwilling helpmate. It was no use getting annoyed; the old woman never took any notice anyway, she thought rebelliously.

In fact Nell felt sorry for her mother – deserted by her husband and left to bring up two small children, while Nell's father was God knew where. She felt sorry for her even as she screamed at her, sitting there like a prison hulk, stewed to the gills. Mrs Gwynne was useless, dependent on her daughter even for the few groats to buy her drink. She was weak, finding in her gin the escape she needed, so as not to face the truth of a life without hope. Sometimes Nell could sympathize. But at times this immobility got on her nerves.

47

'I'm bleeding sick of you and your bottle-swilling sessions. Why the hell can't you *do* something? *Anything* but just sit there like a bloody statue. By the Mass, Mam, if you don't move. . . .'

Her mother sat silently, sunk in apathy, as abuse tore her character to shreds. Yet she appeared to tighten in anger as Nell reached the end of her tirade and stood over her, breathing stertorously. Mrs Gwynne twisted in her chair and squinted up at her, one eye narrowed in hate. Her voice was thick.

'Get back to your whore-house where you belong, you little bitch – and leave me alone.'

Nell's eyes blazed out and she lifted an arm to strike, but dropped it with a gesture of weary defeat. What could one do with a drunken old woman who had lost hope and just wanted to die?

She picked up her cloak and looked steadily at her mother, her eyes heavy as lead.

'I'll be back late tonight, Mam.'

Mrs Gwynne silently stared down at the table top. Nell's heart softened as she looked at the huge bulk of her, sunk in defeat. Even as she pressed the copper coin into one flaccid hand she knew her sister would despise her for it.

'Get yourself a bite to eat, Mam,' she said briskly, knowing that it would go on gin instead. She stood staring at the motionless figure for a second and then turned away. The door banged behind her.

It was the night of the Restoration. London had gone hysterically, unbelievably, mad. Hardly any of her citizens were at home tonight, hardly any of them were sober. Huge bonfires sparked in the night in nearly every street, lighting the dark city from end to end with dots of light flickering across from Cheapside, through Temple Bar to Strand Bridge, and curving up Ludgate Hill in an arc of flames. Lurching bands of revellers wandered up and down and in and out of taverns, waving bottles in the night air and singing raucously,

'The King enjoys his own again
My Lady in her gown,
And all the curs'd apprentices
Have took o'er all the Town.'

The Londoners were enjoying themselves as they knew best.
The mob, terror of kings, lords and people, was out beating
up any who seemed Puritanically inclined, Catholic or foreign
in any degree. The windows of any houses occupied by one
thought to be a Puritan were smashed in joyfully, to shouts of
drunken mirth. Several groups of sturdy watermen, chairmen,
and London riff-raff, roasted huge sides of beef in the streets
and stopped passers-by, making them kneel to drink the King's
health.

At Lewkenor's Lane, in common with the rest of London,
the atmosphere was loudly boisterous. Two lanterns stood
either side of the low door in the dark to guide bleary-eyed
revellers into the charms of Madam Ross's establishment;
by the door, also, stood Benjamin the water-carrier, with huge
arms folded, ready to eject those whose ribaldry overstepped
even Ma Ross's liberal limits. Customers came and went in a
steady, if drunken, stream. The small tavern downstairs was
packed with singing, shouting people, the air smoky from the
cheap, tallow candles on the walls and stuck in bottles on the
tables. The smells mingled with the odours of close-packed
humanity.

Slatternly, grubby maids in mob-caps ran about like mad
hens with huge wooden trays of ale, small beer and occasional
glasses of cheap Rhenish wine. Tonight the place was packed
with extravagantly-dressed gallants, newly returned Cavaliers –
or at least so they all said. Tonight, in the hysterical city, any
who claimed they had been in exile with His Majesty were
treated to drinks and fêted as heroes. Many a woman was to
prove tonight, in this heat of happiness now released, that she
would hold nothing back from a poor follower of the House of
Stuart. Behind the counter opposite the door, beneath the
newly-mended gilt mirror, sat Ma Ross herself, picking a tooth

with one black finger nail and seedily speculating on the sight before her.

She was a buxom woman of about forty-five years, sparkling with cheap jewellery of the 'brass and glass' variety sold in St Martin-in-the-Fields. A huge blond wig sat crookedly upon her head, above a pair of small, greedy eyes sunk in a face elaborately rouged and painted to hide the scars of pox. Tonight, for the occasion, she had donned a gown of hideous purple satin which threatened to burst at the bodice when she leant forward.

Madam Ross did not soil her hands with any work. Nor was she available upstairs now; the days when she had possessed a body worth offering were long past. But she had made enough in the balmy days of the first Charles's reign to set up this establishment which was now welcoming his son's return. Plastered in make-up, surrounded by a bevy of elderly admirers, she sat dispersing Rhenish and bawdy humour.

Her lips set in a satisfied line as she looked at her successors in the noble trade of gentleman's 'ladies'. With trade like this, she could retire in a few years, and good riddance. She leant forward to bestow a kiss on the powdered cheek of the elderly gallant at her side, and saw a small figure sitting on the lap of a husky captain at one of the tables. The girl took the wineglass out of his large hand and downed it in a gulp. Clasping her arms loosely round his neck, she gave him an inexpert and very wet kiss, and whispered in his ear, naughtily tweaking his moustache with one hand circled round his collar. The soldier laughed good-naturedly and pinched her bottom.

Madam Ross was slightly peeved. The child had been engaged as a maid, nothing more. If she was, in fact, old enough for whoring, in Ma Ross's view she should say so and let there be an end to all the nonsense, for then an amicable business arrangement would fix a fee for Ma Ross and they could all be easy.

But if the crafty little slut thought she could neglect her work and pocket any proceeds from such dalliance herself, she had another think coming. Ma Ross put down her wineglass moved her magnificent bulk, and stood up, smoothing down her bulging front.

'Nelly,' she called tartly. 'Come over here, girl, and give me some attention – if you can spare the time,' she added with sarcasm.

The girl gave the soldier a parting kiss, and tossing back her shock of auburn hair, came over towards her mistress. Madam Ross eyed her speculatively. The girl was filling out nicely, she saw with a quick glance. Seeing as most girls were married at fifteen – and few pure as milk when they did so – it couldn't be long before this little jade would be ready to earn a dishonest penny or two.

She spoke briskly. 'Get a mop and go and clean out the chambers. And while you're at it you can stick some new candles in the sconces. Don't forget to light them and leave the rooms looking cosy.'

She turned to survey the carousing groups, amongst whom could be glimpsed her own scantily dressed lovelies. Two at least, with dresses pulled off their shoulders, sat unconcernedly sipping Rhenish, displaying pretty legs under skirts swept up to the knee. There were about ten girls in all; some drinking at their man's expense and Ma Ross's exorbitant prices, others going further to make a customer stay longer.

There was a burst of masculine laughter when one voluptuous blonde, laughing wickedly, pulled her dress up to her white thighs as she sat on the table swinging her feet, and kicked her middle-aged admirer up the breeches as he bent to retrieve a coin. One young spark put his arms around her and whispered something in her ear at which she laughed and blushingly refused an answer. Her mistress rubbed her lips together in satisfaction.

'The chambers will be wanted in a half-hour or so, if I'm not mistook. With the wine that's flowed tonight they'll be as hot as coals come eleven.'

Nell had often been sent to clear out the upstairs rooms but usually in the mornings, when they had been vacated. She had never – beyond giggles and whispers from various girls, and once a tale from Mit the kitchen-maid at which she had laughed – heard what exactly went on within them, though as a child of St Giles' she had some good guesses. Now she merely bobbed an obedient curtsey, and a minute later she went past Madam Ross up the stairs, clutching a mop and a bucket of water. Madam Ross watched her ankles as she went up the stairs and chuckled.

'S'life! Let her have a glimpse of where she'll be working and I doubt not but that a little talk in a year or so, to clear up doubts and questions, will make her jig with the others quite happy. God knows her sister has had enough experience at the art!'

Nell finished cleaning three of the six rooms, stuck new candles in the holders on the walls, and left the fourth half done as she went out into the passage to rinse her mop. It was quiet in the passageway. She leant on the mop handle, wiped her brow wearily, and was just about to return to work when she heard a low voice and a feminine giggle from round the corner of the landing. Without quite knowing what she was doing, Nell took her sodden mop in hand and backed into the room, closing the door behind her. Standing by the door she heard slow footfalls come along the passage outside, and then a voice murmured, soft yet distinct. 'Now let's see, my pretty, how you play when I jerk your strings.'

In answer there was a mocking laugh, suddenly quenched by a series of rustles and a gurgle from a woman's throat. Then the latch on the door turned.

Nell cast a panicked look around the bedchamber. Quick as a flash she ducked behind a high wooden dresser, kneeling down. As the door opened, Nell found herself sitting very uncomfortably on a wet mop in the dust behind the old dresser, but she soon forgot her discomfort as she watched two people stumble into the bedchamber. Laughing as they went, leaning on each other and swaying about, a young man and a girl kicked the door to behind them.

Nell recognized the young man; he was little more than twenty – a student she guessed, for they often came to Ma Ross's when they were flush in the pocket. He clutched his companion with fingers clasped tight, and his eyes ran over her yearningly.

The girl, too, Nell knew well; Sarah had only just joined Ma Ross's happy band, but had proved already that she could provide a heady evening's entertainment for any high-spirited man with the temerity to take her on. With a toss of her blonde hair, Sarah strained up on tiptoe and twined her arms around the young man's neck.

His mouth feverishly came down on hers, as with a sigh of satisfaction he grabbed her to him. Nell, looking over the dresser, saw a red high-heeled shoe drop off Sarah's black-stockinged foot as the young man lifted her up and carried her in his arms over to the bed.

Groans of contentment came from the girl as his hands roamed over her hungrily; his mouth dropped kisses over her throat and down to the white bosom that heaved in growing desire as her clothes were pulled away. His actions were violent, almost animal, in his savage intensity to lay bare the prize. There were sounds of heavy breathing, sighing and torment as the two bodies on the bed tossed together. Sarah began to speak wildly, to urge in desperation, 'I can't bear it, no more – no more. . . . '

The words came in shrill, moaning tones that rose up and up – and then were suddenly checked. Her arms clasped rigid around the young man's body, though his moved urgently. Then they both lay silent on the bed, exhausted by their exertions. The man rolled away from her and lay to one side, mopping his sweating face with his kerchief.

With mob-cap askew on her head, the small Cockney girl behind the dresser watched in awe. She wondered if they had finished or would begin again, and thought in sudden terror that they might stay all night, in which case she would be trapped. But the young man sat up presently, and tucking his shirt back in his breeches, bent over his sweetheart and gave her a light kiss. 'Pull the clothes about you, my dove. 'Tis mighty cold in the chamber.'

Sarah sat up on the bed, the candlelight playing on the blonde hair streaming down her back, and over the smooth naked shoulders which were revealed by a bodice now pulled away to lie in satiny folds around her. She made no attempt to cover herself, but lolled seductively, her breasts standing out hard and firm like young plums. She smiled at her gallant, pouted her lips, and spoke to him softly. The young man knelt forward on the bed and shook free the tassels so that the bed curtains closed on the scene.

Nell gazed at the red velvet curtains. The occupants of the bed would be fully engrossed for some time, she thought. Reaching the door, she turned the knob soundlessly and slipped outside.

In the passage she walked along in a dream, full of what she had just seen and not quite sure whether she liked it or not. The passion and savagery of the man she remembered with shock and dismay, but she also recalled the sighs of Sarah and the look she had cast at her lover when she had sat up in the candlelight. Life was curious, decided Mistress Gwynne, as bucket in hand she descended the stairs with a clatter, back into the moving drunken throng of people.

CHAPTER IV

Beware the fury of
a patient man.
John Dryden

A few days later, when Nell arrived at Lewkenor's Lane to begin work prior to the customers' arrival, she found her redoubtable mistress waiting for her, arms akimbo.

' 'Faith, Mam,' she said in confusion, 'I made sure not to be late but I was stopped by that malapert slut Rebecca Bates who lives next door. I swear she runs on like a parson. I'll just get the broom out and. . . . '

Madam Ross raised a plump hand to stem the words. 'Mistress Gwynne, I want to talk to you about your future employment here.'

Nell looked up sharply. So the old cow was going to turn her off, was she? Blunt, if nervous, she said sharply, 'If you have no further need of me, Mam, I can find work elsewhere. There's a score of taverns opening up now the King's come back, and I dare swear I shall find a job, and that's not the backside o' the truth.'

'You misunderstand me, sweetheart,' purred Madam Ross, the smile that creased her painted face also cracking, as Nell noticed, the film of complexion-paint on her dingy cheeks. 'You are growing up, child, and you are, if I dare say, becoming mighty handsome.'

Nell looked suspicious. What was all this leading to? Ma Ross never went out of her way to be agreeable – unless she wanted something. She must have sensed the girl's suspicion, for suddenly Madam Ross laughed and laid a heavy hand on Nell's shoulder, to her intense annoyance.

'I vow, sweetheart, you need not look so. I merely wondered if you would like it, were I to offer a fine gown in exchange for that mob cap and skirt of linsey-woolsey you wear here. . . . '

Nell remained puzzled.

'Would you like to join us properly – to join the other girls ?' asked Madam Ross boldly. 'Though you can't really take 'em upstairs for a tickle yet, you could make yourself pleasant down here for a few months, and then later, who knows ? 'Twould be your apprenticeship to the trade.'

Nell's mouth dropped open, as her fat mistress's intention became clear. 'You mean become a whore for you, don't you, Madam ?'

'Why not ?'

The girl looked down at the floor, twitching her apron between her fingers. She didn't know what to reply.

Madam Ross watched her shrewdly, and began to use her powers of persuasion. ' 'Twould not be for some months yet, child. You can learn the ropes first, easy as you like. What a job for a girl such as you! A fine gown, an easy evening with the wine – and with the gentlemen. You do like the gentlemen, don't you, sweetheart ? I have noticed it often.'

Nell still said nothing.

Madam Ross was getting impatient. Lord, why was the provoking slut so coy ? Everyone knew who her mother was and *what* her sister was, so why the pretence ? It was the best thing she could do in her position – at least she could get some money for it, which she wouldn't in any other way. Pox on her! thought her mistress. No one in this district was a virgin after the age of fifteen. Was she trying to force the price up ? Madam Ross decided to go carefully.

She patted Nell on the shoulder. 'You think it over, sweetheart. Pity that beauty should go to waste, is't not ?'

All that day Nell saw everything through a haze. As she knelt on the stone floor, raking out the ashes from the fireplace before lighting a fresh fire of the new, smoky sea-coal which now London's citizens grumblingly used, she thought of the rise in status that would be hers. Now she was a skivvy, little better than Mit the slavey, who lived the life of a drudge, kicked around by everyone. If she agreed to Madam Ross's proposal she knew what she could expect: a fine gown, second-hand from the stalls at Houndsditch, where those of gentle blood but fallen on hard times sold their clothes. Goods passed on from previous owners, certainly . . . but still grand beyond the dreams of a girl from London's back alleys. She would actually look a fine lady, though Ma Ross's customers would know what she really was.

It was the word 'whore' that stuck in her throat, that made it all seem so sordid, so finally, horribly real. She remembered the scene she had viewed a few nights before. Did she want to become like Sarah? To accept the animal lust of men in a darkened bedchamber? She didn't know. But was whoring, after all, so very bad?

For, after all, Barbara Palmer, His Majesty's mistress, 'twas well known, was nothing more nor less, yet she was received everywhere at Court. And besides, what did life hold for Nell if she refused? She might be sacked, and even if she were not, what could she do to extricate herself from the life she now loathed but could not escape? The most she could expect was years as a domestic, with marriage if she were lucky to a huge water-carrier or workman, a lover with the hug of a bear and the mind of an ape. She shuddered as she emptied the slop pail out of the window and returned downstairs.

She saw White Jonathan seated at the wooden settle in the corner, moodily tipping sack down his throat, his expression thunderous and his thin nostrils pinched with anger. He looked totally unapproachable and preoccupied. At the counter, arguing in low voices with Ma Ross, were two seedy gentlemen, haggling over a mysterious plain saddle-bag that lay on the counter between them and rattled when one of the men poked it to demonstrate a point. 'Come on now, Ma,' one was saying, 'hand over the clinkers, will you? Got you a luverly haul of pretties, we 'ave, worth at least a five-fingered run. Pink me, if we ain't! Fit for a Queen – or a King come to that – seeing as 'ow it's respectable to talk about Kings agin.'

As Nell came down the stairs, the man looked up and saw her. He grabbed at the bag immediately and clutched it to him possessively. Ma Ross laughed in a cracked chuckle.

'Fie, if you're not afraid of a tavern wench, Hugh! I dare

swear you won't stir abroad for a twelvemonth, now the hussy's seen your ill-favoured features. For a gull nabbler, you're a poor-spirited rogue.'

Hugh looked annoyed. 'There's no need to turn on the acid, Ma. If you don't want the sparklers, Bob and me'll take ourselves off.'

'Aye,' spat his companion, 'there's plenty more as will take this if'n you've turned to vinegar. . . . ' He turned to go.

'Lor', don't take on so. I swear I can say naught nowadays, without there being offence taken.' She looked at Nell. 'You can go now, miss – take yourself off and mind you're not late tonight. And,' she added with a slight smile, 'don't forget what I told you.'

Nell took her cloak and let herself out, after casting a fruitless glance at Jonathan, who seemed to Nell to be drinking deep, oblivious of all around him. As she moved towards the door she heard Ma Ross's raucous tones: 'Body o' me! Now we can 'ave a little talk – quite private – so pour out your troubles to old Ma Ross. . . . '

Rose was getting ready to go out that evening. Nell lay on her narrow truckle bed and listening to the girl's chatter as she made herself pretty. She watched her sister step out of her day dress and put on a billowing petticoat of lawn edged with white lace. 'Lord, Nelly,' Rose exclaimed as she moved over to her jewel box, 'did you hear of the fracas 'tween the weavers' and the drapers' lads today at Moorfields?'

Her sister shook her head.

'I heard it from Mistress Culpepper opposite. It seems they had a right set-to, and there was blood and broken heads aplenty. I didn't hear who won, though. They fight so often you can't hardly keep track.' She smoothed on some pale complexion-paint and studied it critically. 'Where are you going Rose?' asked Nell, in wonder at the finery revealed.

Rose clasped a necklace about her throat, and watched it wink in the candlelight. Pity it was only glass, she thought, frowning. Still, times would change now the King was back, she was sure. With a body like hers, she knew she would never want for men. Rose had seen the fire come alight in men's eyes when she smiled at them – when she wanted to smile at them. She could crook her finger and reduce them to adoring servitude. She knew it and delighted in it. Her expression was self-assured as she peered at her face in the cracked mirror on the corner chest, and applied make-up.

'Nowhere special,' she answered, intent on her cosmetics. 'I hear there's a masque tonight in Mulberry Gardens. Mayhap I'll go to it. Some say 'tis a dangerous and lecherous place to go of nights, I own, but I daresay they're just merchants and other such stuffy people.'

Her tone was studiously light. She swept on a dark eye make-up that matched the cloud of jet-black hair inherited from her Welsh father, and transformed her natural beauty into seductive, breath-taking loveliness. Her pouting, deep red lips opened as she eyed her reflection with satisfaction.

'My, you're a beauty, my dear,' she said to her reflection in the mirror, and swept herself a deep mock curtsey. Then she went to the door and shouted down. 'Marry and Amen, Ma! 'Aven't you finished stitching that dress yet? Bring it up, you old sot, or you won't get a groat more for boozing, and so I promise you!'

Mrs Gwynne shuffled up the stairs and entered the room, carrying over one arm the most beautiful gown Nell had ever seen.

' 'Ere you are, luv,' she sniffed, 'and I swear you wouldn't find it better done by a sempstress.'

Rose ignored her and taking the gown, twitched it over her head expertly without disturbing a hair.

'Do me up, Nelly, will you . . . ,' she asked over her shoulder. Nell went forward and began to button up the amazing costume. Rose shook out the heavy silken folds of the gown. White and clinging, its sinewy length wound down her body to curve outwards in a train of milky froth. Across the front of the gleaming cloudy satin, threads of silver wound in and out in intricate patterning of embroidery, studded with seed pearls.

59

Against her dark hair and eyes, Rose's skin showed white and even opaque in its contrast. Her dark eyelashes and full sensuous mouth curved open in a sigh of satisfaction. Her mother and sister stood and looked on, impressed.

'You look a countess luv, a veritable countess,' said her mother.

'A queen,' breathed Nell, stretching out her hand to stroke the shiny folds of luxury.

' 'Tis well enough,' agreed Rose airily. 'It came from off the back of a countess. Jack tore it off 'er 'imself.' She admired herself, arching her shoulder to the mirror.

'But I look better in it than she did, the cow. Jack . . . *appreciates* my beauty.'

Nell was nonplussed. Who was Jack? She glanced at her mother, who merely looked on with an indulgent smile as her daughter got ready.

'We haven't heard of Jack before, have we?' asked Nell shyly.

' 'Pertinent of you!' came back the retort from her sister, who turned and looked at her with eyes hard as diamonds. Nell returned her glance, measure for measure.

'Has Jonathan heard of him, Rose?'

'Mayhap he has, maybe not. He soon will,' said her sister in a voice of forced gaiety, and tied her cloak around her. 'Anyway, what has it to do with you?' In a second she was gone from the room.

Mrs Gwynne looked after her and a solitary tear rolled down from a sentimental watery eye. 'Eh, she looked a picture. To think she's my own daughter – dressed up so fine. . . . '

Wagging her head in amazement, the old woman shuffled back down the stairs. Nell lay on the bed silently – thinking. This explained all. The mysterious Jack she supposed to be Rose's latest flame, and Lord! by the sound of it he was one of the gull dippers who usually ended by taking the cart-ride up Tyburn hill. Mayhap he was even a Tobyman!

This was nothing new in the underworld of St Giles. Many people, she knew, worked only at night and their business was not enquired into by their neighbours.

Jonathan, if he did not already know of Rose's infidelity, suspected it. Nell had no illusions about her sister – she knew her to be good-natured but thoughtless, and more than a trifle hard. She also knew her to be totally and completely selfish. Obviously she was playing Jonathan false. Nell couldn't think how they ever came together at all. They were so different. She recalled Jonathan's face at Lewkenor's Lane. He was not a man to cross lightly, nor was he a man who would treat lightly any dalliance with others by his light o' love. Undoubtedly they were ill-matched, thought Nell wisely, buttoning the matter up neatly.

Lor' but that dress! 'Gawd, I'd do anything for a dress like that,' she thought. Then she remembered the elegance and vivacity of the fashionable Mistress Pepys. Fans, masks, muffs, gowns, gloves, and shoes flowed past her mind in a glorious stream. Then she went over to the mirror and looked at herself, clad in a shabby homespun dress spotted with grease, her hair bundled up under an old mob-cap. She made up her mind to accept Madam Ross's offer to serve drinks to the gentlemen.

'After all,' she said to herself, 'I needn't do more, if I don't want.'

A loud knocking below awoke her out of her reverie. Nell swung her feet off the bed, and went down to open the door. When she lifted the latch she stepped back in surprise. It was Jonathan. The aloofness had entirely disappeared – submerged by his passion. His face was white, his mouth a hard tight line as he looked down at Nell.

'Where is she?' he asked softly, yet with a note of such menace that Nell stepped back in alarm.

'Who . . . who do you mean?'

'Don't trifle with me, girl, you know who I mean!' His voice was an ugly rasp, as firmly moving her aside he stepped into the dingy room. Mrs Gwynne roused herself from the palliasse in the corner. 'What – what d'ye want?' she murmured stupidly. 'Breakin' in – I'll 'ave the Constable on ye –.' After a brief glance at her lolling form he ignored her, and turned, climbing swiftly up the stairs. Nell waited in trepidation as she heard rustlings and the sound of things moving in the bed-chamber, and then he appeared again and came slowly down the steps.

'So. The bird has flown, I perceive. Faithless, common, two-faced whore!'

He swore long and volubly. Nell's mother stared at him open-eyed.

'Call the Constable, Nelly –.'

'Shut up, Mam,' said Nell briefly.

He walked up and down like a caged tiger, his mouth an ugly sneer, his thin face twisted in anger. Nell looked at him and felt an intense sympathy. This curious, ranting figure – what had he to do with such as Rose? And yet, as she looked at the fires smouldering in his eyes, she knew and understood the tragedy of it, with a childlike wisdom. To Rose it was a flirtation, nothing more. Nell had learnt that lust was a hard horse for a man to ride and control; she remembered the savagery of Sarah's lover with wonderment.

She went up to Jonathan and placed her hand on his black sleeve.

'I am sorry . . . ' she stammered, 'so . . . very . . . *sorry*,' feeling the sense of inadequacy even as she uttered the words. 'She isn't worth it, you know. Though Gawd knows she's my sister when all's said and done. . . . '

Jonathan turned and, seeing two great eyes of clear hazel looking up at him pleadingly, the fire died out of his expression.

'I beg pardon, my child, for having treated you so roughly. I fear my feelings overcame me.' He seemed ill at ease and embarrassed.

Nell smiled. 'Don't fret, my lord, I beg you. You'd be surprised at the people who burst in unexpected in this district, especially when the hour's late and they've had a tankard or two. The Leathern Bottle is just down the alleyway, you know.'

She spoke lightly in an effort to relieve the tension in the atmosphere, but already was thinking ahead to the next problem. 'I have to go now to Madam Ross's for . . . for . . . the evening.'

'Might I bear you company for some part of the way?' he said stiffly, his face an austere mask.

Nell flung her cloak round her shoulders and opened the rickety door.

'My pleasure, sir.'

Silently they walked along. Nell did not dare to speak but walked quickly, her cloak wrapped tight about her. Striding along beside her, the tall figure looked down at the cobbles and was grimly quiet. Nell sought to make amends.

'She's not so bad you know – my sister, I mean. It's just she's headstrong . . . likes a good time, you see. There's no harm in her really . . . she don't understand. She's never had much of a life before and she's making up for lost time, if you see what I mean.'

Jonathan's mouth went hard in anger and his hands, as Nell noticed, clenched into his cloak. She went on, feeling she was treading on very thin ice.

'But she's got 'er good points. 'S'death, when I think of what life would have been like without her! You've seen Ma, you know what she's like – well, don't think this is anything new. 'Oons, she's been a drunken old sot since Gawd knew when. I can still remember Rose getting up in the morning while 'twas still dark to go and skivvy at the Leathern Bottle to keep us alive. She wasn't ever a countess, but she stuck enough bread down me to keep me going till now.'

She looked up from her chattering to see a pair of shrewd eyes regarding her with interest. 'You love your sister, child?'

The girl looked down, embarrassed. 'Lor', I don't know. She's a right bitch when she's in a mood. I've known 'er come 'ome late and fling me near through the wall, 'cos I've not kept 'er supper 'ot for 'er. She can scream for an hour or more and I've seen her take a belt to Ma and get 'er moving, which is more than anyone else can say. Gawd, she can make 'erself felt!' She grimaced. 'But . . . as I said . . . she's got 'er good points.'

The thin mouth smiled wryly. 'Tell me where's she gone

tonight ?' The tone was quiet and persuasive. 'I want to know, child. Tell me.'

Nell paused. 'And what if I did ?' she asked softly.

He smiled a little. 'You needn't worry, sweetheart. I have no mind to slit gizzards tonight.' He sighed heavily. 'In truth, my anger's gone.'

'She's at Mulberry Gardens,' she said. I think 'twas a masque she went for, but I couldn't swear to't.' She eyed him narrowly.

'Ah, Killigrew's *Comus* . . .,' he said to himself. Then his voice became abrupt. 'Have you ever heard of a Jack Cassells, Nell ?'

There was a swift indrawn breath, and the girl's face crimsoned. So that was who the mysterious stranger was. 'D'you mean . . . ?' she faltered.

'Yes, Tyburn Jack, my dear; otherwise known as John Cassells, lately captain in his deceased Majesty's regiment, under the Earl of Rochester. Thrice escaped the gallows from Newgate, and last seen, if my sources are correct, in Madam Ross's, trying to sell his ill-gotten gains a couple of nights back.'

'You knew him – before, sir ?'

Jonathan's face grew austere again. 'I knew him . . . once. A long time ago I knew John Cassells. By God, I have reason not to forget him. I think,' he said slowly, 'he is the nearest thing to a rat I have ever, in my experience, met. There are many heads, aye, and some hearts, to lay at his door. . . . '

Nell hesitated, but decided to speak. 'Rose mentioned someone called Jack, sir. She was trying on a gown, you see, and she said that it was a present from someone called Jack. That's all. Just Jack. Gawd, what's she got 'erself into now ?'

Jonathan's eyes glittered. 'So . . .,' he said softly. 'Then you've bitten off more than you can chew this time, my lady.'

Nell pulled at his cloak. 'Sir, sir, what do you mean ? Is my sister in danger ? What mean you, sir ?'

He looked down at Nell and she saw in his face a look of cold, knowing malice. 'I don't care about your sister,' he said

64

levelly, 'but I suggest you tell her, child. Unless she says goodbye to John Cassells, this time she will rue the day she realized she was a woman.'

'Pink me sir, but you're an arrant rogue, I declare.' Nell's hand took a thin chin in her grip as she turned a nervous clerk's face up to hers and then planted a kiss upon the quivering mouth.

''Struth gentlemen, he fair pulsates with passion,' she told the assembled company, and made as if to rearrange her skirts that lay untouched about her ankles. There was a rumble of laughter around the smoky tavern and the girl smiled, showing small, even, pearly, teeth.

'I vow he tried to take me here on the table –.' she said loudly, fanning herself briskly with a lace kerchief.

'Madame, Mistress, I swear . . . I didn't. . . . '

'Ah,' she wagged a knowing finger at him, as his face grew steadily redder. 'Virtue's atop, but what goes on under the table, eh, saucy lad?' She picked up his ale before he could stop her and drank it to the dregs.

'Mistress, I think you forget yourself,' he said stiffly, endeavouring to drown the laughter all around him.

She leant towards him as if to kiss his ear, and hissed wickedly at him in a shrill undertone. 'Mayhap if you buy me a drink, and yourself a new one, I could find a new friend to play with, sobersides. . . . ' His eyes blinked. 'I . . . I . . .,' he muttered hoarsely.

A pair of hands pulled at his neck-cloth, while she screamed, 'What, when can we go upstairs, did you say? I'll have you know I'm not a jill-flirt, sir. Indeed! The idea . . . !'

Laughter again echoed around the tavern. The young clerk re-knotted his neck-cloth hastily. 'Two . . two . . . of Bide's ale there!' he shouted quickly at the nearest serving-maid. Then he caught Nell's mouth forming a silent word. 'Rhenish . . . er, to be sure . . . Rhenish!' he squeaked with a note of desperation in his voice.

The girl took a seat, and they both sat and drank the wine

while the attention drifted from them to other things. The clerk sipped nervously, staring straight at the glass as the cheap wine went down his throat. Nell downed hers fast – in her case it was only coloured water, doctored to look like wine; but the customer never knew that, when paying the price of Ma Ross's hospitality.

She stood up and blew him a kiss. 'Farewell my love . . .,' she cooed. The clerk made no answer, but his mouth tightened as he watched his fair tormentor walk briskly over to the door by the counter and go through, slamming it behind her.

As she leant against the door, breathing heavily, Nell's eyes sparkled with delight at the new game that was hers. She was in the dirty kitchen at the back of the building, now deserted by Mit, the small maid who drudged in there all day. Going over to the draining-board by the rusty copper, she picked up a pan newly scoured with sand, and looked, mesmerized, at her reflection. It was that of a transformed being.

Nell remembered the glorious afternoon that had been hers, after she had told Madam Ross the welcome news. First there had been the glorious bath in real hot water, brought upstairs in buckets to a huge tub in one of the chambers, with real body perfume such as, Sarah told her, Barbara Palmer herself used. Then, amidst a bustle of maids and with the help of the redoubtable Ma Ross herself, came the trying on of a gown from among the many of all sizes that jostled in a wardrobe kept by the old harridan for the fitting out of her protegées. Lemon yellow, and simple, it admirably set off Nell's fair skin and her auburn hair, that, with the aid of curling tongs, Ma Ross had twirled up and set high on her head, caught by a matching satin ribbon. It was styled *à la bergère*, piled in a coil at the back, and pushed out at the sides by the use of several dexterously placed combs to coax delicate curls to fall parallel with her face, framing it and setting it off to a fault.

As she gazed at the face of the burnished pan, she saw staring back at her, not the maid of earlier days, but a young woman of at least three years older than her true age. She looked no longer a scruffy girl from the backstreets, but a lady of fashion; in such a gown, her body seemed to invite attention as it had never done. Ma Ross certainly knew her job well – there was just enough subtle grooming, and not too much. She still looked fresh and young – purer, Ma Ross had noticed, than many of the painted harpies around her. And though the finery would have to be returned at the end of the evening, the spell was upon the girl as she stood in the kitchen, breathless at the transformation.

As they had laughingly decked her with the uniform of a new trade, Nell had been initiated into the art of whoring. The girls around her, who before had ignored a small servant wench in a mob-cap as they had disdained the company of the kitchen-maid, now took her to their hearts as one of themselves. They spent over an hour in the dressing of her; pulling the bodice down at the front, hitching it up at the back, adding ribbons, flowers and various tawdries on finger and wrist and in the hair. Nell was prodded and pulled till she knew not whether she stood on her head or her feet, as they giggled and commented, turning her this way and that.

The small girl regarded them with wide open eyes, seeing extravagantly rouged faces, with luscious lips pouting red, and kohl-rimmed eyes giving a dusky appearance to bewitching features; and, as they spoke to her, she came to know them as people and not as painted dolls.

There was Beatrice, a tall, imposing girl with long, straight, black hair and a smile a trifle wide for true beauty. She seemed quite composed as she told Nell matter-of-factly that her mother, father and two brothers, had been butchered during the war by Cromwell's soldiers after the famous capture of Basing House, one of the last strongholds for the King. Her father had been an ostler, and the unruly, drunken, soldiers had accused him of helping the malignant cause and flogged him to death with his own stirrup-leathers – and then raped his wife before putting her to the sword. Beatrice had hidden, quivering, in the stables, behind some bales of straw, where she remained undetected, and only came out when night fell and the soldiers had finished their looting. She never found the bodies of her family. The whole place was littered with corpses, and the stables smashed up beyond repair. She had walked and begged her way to London where she had soon drifted into the trade in which Nell now saw her employed. But she shrugged and told the girl that Ma Ross paid well and that life was too short to worry about one's misfortunes.

Martha, a short, plump wench, had been married, but her husband, a waterman, had died of the Thames Plague two years before – and Martha, also, had drifted into the echelons of Lewkenor's Lane. A quiet, refined girl named Edith seemed sadly out of place amidst these carefree young girls; she was pale and appeared to be nervous. She was whitely pretty but seldom wore much make-up. She hardly spoke, and sat staring out of the window as they crowded round, but Beatrice told Nell in an undertone that Edith's father had been a Quaker minister who had been kicked to death by a troop of Ironside cavalry; in Worcester, she thought it was, after the young Charles the Second had lost his first battle there. Cromwell's promised religious toleration did not include Quakers, who were baited and assaulted at will by self-righteous Puritan soldiers and citizens.

' – And I am the only willing whore here,' shouted Sarah gaily, twirling a pair of stockings above her head and arching her shoulder to the mirror, while she gazed at her reflection. 'And pleased to be here, and so I promise you. My family is not dead – more's the pity! My father is one of those gloomy Presbyters – my grandam sailed to the Americas thirty odd years ago. And lucky was England to see the back of the old misery, I make no doubt, judging by my *father*.

'No, I left home because I wanted to, and they were as glad to see me go. So, I am a whore – and happy to be one!'

As Nell had waited for the customers to arrive, she fingered the large, vulgar patch stuck firmly to one white temple; like the mark of Cain, it was the symbol used to denote whoredom in London. She felt her stomach flutter, for she faced the unknown.

The evening had been enjoyable so far. She had been pleased

at the attention paid her and she seemed too young for any outrage to happen. She had already won a customer or two to help fill Ma Ross's till; she was doing her job well, and it had been easy to exchange comments with huge, good-natured soldiers, and shy young citizens, too embarrassed to reply. She found she had the gift of repartee; love philtres were not necessary to arouse the men as they looked at her, she saw with a new thrill. The only fly in the ointment was White Jonathan.

They had become increasingly friendly since that dark night when Jonathan had discovered he had been cuckolded. He came frequently to Ma Ross's, and always his eyes would search for a small, grubby figure with a snub nose and freckles. And he would take her into the corner, where they would talk about nothing in low voices and laugh together.

Ma Ross was surprised. 'I see White Jonathan's taken up child-care,' she told Sarah acidly. But she never said it to his face. Jonathan seemed to have a strange relationship with the girl. He treated her with indulgence, bringing her small sweet-meats and listening to her chatter with the amusement of a fond parent. But when he looked at her, his eyes seemed to cloud with something deeper. He looked worried as he listened to her. One night he said, 'You are so like your sister, Nell, and so unlike her. It is passing strange, for though you are sisters, you are the one with a vastly more interesting character, despite your years.'

And she had been glad, knowing he preferred her to Rose, beautiful though she be.

She mimicked the gentlemen who came in, and he would smile slightly when she imitated the exaggerated compliments of the elderly gallants or the clumsy attempts at love-making by soldiers whose hands were more used to clutching a pike. And when Ma Ross was out, she would waddle towards him, leering gently, as she inquired, 'More Rhenish, sir, or shall we go upstairs?'

His mask seemed to drop when he was with her, for she was a child against whom he need not guard himself.

He never inquired about Rose, and Nell was relieved, for she knew the affair with Tyburn Jack was still going on. Nell had not met John Cassells; neither had her mother. Rose would dress up fine in one of many gorgeous dresses she had been given by her lover, and sally forth to the night-life of London, usually not returning until the early hours. The most she had seen of Rose's new *cher ami* had been one dark night when she had awoken to hear voices in the street outside, and had peered out of the tiny casement under the eaves. Looking down, she saw her sister crushed in embrace with a dark figure in a plumed hat which tickled Rose's cheek. Nell had heard her giggling. He had released her finally, and as she stepped back into the house he had looked up at the night-sky. For a second, Nell had seen a coarse-featured face, with a bar of moustache running across it, and then it had gone and she had sped back to bed, feigning sleep when Rose crept up the creaking stair.

Jonathan had never seen Rose since he had found out her infidelity, and Nell had never dared mention him to her sister, for Rose was obviously embroiled in a passionate affair, throwing caution to the winds. Certainly Cassells seemed to treat her well; her purse jangled with golden coins which she spent at a furious rate. Rose's low bedchamber was crammed with fans, masks, fur-lined cloaks and expensive perfumes. Even the family had benefited, and Nell's stomach felt fuller than it had for an age. Rose would come home and tell Nell of the places she had been and the people she had met. Once she had spent an evening with the Duke of Buckingham and Sir Charles Sedley, and Nell had been as thrilled as Rose, when told of the evening and the elegant entertainment.

Now Nell seemed to be following in the same tradition.

Jonathan was already there when she came down the stairs, watching the first customers arrive, in fear and excitement. Carelessly, she had danced down the steps and arrived at the foot all in a rush, flushing with anticipation. A tall figure leaning against the counter had turned idly, tankard in hand, to see who it was. For an instant their eyes met – Jonathan gazing at her coolly, Nell pink with embarrassment. His brows went up, and he looked her up and down from the crown of her burnished, brushed head to the toes of her newly beaded pattens. Nell had felt as if she were being stripped naked. Then his mouth twisted in a sardonic smile, as he summed her up in a phrase.

'Like mother, like daughter, like sister, I perceive, Mistress Gwynne.'

She had gone white and all her brightness evaporated as she looked at him numbly, feeling as though he had slapped her across the face.

'I . . . I . . .,' she began.

'Pray don't worry, my dear! Dressed so modishly, you doubtless think that the opinions of such as myself are hardly worth consideration.'

'That depends,' replied Nell, with eyes hard with anger, 'on your own respect for your opinions, sir.'

He shrugged, and walked away across the tavern, where he sat in a corner taking no further interest in her at all.

That, thought Nell, had been the worst moment of all. She peered at her reflection, laying an uneasy hand on her lightly rouged cheek. Did she look over-dressed, cheap and unclean? Was she at this moment . . . a whore? A pretty girl in the rising blush of youth gazed back worriedly from the pan's mirrored reflection. But in the scared eyes that stared at her, there lay a gleam of recklessness, a desire to taste the unknown. All of a sudden Nell gave a short laugh, and put the pan down as if satisfied.

' 'Od's Death, mayhap yon fine gentleman might prefer me virtuous, but I'll be hanged if I'll go back to skivvying. I warrant virtue comes at a lower price.' Yet she felt sad as she defiantly said the words.

From beyond the door, amidst the babble of voices and clinking of glasses, rose a shrill, harsh cry that Nell knew well.

' 'Faith, where's the wench? Nell . . . Nell . . . !'

Hastily the girl patted her curls into place and shot through the door to her mistress's command. She made her way through

71

the press to where Ma Ross stood at the counter, surrounded by a motley bevy of aged roués. Several old gentlemen ogled the girl and smiled, showing broken and blackened teeth, and one asked Madam Ross for the name of this new bird in the dovecote with a nudge. She felt her colour rise as she curtseyed in front of her mistress.

'Where've you been? No, don't tell me, there isn't time – I've got a job for you.' She pointed across the tavern to where a figure in pink velvet sat unconcernedly drinking brandy and eyeing the voluptuous Sarah at the next table.

'That, sweetheart, is Sir Cyril Dimchurch. He has just arrived, and, by the Mass, he's stopping now he's come. His purse fair bursts with gold – he doesn't know what to do with it, and he's got,' she leered at Nell, 'a roving eye.'

'Sarah's going up to the chambers soon, from the look of things, so go and entertain the old sot, and pour some more wine down 'im afore 'e goes. 'Twill be a test for you, sweetheart, to see how you're doing.'

Clutching a brandy bottle, Nell made her way across the musty chamber to the gentleman sprawling at a table. As she came towards him, he looked up; and as he saw her, a smile creased his powdered cheeks. He was a thin, weedy gentleman, who would, Nell thought in distaste, never see forty again. Bags under his hooded eyes, and lines scouring his thin face, betokened a life of dissipation as yet unsatisfied. He waved a hand at Nell and fluttered his lace handkerchief, and she caught a whiff of sickly perfume.

'A plum,' he murmured, 'a peach . . . dropped from heaven to such an unworthy mortal beneath. To what do I owe such a pleasure?' He raised a spyglass and gazed at her bosom, sighing gently.

She curtseyed unsteadily. 'The compliments of Madam Ross, sir, and would you care for another brandy?'

'So kind, so . . . thoughtful,' the handkerchief waved languidly, 'do *you* pour me out a glass, child and . . . one for yourself, sweeting. Your cheeks are burning with thirst, I swear.'

Nell swallowed hard and poured out two glasses of brandy. Of all the nerve! she thought in indignation. Burning with thirst indeed! She had never heard such nonsense!

He sat and watched her pour out the glasses of brandy, then he picked up a glass and sipped it, looking at Nell standing uncomfortably in front of him. He patted his lap invitingly.

'Come,' he said simply.

Her heart beating faster, Nell picked up her glass of brandy and perched gingerly on two rather bony velvet-covered knees. The first nervous gulp of brandy set her coughing and spluttering. It burnt her throat and made her eyes run. He laughed good-naturedly.

'Don't spill it on me breeches, sweetheart, or I am undone. They come early from the tailors just this morning.'

A hand crept around her waist, and she felt herself being drawn firmly right on to his lap while an arm held her rigidly tight. She tried to still a rising tide of panic and glanced swiftly over to the counter; but Ma Ross, after seeing in satisfaction how things were going, had turned back to her elderly admirers. She didn't like this man with the soft voice and powdered cheeks, she didn't like the look he cast at her from under hooded lids – and she didn't like being held so she couldn't move.

He kissed her on the neck, as he sighed languidly, 'So fresh . . . young . . . so firm, and as yet . . . untasted.'

Nell laughed nervously. 'I declare, sir, you are a bold gentleman . . . . 'Ods my life, I swear I have never met such a prodigal rogue.' She tittered, assuming nonchalance.

He laughed, but unlike the clerk seemed completely unaffected by such rough badinage. He pulled her to him and began to kiss her, on the neck, on the shoulders; and finally, taking her chin in his other hand, he held her face and kissed her full on the lips. Nell felt sick. She did not know how to deal with the situation. She had never met such an accomplished gentleman before, of such obvious evil intent – and could not think how to deflect him.

His smile was mirthless as a hand crept up to paw a rising

breast. 'No more wit, my sweeting; enough of talk! Let me pluck those fruits that hang before me.' He began to pull her dress off her shoulder. Wildly, she sought to replace it and struggled to get from his grasp.

'Indeed, sir, I am stayed for,' she gasped, trying to get off his knee. 'I am not at leisure to stay. . . .'

'Why so shy, my pretty, so coy . . . ?'

Then his hand began to unlace her bodice. She struggled frantically to get free, but all around her people were drinking, immersed in their own affairs – and their own women. No one seemed to notice her, and, she thought, if they did it would make no difference. They had seen such things often enough before.

Sir Cyril was beginning to get angry at her reluctance. 'Enough of games, sweetheart,' he whispered breathlessly, as he held her close and breathed sour breath into her face. 'There is . . . a time . . . when all pretence must . . . cease.'

She put her hands out to stop him, but his face, with eyes malevolently glowing, came closer, ever closer.

'I believe the young lady has had enough of your charming company, Dimchurch,' said a soft voice.

Loosening his grasp, the nobleman turned and looked up at Jonathan. Nell took her chance and scrambled off his lap. He did not look at Nell for a second. She stood, white and shaken, as the two men gazed at each other like two cats ready to spring. Sir Cyril got up carelessly. He was tall and loose-limbed, bigger in fact than he had appeared sitting down. Gradually the tavern's customers became aware that something was wrong and turned to watch them.

White Jonathan bowed stiffly. 'At your service, sir.'

Sir Cyril stared at him, pale with anger.

'And who, may I ask,' he purred gently, 'are you, young sir ?'

Jonathan smiled. 'One who has a care for the young, sir, nothing more. Doubtless they need protection sometimes ?'

'Protection sir ? I fail to understand you,' Sir Cyril was quiet and deadly.

Jonathan met his icy glance. 'I think you do, sir, but let it pass. Mayhap the brain is tired, as one gets older. Do not distress yourself, I beg. I have also a care for those with . . . grey hairs and palsy. . . .'

Sir Cyril's eyes blazed and he laid a hand on his sword hilt. Jonathan watched his action calmly and finished without haste. 'One must not over-tire oneself when advancing years are upon one, Sir Cyril.'

Madam Ross bustled over to the scene. 'Gentlemen, gentlemen, I beg . . . !'

They both ignored her. Sir Cyril walked straight up to Jonathan and waved a handkerchief under his nose.

'I would,' he said thickly, his voice quivering with passion, 'call you out for such words, sir. But,' his nostrils pinched in distaste, 'I only fight with . . . gentlemen.'

There was a flush of wrath in Jonathan's face. The back of his hand swung round at a vicious speed and whipped straight across Sir Cyril's jaw. He dropped where he stood.

Behind him Edith screamed and dropped her wineglass, wine dripping down her gown.

Muttering fiercely, Ma Ross knelt down and helped the prone form to a sitting position. A tooth dropped to the floor as Sir Cyril dabbed at his mouth, running with a slight trickle of hot, sticky blood. He looked up at Jonathan, who regarded him coolly, and tried to straighten his periwig.

'You will regret that, sir!' His voice rose to a scream of hysterical anger. 'You will regret that you were ever born, that you dared to lay hands on me, you gutter-bred scum.'

Jonathan's gaze was frosty. He sneered as he straightened his cuff.

'I doubt it, sir.'

He took Nell firmly by one arm, and ignoring Ma Ross's curses, strode out of the chamber.

As they walked back along the deserted streets to the Coal Yard, Nell glanced sidelong at her companion, who had flung his cloak around her but had since said not a word.

She laid a tentative hand on his sleeve. 'I . . . I'm sorry, sir,' she murmured.

'There is nothing to be sorry for, mistress,' he replied tersely. 'Pray hurry along or you will catch an ague in this night air, I doubt not.'

All of a sudden, all reserve went and Nell flung herself into his surprised arms, sobbing unrestrainedly.

'It was horrible,' she wept, 'he wouldn't let me go and he was pawing me, feeling me like a lump of meat . . . I . . . I . . . couldn't get away, or stop him, or . . . or . . . anything.'

His arms, at first rigid, came down around her, soothing her like a baby. He waited until her sobbing had stopped and then, as she sniffed and hiccoughed into her handkerchief, put his hands on her shoulders and drew her to face him. His gaze was stern but understanding.

'Nelly, you silly child, couldn't you see this was bound to happen? When you don the uniform of a whore, you become a whore, did you not realize? Men like Sir Cyril would think you welcomed, and were paid for, such advances as he has just made.'

She was quiet.

'You can't accept a job and then ignore its responsibilities, child. Yes, I know you felt like a lady dressed up fine as a peacock, but it won't do, Nell. You'll see your beauty disappear, slowly but inevitably, tightening and hardening with greed; your eyes gleaming for money, not love; your face wrinkled and old, sapped with dissipation. Do you want to end up behind a cart's tail, being flogged in London's streets? Do you want to join those filthy, painted whores in Fleet Alley, leering at every passer-by and thrusting a wrinkled, rouged breast under everyone's eye? Aye, I know 'tis disgusting, sweetheart, but you've got to know.'

Tears brimmed in her eyes, staring at him in shock. He paused and sighed.

'What you need, child, is someone to look after you till you can look after yourself. I only wish I could do it myself.'

She gasped breathlessly. 'Sir . . . could you . . . look after me?'

He shook his head almost with violence. 'No! For one thing you are too young, and for another. . . . Well, sweetheart, I may

76

as well be frank. Sir Cyril Dimchurch is a powerful man, with friends in high places. Albemarle is a personal crony of his. Those were no idle threats back there; before a couple of days are out, the Constable will be after me with a warrant of arrest. I must leave – go away – now.'

'Where will you go?'

'France,' he answered crisply. 'There are still some friends in the Palais Royal who remember my name and can extend a helping hand . . . for a time at least.'

She clutched his arm in desperation. 'But how long will you go for?'

'As long as Sir Cyril's memory still rankles or London's constables remember me. I have no desire to taste the inside of Newgate prison.'

'But it's my fault . . . all my fault . . .'.

He looked at her seriously. 'Nay, don't talk nonsense, child! How were you to know such things? It is hoped, however, that you know better now.'

She flushed. 'I do, sir, believe me, but what can I do now? Ma Ross wants me to tout for 'er and the only alternative is skivvying again.'

'I will have a word with Madam Ross, child. I think you will find you have no further trouble.'

'But . . . but . . . how can you be sure she will listen, sir?'

He smiled in the dark. 'She will listen,' he said, 'or 'twill be the worse for her.'

Nell looked at him with a new respect. They turned down Drury Lane and into the Coal Yard. As they stopped at the door, Jonathan looked up at Rose's window, which was candle-lit, and a grim smile flickered over his features. though his manner was kind as he took his cloak from Nell's shoulders.

He bowed over her hand. 'Adieu, Mistress Gwynne.'

He pressed her hand and she returned the clasp fiercely.

'Goodbye, sir,' she muttered huskily. He vanished into the dark.

CHAPTER V

What state of life can be so blest
As Love that warms a Lover's breast?
Dryden

King Charles the Second was bored. He sat in his closet, alone in the candlelight, playing idly with a quill pen.

Outside, the Thames flowed sluggishly, lights flickering from the dark river as the full moon caught the flow running past the moorings by the backstairs. It was late, but he had only just said good-bye wearily to the pressing, chattering mass of courtiers, and his own brother of York, who had thronged around him for the whole evening.

At last he could rest. Here in this closet, with its thick carpet, and books lining the walls, he could discard his kingship and relax. No one was allowed in here; only he and his page of the backstairs had a key, and not even his brother had seen the inside of the sanctum that was littered with his most private things. Models of ships, his passion, stood on bookcases; and a large, exquisitely detailed facsimile of his pride and joy, the *Royal Charles*, stood on his desk. On the walls hung his treasures, the paintings of Holbein and Titian, for Charles, like his father, was a patron of the arts. At intervals, on cabinets and tables and on the mantel, stood the King's collection of priceless porcelain and crystal, vases and glassware in careless array.

In the quiet room could be heard the murmured tick of the several delicate clocks and watches which Charles never forgot to wind, and of which he was very proud. In the corner was a jumble of scientific equipment. Glass tubes, bowls, and orbs, lay in a heap by a magnificent lodestone, near to a small collection of phials and bottles containing the medicaments Charles loved to experiment with, jostling for space on a plain and dusty table. The King was contemplating, not for the first time, the wilfulness of women.

He had just had another tiresome quarrel with Barbara, known to the rest of the Court and to the world as the Countess of Castlemaine. The King smiled slightly as he remembered the screaming, magnificent creature who had raged before him, stamping her foot in fury. Barbara, he decided, was one of those few women whose beauty increased in anger and did not diminish. With her head tossed back, her eyes flashing, and her glistening hair in a cloud about her as her bosom rose and fell uncontrollably, the King thought her at her most attractive.

Another quarrel; how many had there been since she had become his mistress, and his whole life, two years before? He could not remember. There had been so many and for such silly reasons. She was, she had told the King, *enceinte* by him; and as she carried his child, she thought it only right that she should be rewarded. Rewarded! Charles laughed softly as he remembered all that the rapacious lady had screwed out of him – jewels, carriages, money; her apartment in the Palace was finer than the King's. Her huge debts he paid regularly, in order to enjoy that lady who never failed to excite him sexually, but whom he found so troublesome in other ways.

This time she had demanded a dukedom. In vain he had pointed out that such a thing was impossible, that when her cuckold of a husband had been made an earl at the end of the previous year, so that *she* might be a countess, there had been such a to-do in the Commons that he had only achieved it by getting the title passed in the Irish Peerage.

Yet now she wanted to be a duchess. She would be, she reminded him, the mother of his child. Besides, she needed a recompense for all the trouble of childbirth that *he*, she had screamed, had caused her. He had waited in vain for the tirade to cease, and then he had left her, before the anger dissolved into the tears he hated so much and could not resist.

Why, he wondered, could not life be easy?

The King did not usually give way to malaise either of the mind or the body. Of all the Court, he, its master, stood the rigours of the life best. He alone, after carousing all night with his brother and a crowd of friends would be up at dawn, striding through St James's Park so that his courtiers panted to keep up with him.

He knew why he was depressed. Here, in the midst of the bright and glittering Court, he was, he knew, alone. And, to make matters worse, he could never indulge his dyspepsia privately, always he had to live in public, always he had to smile. Even his meals were taken in public, before virtually anyone who wished to stand and gaze in the Palace Banqueting Hall at the King eating like any other mortal.

The very food was always cold by the time it reached him. Life as a king, he decided, was not all a bed of roses, but then he had never imagined it would be, not even when he rode into his hysterical capital eighteen months before.

Any visions of a life of ease and plenty had been quickly knocked out of Charles by a childhood of civil war, and a life of early kingship spent in chilly surroundings in Europe amongst people with whom little money usually meant a poor welcome. Now he was king, lord of all he surveyed. That, in theory, was the case. But now the honeymoon was over, he and his people were settling down in an uneasy partnership. It was not, as he knew it could never be, an easy matter. His followers had thought when they entered London that it would be as if the Civil War had never been, that they could reclaim their lands and their fortunes, and live as if it were still 1640. Charles knew better. Twenty years and a great deal of water had flowed under London Bridge since then.

Ever since he had arrived, he had been besieged by petitioners demanding restitution of lands, pleading for Court office or claiming old appointments their family had held under the late King. One woman even claimed damages because her son had been bitten by Charles the First's spaniel at Oxford twenty years before.

Charles had done his best and had made sure that the adherents who had shared exile with him were not forgotten, but he could not satisfy all. The landed estates had often changed hands several times and could not be recovered, the Court appointment was often already filled. Charles came to dread the pathetic crowd of threadbare supplicants whom he saw when the velvet curtains parted and the gilded doors opened for him to pass through, and he hated even more the fact that he could so often do nothing for them.

To ignore these people, who had given their all to his father, hurt him deeply, and made him more coldly angry still with such harpies as Barbara Castlemaine. He was angry, too, with those extremists who demanded a blood-bath as the symbol of the restitution of the monarchy. Charles was not vindictive, and had not wanted his reign to begin in such a way. He was agreeable that his father's murderers should be punished; but for the rest he wished for pardon, for a reign under which life should again be easy. Restraining the violent Parliament, so anxious to welcome him with sacrificial glee, had been a hard business. Sighing, Charles wondered again why people had to make life so troublesome.

State duties seemed to ensnare him, and he had a momentary vision of his Chancellor, now created Earl of Clarendon, standing reprovingly before him. Clarendon meant well, but he was so pompous, so overbearing. He could, and did, antagonize people, and it was often left to the King to smooth down the ruffled feathers and restore tranquillity in Whitehall. To be a king was a tiring and thankless task. One received in reward little but demands for payment and a bunch of syco-phantic friends, most of whom Charles loathed. Charles knew what he wanted – the virile Stuart King wanted a wife.

It was, he realized, expected of him that he should marry and beget heirs, and also that an advantageous alliance might be made for England through the match. But Charles hoped for something more. His memory ran back over the women in his life – and there had been many. He saw again the small, dark Lucy Walter whom he had seduced at the age of eighteen, and whose son he had now received at Court; he thought again of the voluptuous Hortense Mancini, marriage with whom had been refused during his exile, as a match with a beggar, how-ever royal, was beneath her.

6

And he thought of his sister, Henriette Anne, Minette, who had married the Duc d'Orléans, and who had left him to go back to France. She was, he knew and she knew, the person he loved most in all the world. He looked at her miniature which always lay open on the desk before him. But then his thoughts returned to Barbara.

While she never failed to rouse him, she never failed to disgust him at the same time. Charles was a shrewd judge of character, and he had no illusions about Barbara. She was calculating, thoughtless of all but her own comfort, and sometimes downright cruel. She was so vulgar, thought the King in sudden anger, as he remembered her harsh voice screaming at him earlier. Bright, vivacious, and sparkling, she looked every inch a fine lady, but when roused or crossed her veneer was scratched, and she cursed and swore like any fishwife of London's backstreets. Charles was beginning to find Barbara a trial and a brake on his enjoyment of life.

She was just a body, he supposed dispassionately; he knew that he did not love her, but would still probably want her, desire her, for years, despite himself.

Minette was different. He adored her passionately, protectively, with all the force of which he was capable. If anyone should ever hurt Minette. . . .

Every night he wrote to her, and, she had told him, he was her main reason for living. But his love for her was fraternal, smooth and steady, not heightened by those excitements of the flesh which life demanded. He seemed either to love or to lust, never both.

'Mayhap a wife will give me that intoxicating, elusive blend,' he said aloud in the quiet room, above the ticking of the clocks. But he knew that the need was great. In this world made up of hard work for the State, and the spite and intrigues of a multitude of self-seeking people cloistered up in a court of envy, life was in danger of becoming *ennuyant* – a thing Charles abhorred. He wanted to love deeply with every fibre of his being, to submerge himself in someone who could give him everything that would make life have a meaning which as yet he knew it did not possess, and perhaps never would.

He shook one locket from under his shirt and placed it with another lying on the desk. Side by side, Barbara and Minette gazed up at him; Minette petite, looking lovingly at her brother, Barbara frankly sensuous, smiling insolently up at him.

'Ah well,' he sighed, closing them both, 'in truth when the Almighty created women He let loose a curse and a blessing on the world.'

The door was opened, and a small dark figure peeped round it and said, 'The young . . . er . . . lady is here, Sire,' and then retreated, closing the door again.

Charles smiled to himself. It was a girl from the Duke's Theatre whom he had seen that day. Getting up, he strode across the room and went out, locking the door behind him. He stopped on the threshold of his bedchamber to look. A girl, heavily rouged and painted, in a gown so low as to be almost superfluous, smiled across at him. Charles looked appreciatively at the seductive figure with the full breasts straining at their restrictions, and the overtly sensuous look cast back at him while the girl coyly simpered.

' 'Odsbud, Your Majesty, I'm sure I never expected such an honour. I protest I am quite took aback! 'Twas such a surprise when I received your missive. I vow I nearly took faint. . . . '

Charles walked across the bedchamber towards her, deciding that life was not so bad after all. There were advantages in being a king.

PART II

LONDON 1663

CHAPTER I

Your charms in harmless childhood lay,
Like metals in the mine,
Age from no face took more away
Than youth concealed in thine.

But as your charms insensibly
To their perfection pres't
Fond love as unperceived did fly,
And in my bosom rest.

Sir Charles Sedley

'Turnips, buy your turnips here, my masters and ladies all. . . .'
A girl's strong voice rang out amidst the rattling and noise of
the London street. Clustered at the corner of Seething Lane,
a row of four stalls – carts piled high with produce – plied their
trade, each owner seeking to out-bawl his neighbour, so as to
make himself heard above the rattle of the coaches and sedan
chairs jostling across the cobbles, and the shouts of the
'prentices selling their masters' wares, with the reiterated
'Buy, buy, buy!'

But the speaker who had just waved a turnip enthusiastically
over her head, and offered her goods so loudly, was a beautiful
young girl with plentiful auburn hair caught up in a snood
close to her slender neck, which arched now as she lifted her
pretty head to make herself heard. Mistress Nelly Gwynne
had set herself up in business. Hands on her hips, she now
gazed with scornful look at the uninterested citizens trudging
by, and gave the cart a hefty kick.

'Lor', Hobey,' she said over her shoulder to the old man
leaning against the stall, 'don't they fair make you want to spit.
Four hours I've been out here, and for what? Two turnips!'
Her tone was disgusted. 'They crawl by as if they're on their
last legs. 'Oons, I swear they're dead from the neck up, thick-
skulled lot. Devil take them, I say!'

A rat-catcher walking by, with his victims suspended by their tails from the pole over his shoulder, stopped and winked at her, hearing her complaints.

'Exchange trades, sweetheart?' he offered. Nell shuddered and shook her head.

'I just come back from Mistress Cudlip's delivery, Nell; that's two groats at least, you know.' The beggar sounded pleased.

'Two groats?' retorted Nell, in an outraged voice. 'We'll hardly get rich on that, will we? Hardly get a decent meal for that matter. Gawd! Who'd earn a living like this?' She stamped her feet on the cobbles, for the December day was cold. The wind was bitter and cut through the cloak she was wearing, thick as it was.

'When I bought this stall-load of curs'd rubbish I never thought it'd be easy, but 'S'life, I never saw it being so hard to sell them. A pox on these vegetables! What's the matter with these people, don't they ever eat? This stall's soon going to be as rotten as that body of Cromwell's they dug up and hung on the gibbet at Tyburn!'

She looked up at the sky and saw it already turning grey, in readiness for the dusk. She would not sell much more today, she knew. Two weeks she had been at this God-forsaken job and she had hardly sold a thing. Still, she wondered, what else could she have done when she'd been turned away from Madam Ross's. She could hardly live off her savings and there seemed to be no jobs going. Besides, she had thought an open-air life would suit her.

Carts full of produce came in from the country every day, and they usually did a thriving business. London was surrounded by the countryside; it was little distance from the farms into the City, so the fruit was always fresh. All the money went on a stall and some produce to sell as best she might. But they had sold scarce a thing. Now they were living off the remnants of Nell's ever-dwindling savings. She hadn't, she supposed, got the selling knack. Old Hobey's deliveries to regular customers were a help, but they couldn't make ends meet on that.

Then she saw a likely customer coming. He minced along idly, fanning himself gently with a luxuriously feathered hat to drive away the smells of the street, and eyeing the shouting stall-holders with ill-concealed disgust. Then his gaze was taken by the young girl leaning over the stall, piling turnips in a heap. She looked up at him and smiled slightly. The gentleman approached and viewed the goods on the stall. Over plump jowls, he peered at the vegetables.

'The turnip.' He picked one up. 'A homely root, staple diet of horses and er . . . of men. Which only shows to me yet again what little difference, I swear, there is between them. Both so gullible, so easily led.' He sighed.

'Threepence a measure,' said Nell flatly.

'Hmm . . .,' said the gentleman, apparently lost in thought.

Nell watched him icily. She knew what he wanted, just like all the rest of his kind. They came to dally – but they never bought. All they desired lay not in her turnips, but in her, and she knew well what their intentions were. They would try their repartee on her; they might even try bolder tactics.

The day was far advanced; Nell had sold nothing and she was tired and in no mood for such as he.

'Would you care for a regular delivery to your house, sir? It can be arranged –.' She looked at Hobey, who immediately stood up.

'Do you make the deliveries, my dear?'

Nell smiled. 'No,' she said. 'I deal in vegetables sir, not' – she plucked his hand from her sleeve – ' in Cupid's passions.'

The gentleman blinked. 'Ah . . . yes. Quite so, Madam, an admirable view, no doubt. But sometimes to mix a little business with pleasure can be diverting. . . . ' He leant across the stall towards her, his eyes twinkling wickedly, his hand stretching across to paw her breasts.

A hand came out and slapped him hard across the face. He staggered back, purple with rage. The girl stared straight back, unperturbed.

'As I said, sir, I run a vegetable business. You can keep your handling for your bawds, an' I thank you.' She picked up a turnip, and tossed it lightly from hand to hand. 'Take yourself off before I throw a few of these . . . homely roots, I think you called 'em, at your head. If you please, sir.'

Bursts of guffawed laughter echoed around, as the brawny stallholders amused themselves at the gentleman's expense.

'Yon wench has got a fine swing, have you not, sweetheart?' shouted a huge seaman standing by.

'Good enough to take you on, an' you want it,' answered Nell shortly.

The gentleman gave Nell a long, withering look, and as the laughter increased, turned abruptly and walked off in crimson wrath.

Hobey whispered urgently. 'I don't know who that is, Nell, but from his finery you've just hit a very rich cove around the chops. . . . '

Nell snorted in derision. 'Then he may count 'imself honoured. And I'd do it to Old Rowley himself, if he tried it on in a like manner.'

Hobey shook his head wonderingly.

Certainly the child had grown up, he thought as he looked at her, standing hands on hips, looking irately at the disappearing figure of the discomfited gentleman. Nell had thrown off the shackles of childhood for good. She would be fifteen in a twelvemonth, but she already looked a goodly seventeen, and her fine rounded arms, now placed akimbo, could easily repulse any unwelcome attentions, wielding a hand that could give a stinging smack around the face. Those pretty fingers, too, could claw a red furrow down each cheek.

Hobey had seen the looks cast at her by men as she walked down the streets, her shapely thighs moving gently and undulating as she walked. He had heard the indrawn breaths and the soft comments, and, reluctantly, he decided the years had brought a change. He was no longer her protector.

Now an elegant fop stopped in front of the stall and observed her figure appreciatively. Hobey watched her face, but it was not wearing the aggressive expression reserved for those who came to finger her wares, make false proposals and spend not a penny. She was smiling. Faith, thought Hobey, she's fair inviting him.

He was a magnificent figure. Portly and imposing, he stood looking, not at the turnips, but at the girl behind the stall. Nell recognized him with a shock which touched a hidden chord in her memory. It was Mr Pepys.

He was more fashionable, she decided, than when she had seen him last. Now he had thrown off any of the light chains that had hitherto bound him to a Puritan mode of dress he had found repulsive. Before, he had been cautious and subdued – a man with a secret, harbouring hopes the State would deem treason, and, accordingly, sinking his desires beneath the coverings dictated by the times.

Now there was no call for concession. In the splendour of England's re-awakening, Mr Pepys had blossomed like some exotic bloom. He sported one of the new periwigs, imported from France and worn by the most daring gallants, and it was extravagantly curled, and faintly but expensively perfumed. His coat was of brocade so covered with embroidery that Nell could scarce see the stuff beneath. Great skirts, stiffened with whalebone, shimmering with silver thread, stuck stiffly out revealing the gorgeous waistcoat beneath. A large hat, drooping a white ostrich feather on the brim, swept down his back.

With hands nestling amidst ruffles of gold lace edged with black, he fingered one of the turnips as he eyed the girl speculatively. He did not recognize her; Nell saw in an amused moment that he did not remember the time four years before, when he had been so kind to a poor little brat from the gutter at Lewkenor's Lane. She had never forgotten him; not though ten years should pass would she forget him, and she realized that it was since she met him that life had changed. Mr Pepys had brought the fresh breeze of ambition into her existence that day and it had never left her.

She would never forget . . . but he? He did not remember.

Indeed Mr Pepys' mind was firmly fixed in the present as he smiled at the beautiful girl in front of him. She bore little resemblance to a thin, half-starved urchin he had carelessly helped one forgotten day, some years before. He looked at her as though for the first, delightful time. For Samuel Pepys, unlike Nell, had not changed.

'Could I take a couple of measures, sweetheart?' he asked softly.

Nell weighed them out and then piled them into the capacious pocket of Hobey's apron.

'Twill be sixpenn'orth you have had, sir, and we will deliver for you.'

Mr Pepys bowed.

'As I only live in Seething Lane, mistress, your delivery should be short, of which I am glad, seeing your companion's ailment.'

Hobey stared at him balefully and spat noisily on the cobbles. 'Cheesecurd!' he snapped quite audibly.

Nell ignored him. 'Whereabouts, sir?' she asked eagerly.

'At the Navy Office, to the end of the lane, sweeting,' he answered, indicating the smart street behind him. 'I am Clerk of the Acts to His Majesty's Navy.'

The girl bobbed demurely. Her eyes twinkled. My, you have come a long way, Mr Pepys, she thought, seeing his prosperity with satisfaction, and remembering his past kindness. She looked him up and down with pleasure, knowing he would be happy to have achieved so much – and that merely to dress as he did must be a source of the greatest satisfaction to the aspiring macaroni who must always have been latent in him.

'As 'tis only a short step, mistress, would *you* care to bring them? I am sure in such cold weather you could imbibe a hot posset to your certain advantage.' He looked straight at Nell's full breasts, not completely hidden by the folds of the cloak draped around her shoulders. 'Or perhaps a glass of mum?'

She curtseyed.

'No, an' I thank you sir. . . . '

His face fell.

'But perhaps another time . . . as my stall remains here for the present . . . ?'

Mr Pepys' face lit up.

'Certainly, mistress, my word on't. I make no doubt but that your turnips are the choicest in London.' He fumbled in his pocket and gave her a shilling. 'Please keep the change for future purchase, sweetheart,' he murmured.

Nell bobbed a quick curtsey. 'Thank you, sir.'

Hobey hobbled forward, sniffing. 'Ready?' he asked the customer balefully.

Mr Pepys gave Nell a last, wistful look. 'Till we meet again, mistress – .' He bowed.

'Till we meet again, sir.'

He walked off briskly with Hobey following him, muttering loudly about dalliance, cold weather, and innocent maids.

Nell watched him go and clutched her shilling.

'Again you have helped me, my old friend,' she said to herself, knowing that she had food and to spare for at least another day. They would not starve this cold winter night – though they might another. She had pulled a sheet canvas over the turnips and battened them down ready to leave when Hobey returned. Dusk was fast falling now. As she was fastening the ropes of the cart, a pair of hands came down over her eyes. She gasped in surprise. The fingers blocked out all the light.

A voice in her ear said, 'O mistress mine, how art thou changed!'

Whirling round, she grasped at the hands before looking up at a tall figure. A long, thin face gazed down at her in grave amusement. It was Jonathan.

Instinctively she ran into his arms and clung fast, burying her head in his cloak and sobbing with joy. Jonathan was taken by surprise and awkwardly protested.

'Why how is this, Mistress Gwynne? I swear, when I saw you at the end of the street, I took no doubt you had grown up. Methought I had left a child and found a woman.'

'It has been so long . . . so long,' she gasped breathlessly, 'I thought you were at the bottom of the ocean or the end of the world. . . . I never thought to see you again. You never sent word. I thought you were dead.'

'Aye. Dead and forgot.' Immediately she hotly protested, just as he had hoped.

'Never! Never for a thousand years could I forget! I have thought of you, aye, and remembered that dreadful night when you had to leave because . . . because of me. Every day for the past three years I *have* thought of you! How could you think otherwise?'

Her nails dug into his coat sleeves.

He tilted her head so that he could see her face. 'Peace, child! Let me look at you.'

He drew in a long breath as he saw the change time had wrought on her. He had left a child, small and ill-cared-for, uneasily wearing the heavy mantle of maturity. But he returned to a stranger. She looked up at him, eyes sparkling from under long, dark lashes, mouth slightly open to display the most perfect set of small, white teeth he had ever beheld. A pair of tiny hands gripped his velvet sleeves, but he put her from him to look at her better. Gently he pushed back the cloak from her brow and gazed in wonder. Her dress was plain, of wool, dyed green, rucked into creases by her day's toil; but neither it, nor its shabby condition, could disguise the slim legs and exquisite form that moved gently beneath its folds. The stomacher of black cord was pulled in tight, revealing a waist no thicker than a willow wand and supporting a pair of fine breasts that stood out proudly. Then up, up a slender white throat to a face framed in a mass of soft, curling, auburn-chestnut hair, wound thickly into a pile at her back. She pushed a strand nervously under her snood with a quick finger, as she saw him looking at her.

'Why, child,' he said slowly, 'but you're beautiful.'

Hobey returned to find his young mistress standing with both arms outstretched, her hands in the grip of a tall stranger he had never seen before.

'Body o' me,' he sniffed in resignation, 'they never stop coming, do they?'

Jonathan took her to a nearby alehouse and made her sit

down, abruptly ordering brandies for them both. Nell wanted to hear all about him and where he had been, but he was brusque.

'In a moment, in a moment.' His voice was impatient, as she had heard before when he was worried. 'When I left, you were still working for that old hag Ross at Lewkenor's Lane – and I made sure that your duties ended at the foot of the stairs besides. And now I find you on the streets – on a cold December day too. How is this?'

'I left Ma Ross two months back,' said Nell, twisting her fingers nervously, 'or rather I was chucked out. After you had left I carried on just as usual and old Ma Ross was that pleasant I thought the future was set fair. You might say she was nervous – even scared.'

Jonathan did not seem surprised.

'But of course things changed. 'Twas after a twelvemonth had gone by that Ma Ross took heart – said you were dead and all. Faith, did the old hag change her tune! And about the same time I started having trouble with the men. I warrant you that bawdy house is filled with the most frustrated boobies in London.' Her eyes danced. 'I kicked 'em off faster than you could kill fleas in bed, but it wasn't any good. Old Ma Ross made things worse. She told me if I didn't want to have a dabble or two, I could get out, as she made no mistake but that you were dead, and I could play the virgin elsewhere but not on her premises.'

Nell smiled ruefully. 'You couldn't really blame her, the old sot. I had – as you said – *changed*, and Ma Ross said she wasn't going to act like a popish Mother Superior no longer; protecting girls had never been her job. I agreed; readily it hardly seemed fair not to.'

'But what have you been doing since then, child?'

'I had a bit of money saved up, which Mam hadn't got to for her brandy yet, so I bought a cart and a load of curs'd turnips. Pox on them! I swear I've sold no more than a handful, so Hobey and me – that's the old man's name – we've been living off my savings. Now they're all but gone. I don't know what's to do. Mam's been laid up with a tertian ague and only just got on 'er feet again, and you know what Rose is like, Jon. . . . '

'How is she?' asked Jonathan idly.

'Oh, Rose? Well enough, I suppose. But really, Jon, you must have been addled in the head if you thought you could continue long together. Looking at you and then her . . . . She is not for you, Jonathan.'

'No,' he agreed ruefully. 'And how many fine gallants has she had since?'

'Lord, dozens!' said Nell cheerfully.

He smiled at her – the comment no longer had any power to wound, and he appreciated her candour. Then, after renewed pleas, he told her of his experiences in France.

She heard how he had been to Paris and been received by several ne'er-do-wells. Johathan did not specify further what his business had been, but swiftly changed the subject to gossip of the Palais Royal, the Cathedral of Notre Dame and the Palace of the Louvre – treasures of a nation now being stirred to life by France's brilliant young monarch, Louis the Four-teenth.

Nell was enchanted to hear of a visit Jonathan had made to Saint Cloud where Monsieur, the Duc d'Orléans, and Madame, his wife, lived in a gorgeous palace. Madame, as all London knew, was Minette, their King's adored sister, exiled, in a loveless marriage, from England.

'Were you introduced?' asked Nell eagerly.

'I? Would the brother of Louis, the Grand Monarque be introduced to such as I? No. But I saw them walking in the gardens, or rather 'twas Madame I saw – with her ladies, and a small spaniel dog which I was told her brother Charles had given her. She was quite beautiful. Not seductive – rather innocent I felt, and even unhappy. 'Tis known that her husband cares not for her but only for his young boy friends. Perhaps she, too, felt homesick for England, as I did.'

'Why did you not come sooner, Jon, or even send a message?'

asked Nell plaintively. 'I looked in vain many a time, you know.'

'I could not come until I knew 'twas safe to come. And I dared not send a letter for they could so easily have traced me and implicated you, child.'

'Then why did you come now?'

'I heard my dear friend Sir Cyril Dimchurch had passed on to higher – or should I say *lower*? – things.'

'But that was near nine months ago!' protested Nell, remembering the news she had heard so gladly.

'It takes time for news to filter across the Channel, Nell, and I had some . . . affairs to wind up. But, i'faith,' he finished briskly 'now I'm back, and we can all be merry again.'

Her eyes filled with tears. She put her hand impulsively on his, on the table. 'Three years – is a long time. Things and people change.'

He looked down at the hand lying on his and then up at a beautiful girl, who gazed at him from eyes shining with tears.

'Aye,' he echoed soberly. 'Time past is time lost.'

Madam Ross was busy doing her accounts, perched on a high stool at a corner of the counter, when Nell and Jonathan walked in. She did not hear them enter but sat counting golden coins, one by one, into a selection of dirty bags, until Jonathan stood over her. The tavern was empty for it was early morning, and the ale slops still lay in heavy pools across the tables.

'How now, Madam Ross? I bid you good day, Ma'am,' he said, and the old woman looked up, turning pale under her paint as she saw who it was.

'You, here?' she muttered, as though she could not believe her watery eyes.

'As you see, Madam.' He bowed smoothly. 'You may throw off the mourning weeds, which I am persuaded you must have donned. For indeed, I am not dead, or at least so I believe.' He indicated Nell with an elegant movement of the wrist. 'I believe you have a vacant situation for my friend. You have not met, of course. May I introduce Mistress Gwynne?'

Nell gaped at him, amazed, but curtseyed as if from politeness.

Ma Ross was staring at Jonathan, sucking in her lips. She remembered the men flocking around Nell; she remembered the falling off in business as they pursued her, rather than going upstairs with Sarah or Beatrice or any of the others. They seemed to see her as a prize – the unattainable, a concept which paid Ma Ross not a penny groat. She would *not* take her back and she was furious that Jonathan should ask . . . yet she was scared.

'No,' she said flatly, and her flaccid mouth set in a hard, mutinous line.

'Ah, Madam. . . . ' Jonathan took one plump hand in his and raised it to his lips. 'Are you sure I can't persuade you?' All at once the grip grew steel-like, closing around her fingers until she wanted to cry out in pain. But he still looked at her blandly, though there was a light in his eye.

'No!' repeated Ma Ross with such a glower that Nell quailed to see.

'You *will* change your mind, Madam,' he said quite quietly, but with menace.

Nell saw that Madam Ross understood the unspoken threat. She saw a flash of fear for an instant in those shifting eyes.

'After all,' he continued, 'you have not tried her out yet, have you?'

Ma Ross felt as if her hands were being crushed. 'No,' she murmured, 'no, no. . . .'

'I feel sure after consideration you will agree, Madam,' continued Jonathan softly. 'You can always benefit from assistance to clean your attics – and your cellars, of course.'

Madam Ross appeared to make a supreme effort, though her powdered jowl wobbled aggressively.

'To be sure,' she faltered. 'If there is a job. . . .'

'Oh, there is a job, Madam, I am positive. And Mistress Gwynne will be admirable – to serve the drinks, no more nor less – eh Madam?'

'I dare swear it can be arranged,' said Ma Ross sulkily.

'To be sure,' agreed Jonathan pleasantly, releasing her hand. She rubbed it hard to restore the circulation and scowled at him.

He did not appear to see, but went on idly, 'And Mistress Gwynne has an added qualification none of your other girls enjoy, except perhaps for the enchanting Sarah, of course.'

'What is that, pray ?'

'Why, my reference, Madam, my reference.'

In later years, Nell was often to look back on that occasion with amazement. She had not understood what Jonathan had said, but she had seen the fear in Madam Ross's eyes, and felt the tension as hidden barbs of threats and purring double-meanings passed between the two. But she had dismissed it from her mind, content to have her job back, and pleased to be returned to an occupation of doubtful morality but of greater warmth in a cold December. In later years, she was to think wonderingly of her slowness of wit.

But troubles seemed far away. Within days, it was as if Nell had never been away. Ma Ross was not one to harbour a grudge. Like all the poor of London she accepted what life sent when she could not change it and she saw how Nell did in fact attract custom to her tavern. For Ma Ross conceived the idea of Mistress Gywnne standing at the entrance to Lewkenor's Lane of an evening, holding high a lanthorn to entice in the gentlemen. 'A pretty thought,' she mused with satisfaction, seeing her bawdy-house fill yet again each evening.

For Nell it was not enjoyable. It made her arm ache. 'Like a benighted statue, I swear I feel,' she would say to Benjamin, the grinning water-carrier, who stood solidly, gazing down her bodice in appreciation. Lewkenor's Lane saw a steady procession of men attracted by Ma Ross's protegée and welcomed them indiscriminately with open arms.

The only notable absentee was White Jonathan. Since he had returned, Nell had seen him but seldom. Occasionally, when she left Ma Ross's in the early hours, a dark figure would detach itself from the shadows and come forward to take her hand – and then they would talk, and walk to the Coal Yard slowly, enjoying the night air. But so often no figure was there, and when she asked him where he went, he merely chucked her under the chin and laughed easily, telling her he was but making his living.

'But what at?' she demanded furiously.

He wagged a reproving finger and said nothing. She knew she might as well keep her breath to cool her porridge but still her curiosity assailed her. What was Jonathan doing – where did he go of nights? Nell had disturbing suspicions. And she had other reasons to feel guilty.

She tried to shrug them off, tell herself it was none of his business, that it would do no good and likely a great deal of harm, but still her conscience pricked. For her sister was with child – and the child belonged to Jack Cassells.

Nell tortured herself with guilt, that she had not given Rose Jonathan's warning. She determined to tell Rose to stop seeing John Cassells. But each night she vowed the same thing and in the morning looked at her sister out of wide, scared eyes, saying nothing, so that her mother had sworn she was sickening for the sweating sickness and Rose had teasingly asked her who her new lover was, that he gave her such pain. Nell stayed silent, for how could she tell Rose, beautiful Rose, who to see and not to see? She dared not say anything, persuading herself that if he were so wicked she would find out soon enough.

Rose bloomed these days in the way she had always wanted; now indeed she made up for past privation. The flow of gold kept Rose's heart securely in the pocket of John Cassells. When Nell had told Jonathan her sister had continued her flighty paths of infidelity she had lied. For three whole years Rose had stayed with the one man – it was near impossible to believe.

Cassells shied away from contact, seemingly, with any human being – his occupation remained unknown and he lived in shadows. Only once, when Nell had returned very late from Ma Ross's after a brawl in the tavern, had she unexpectedly found her sister in Coal Yard Alley, locked in the arms of a stranger who swore viciously as he had heard her approach and whipped out a short-sword.

Rose had started and then sighed in relief as she had seen who it was. The sword had dropped in Cassells' hand, and he had laughed softly when told by Rose it was only her sister.

Nell found herself being greeted by a low, mocking bow and a pair of thick lips brushed her hand. Nell found herself looking at a coarse, swarthy, face with a dark moustache and a pair of cold hazel eyes. In complexion, he had more than a look of the King, but immediately Nell had seen the coldness in the eyes and sensed the menace behind the soft laughter as he had greeted her. She had been amazed her sister could find him attractive, though as she saw the ruby ring flashing on his finger as he took her hand, she had wondered if that were why.

That night she had been more worried, seeing again that swarthy face, and remembering, 'your sister will rue the day. . . .'

As her pregnancy advanced, Rose changed. She crept about holding her stomach, clenching it with sweating hands and looking wildly about as if to put off a doom that grew inexorably nearer. Nell could not understand her sister's new panic and misery. Was it, after all, so bad to have a baby?

Rose's explanation was saddening. 'I only have one thing to sell and I'm not going to stand by and watch it ruined, while a brat kicks the belly out of me. Look at Ma! Would you want to end up like her? And if I do have it, what future have I got? No one wants a girl with a child clinging to her skirts. It's like a notice saying "used before". Oh Nelly, this is Jack's child and I have nobody but Jack – you know that. If he leaves me now, I'd be better off if I caught the Thames Plague and died of it.'

She put her hands up to her face. 'I'll grow wrinkled and fat and pox-ridden. No one will want me then. I'll end up in the Fleet ditch and you know what happens to those women.'

Nell had seen them before – women stumbling along behind a cart, with matted hair falling over their faces while a lash cracked down on their shoulders; being publicly whipped through the streets. The law fell quickly on these women of the backstreets, who were shrilly denounced as notorious prostitutes when their beauty had faded and they were driven to solicit custom more brazenly. Such public spectacles, like the executions, were the favourite amusement of the citizens, as Nell well knew. And Rose waited for her belly to swell and her figure to lose its lustre.

'But Rose,' Nell protested, 'you're still young –.'

'You age fast in the Fleet Alley.' Rose looked at Nell, her eyes hard and gleaming. 'There's only one thing for't, Nelly. This is Jack's child and I have no other man. He'll have to own it – and marry me.'

'*Marry* you?' said Nell, surprised.

'Why not? There's plenty worse than me, I'll warrant. Many would be glad of me, I know.'

'Yes, but –.'

'It's my only chance, Nelly,' said Rose with anger. 'The only chance I have.'

Yet Cassells did not care, it seemed. Rose would feign unconcern and laugh nervously while she laced herself in tightly, and declare the matter as of no moment when she sallied forth to the delights of London at night. But Nell was not deceived by this brittle sparkle, for she saw the figure of misery as it hung over the basin every morning in the cramped chamber they shared.

Rose could not help herself. She seemed to have lost her senses. Still her extravagances mounted; now she talked of wanting a diamond necklace to place about her neck to match the drops given her only a week ago. And Cassells obliged, though he did nothing to help his lady rid herself of an unwanted child or make her an honest goodwife.

To confide in Jonathan would have been such a comfort. But she searched the dark streets for him in vain.

CHAPTER II

And honesty's against all common sense:
Men must be knaves, 'tis in their own defense.
John Wilmot, Earl of Rochester

Rose smoothed down the rich folds of parma brocade and pulled on a pair of gloves of French lace. She anointed herself carefully with rose-water while Nell plunged the crockery of the evening meal just finished into a sinkful of icy water to wash up. Her sister looked happy, indeed gayer than Nell had seen her for weeks past, and calm and serene as never before.

As Nell rolled up her sleeves, she began tentatively: 'Rose, I was talking to Sarah today, whose aunt has a farm . . . up at Bristol, Sarah said, where a girl could go and. . . .'

Rose turned pale. 'God, Nelly, you didn't –.'

'No, no,' said Nell soothingly. 'I but told her I had a friend in trouble who would be grateful – and able to pay – for a secret refuge from the world for a couple of months, to have a baby and see it adopted by some cottager or other, till it could be looked after by its mother, of course.'

Rose shook her head violently. 'I want no brats around my skirts – not now or ever,' she said.

'But Rose, surely you would wish to keep the child. Between us, you and I could look after it. It would be *yours*, Rose. You couldn't forget it, surely?'

' 'Od's death!' snapped Rose peevishly. 'Don't be so melodramatic. Talk sense, Nell. How could you bring up a child in this district?'

'We managed, Rose; we're still kicking.'

Her sister snorted. 'It's a miracle we ever grew up. Precious few do around here. Mistress Culpepper has had nine children and not one's reached five yet and well you know it.' But in face of Nell's accusing expression, Rose looked guilty. 'Perhaps everything will come aright. I have great hopes that it will.' Her voice was brisk as she turned away from Nell.

'How?'

'Ah –.' Rose looked mysterious. There was a knock on the door. A sedan-chair stood waiting outside in the dark street, its lantern flickering. The chairman bowed to Rose, and told her it had come as ordered. Rose put up her hood and donned her vizard mask, which all fashionable ladies were now affecting; her hood slipped silkily up around her head.

'Good-bye, Nelly, don't wait up for me.' She swished from the room. Nell looked out of the small window at the chair as it swayed away down the narrow street, its lights bobbing in the dark. Rose seemed to be planning something. She had been vague but not worried, thought Nell, as she dunked the cold pots up and down in the tin sink in the corner.

'Mayhap that cheesecurd Cassells has found 'er a place to have the brat privately. Or maybe he knows an apothecary whose brew will get rid of it for her. At least she seems to be quite happy and that's an improvement.'

Nevertheless Nell still felt uneasy. The next evening Jonathan reappeared, offering no explanation for his absence. Almost as soon as she greeted him she poured out the whole story. Jonathan was angry; angry with Rose, with Nell, with Cassells – but most of all, himself.

'I should have known that skulking rogue would get her into matrons' town. Why did you not warn her, Nelly?'

'I did, Jonathan, but I can hardly tell the sister who brought me up how to run her own life. 'Od's death, she can still knock me across the room.'

'Where is she going to have the brat?'

'I don't know – that's just it. Nobody knows. Rose tells nobody her secrets. But she looked happier tonight. I have a feeling she's going to be looked after by Jack.'

'Jack Cassells never helped anybody except to an early grave,' said Jonathan in a cold, hard voice.

'Why do you hate him so much, Jonathan? What has he done to you? No, don't frown; indeed, I only want to know since it seems to pain you so much.'

Jonathan looked down. 'It is something that lies back in

time when you were in your cradle, Nell. You wouldn't understand. It's all a long time ago. I just have a sadly good memory.' His white fingers curled around his wineglass.' War does funny things to men, Nell. Some blossom under the cut and thrust of battle; some you would never expect become lions, and usually get killed for their pains. War is simply chaos – it's every man for himself. Some rise because of it, but some just go rotten.'

Nell's eyes were wide. 'Did Jack Cassells turn rotten, Jonathan?'

'Don't ask me, Nell; I can't speak about it. Perhaps one day I will, but not now.' His mouth took on a stubborn look. 'It's not a tale for your pretty ears, child.'

Nell stood up, annoyed. 'Pox on you, Jonathan! I'm not a child any more . . . haven't you noticed?'

Her cloak fell back, revealing her figure as she sat opposite him and she tossed her hair free of its hood. She looked up at him from under her eyelashes and smiled.

'Yes,' said Jonathan quietly, 'I had noticed.' His hand stretched out over the table. But Nell clapped a horrified hand to her mouth. 'It's dark already! I swear I'm half an hour late. Lord, that old sot'll kill me.' She chuckled naughtily. 'S'blood! Jonathan, she's that glad to have me back, I swear she scowls at me when I arrive like I was one of Noll Cromwell's puritan preachers come back to see her. It almost makes you feel sorry for her.'

Jonathan got up slowly. 'Nell –.'

'Yes, Jonathan?' Her smile was frankly curious.

His hand dropped to his side. 'I hope your sister will be all right, Nell.'

Nell tied her cloak, but as she left she had a feeling Jonathan had been going to say something else.

There was no moon that night, and the sky was pitch black as Nell left the bawdy-house, little before midnight, and made her chilly way home, her solitary footsteps echoing out in the silent, dark streets. All of London's citizens were long abed for it was not safe to be out after dark, with nothing but the flickering light of the linkboy as a doubtful protection in the winding alleys.

There was no wind, and in the stillness the leaning, gloomy houses seemed almost eerie. The girl would have been glad of the comforting sound of the nightwatchman making his slow round, but, as all London knew, the old men – known to the populace as 'Charlies' – seldom stirred from their warm alehouses before the early hours to make their chilly round, shouting the time in each street as they nervously passed. The old watchmen were careful to keep out of the way of any foot-pads who might be lurking in the alleyways, and Nell knew they were of little help to deter potential molesters. Neverthe-less she would have been glad of the mere sound of a voice tonight. The silence was darkly ominous.

She passed down Lewkenor's Lane and groped her way into Fish Street where the stench, despite the darkness, told her she was going in the right direction. Carefully avoiding the gutter, Nell picked her way through the stagnant puddles in the cobbles and sighed in weariness. The evening at Ma Ross's had been very busy. The old woman had just become aware of the new craze at Court for card-playing, another of the pleasures imported from France by a pleasure-loving King, and now cards as well as bottles littered the tables in the tavern where Ma Ross kept her own court.

Nell had been presiding over a school of Basset all evening and the play had been heavy. The proceedings from games of casino and loo swelled those bags of Ma Ross's which lived under lock and key behind the counter. Nell had been on her feet all evening, exchanging comments and oaths with the gentlemen who lounged at the tables getting steadily more tipsy as the night wore on. Now she was tired and longed for her bed. As she passed under a low shop sign which hung motionless in the still night air a hand came out from the overhanging shadows, grasping her arm, and whirling her around.

She screamed slightly and her hood fell off as she kicked out with all her force to beat off the unknown attacker, thinking him to be one of the cut-purses that came out at night with the rats, and swarmed about the dark corners and alleyways of London.

'Poltroon,' she swore, 'rogue . . . I swear I'll knock your vitals into the gutter, you skulking pocket tipstave . . . !'

A voice cursed softly, and the man tried to place his palm over Nell's mouth to stem her noise in the empty street. She bit it savagely, and it withdrew with a furious oath.

But a strong merciless grip overcame her resistance and pinioned her arms, while a voice, soft yet menacing, grunted at her: 'Soft, my sweeting, there's no cause for alarm. Faith! You're a wild cat. I only wish for a little talk that can do no one any harm.'

Nell remembered that voice. A pair of impassive, cold hazel eyes looked down at her mockingly and there was an appreciative flash of white teeth in the dark as the girl was hugged by two large arms. Then John Cassells swept off his hat so that Nell could see him, and bowed, chuckling. She rubbed her bruised wrists and regarded him with sharp disfavour.

'Do you always greet ladies thus, Master Cassells? Perhaps some like being clinkered in a dark street o' nights; they say London has become a wanton city. I can't say I've acquired the taste as yet.' She paused, pleased at the sound of the small speech she had just uttered.

John Cassells grinned at her. 'I beg pardon, Mistress Gwynne.' From out the large pocket of his muddied riding coat he drew a shabby billet of paper, rubbed at the corners. 'Would you take this to your sister. . . ?' His tone was light. ' 'Tis most urgent.'

Nell held out her hand uncertainly and took the letter. She glanced at it and then held Cassells' eyes with an accusing stare.

'I hope it is for Rose's good, Master Cassells. You have something to atone for, with my sister.'

Cassells' eyes shifted and looked away, but he laughed easily enough. 'This letter should solve all her problems, I imagine. Can you not trust me, Mistress Gwynne?'

'Haply I could if I knew you better, Master Cassells. You seem a very . . . shall I say . . . retiring person, living in shadows, never in the light for more than a second.'

'You make me sound like a bat, I swear, and you wrong me. Such a sinister image.' But he seemed anxious to be gone.

Nell was not favourably impressed. 'If you tell me that you mean well by Rose, John Cassells,' she said levelly, 'then I'll take the letter, but not otherwise, and so I promise you. I have little reason to trust you and even less reason to like you.'

'I have the best possible reasons for wanting to see her. It is for her happiness' sake, I swear. You worry yourself unduly.' He looked meaningly at the packet in Nell's hand. 'It is meant for Rose's eyes alone; it is very private, you understand.'

Nell smiled. To her, Cassells' nervousness seemed yet another sign of his general shiftiness. 'You need not fear, Master Cassells. It is safe – and secret – with me.' She turned to go, clutching the letter, but he grasped her by the shoulder. They were alone in the gloomy alley. He moved close to her, so that she could smell the odour of his breath as he glanced quickly around.

His whisper was sibilant. 'Tell her – the Cat's Paw, at two, and she will understand. Remember that – the Cat's Paw, at two.'

Nell looked at him in bewilderment. 'Anything else?'

'Just that,' he murmured, and vanished into the night.

Rose was sitting in the corner of the dirty chamber when Nell came in and flung down her cloak. No candle was lit and Rose sat hugging her knees, perched on a rather rickety chair. Nell lit the solitary candle on the table and turned to face her sister. She saw in Rose's hand a rather damp handkerchief, and on her sister's face the blotched, tell-tale streaks of grief. Rose sniffed valiantly and her eyes were puffy red.

'Not for a week or more have I had even a word,' she moaned. 'I swear he's clean forgot me. He swore he'd come the night afore last and he never did. Oh Lord, Nelly, I'm lost; I know it now. This brat will be the end of me. It's no use any more, I can't stand it. . . .' She buried her face in her hand, sobbing. 'I shall have to go away somewhere. I shall have to sell all my things, everything.' She gazed at Nell, a tear trickling down one pink cheek. 'I wouldn't mind, Nelly,' she said brokenly, 'but I've only *lived* for such a short time. And tonight, well, you know that I was going to the Duke's Theatre.' She looked down at her rich gown. 'I found I couldn't get into the blessed thing. I'm too . . . fat.' A fresh bout of woe overcame her.

Nell pulled the billet from under her cloak and silently put it in the trembling fingers. Rose looked down at the note as if mesmerized, and then up at Nell in a watery fashion, and opened her mouth to ask a list of questions.

'Open it,' said Nell.

Alone in the house she watched and waited for her sister to come home. The night was far advanced, but no pink tinges of dawn above the rooftops as yet betokened the arrival of a new morning. Yet it was very late – the early cold hours of a new day when the city slept and no one respectable stirred abroad, save perhaps a gallant stealing home from a late party or his lady's bed. Nell's mother had not yet returned from the alehouse. The house was empty and silent as death as Nell walked up and down the low chamber. The flickering candle was nearing its guttering end, and she strained to hear a footfall or the sound of a late hackney.

Rose had gone. Six hours now, it had been, and where was she? Nell stared out at the black opaque windows and knew that somewhere outside her sister was being attended to, or, as Rose had said, 'put to rights'.

What was happening to her? Could she get rid of the child? Nell had no illusions – she knew such things were done in the little alleys and corners of London for the right persons with the right money. But she was afraid for Rose's safety, for the pregnancy was not in its earliest stages. And she did not trust John Cassells.

Nevertheless, as she sat in the cold, murky chamber, in the small hours of the morning, alone, she found her thoughts being driven towards the image of an aloof, austere gentleman, whose cool eyes seemed to bore into hers and grow bigger in her mind's eye as she sat in the dark. The watchman passed up the corner of Coke Alley in the distance, with his little dog barking shrilly, and the muffled clang of his bell as he made the last round. But above it there came a swift hurried footfall, and the darkness in the room was suddenly dispelled as the door was flung open and a light from a lantern flooded into the chamber. Nell blinked her eyes against the sudden glare, and holding her hand up nervously looked at the dark cloaked figure behind the light on the threshold. It stood in the shadow.

'Ma . . . ?' asked Nell nervously. 'Is that you? Where did you get the lantern from, you thieving bawd, at this hour?'

She screwed up her eyes as they got used to the dark. The lantern threw up weird shadows. There was a muffled giggle.

'Rose!'

The figure put the lantern down and ran over to Nell, hugging her and whirling her round and round across the room. Peals of laughter came from her until she collapsed on to a chair, panting and giggling at the same time, rocking back and forth.

'What's happened Rose, did you get rid of the brat?' Nell stopped her sister's movements and held both her hands firmly as she gazed searchingly into her face. 'You look mighty healthy if you have had one of those damn potions.'

Rose's face was flushed with excitement, her eyes glowed with happiness. 'I didn't get rid of the brat. We went to a place near Tower Hill to an old woman Jack knows and she told me it was too late to rid meself of the child. So it looks like I shall have to have it.'

Nell was shocked. 'Oh Rose, no. . . .'

But Rose looked quite unperturbed, and smiled irritatingly. 'Oh, it doesn't matter *now* –.'

Nell opened her mouth to protest.

'Wait, Nelly. So after that we went on to see another friend of Jack's called Jeremiah Cutler at an alehouse at St Paul's and he sent us to see someone who lived opposite the Dolphin in Tower Street. You know the place.'

'Yes, yes,' cried Nell frenziedly. 'But what *happened*?'

'Why, Nell,' laughed her sister, 'can't you guess? I'm married!'

'I can't believe a word,' muttered Jonathan morosely, and he put his tankard down with an air of finality on Ma Ross's rough board table.

'It's true, Jonathan. Rose has got the ring and everything. Apparently they went to an old minister Jack knew – one of these Baptists or something – that was used to be around in Holy Noll's day. Now old Rowley's back, times are hard and the old sot exchanged his old life for a new one of gaming and wenching. I must say it sounds more interesting. . . . Anyway, the old devil is always ready to earn an extra florin or two, and once Jack had greased his sweaty palm there was no trouble. I own I was shocked at first but, faith, it seems Cassells has got some good in 'im. He married Rose and he says he's going to set her up in fine style with apartments in the Strand and her own carriage and all the servants she can need. The bride is that happy I can't begin to describe it.'

'And how is the bridegroom?'

'Oh – Jack? Well, we haven't seen him since.'

'He has just married your sister and you haven't seen him?' asked Jonathan incredulously.

'Well, but Rose says he is finding their lodgings and everything,' Nell defended her new brother-in-law. 'He wants to be able to offer her a home, you see.'

'How touching!' murmured Jonathan. 'I never knew such sentiments existed in Master Cassells' personality, or such delicacy of feeling. Oh, I'm sorry, I forgot. 'Tis brother Jack now, is it not?'

Nell flushed with anger. 'I know you have some reason to dislike Ja– Master Cassells, but this is hardly the time to express them, sir. I'll thank you to remember' – she spoke with a hauteur she could always adopt when the need arose – 'that you speak now of my brother.'

Jonathan shrugged ruefully. 'I'm sorry, Nell. I didn't mean to lose my curs'd temper. I've just got a natural hate for Cassells. But there – they say there's good in everyone, do they not?'

Nell eyed him suspiciously. 'I trust you least when you are accommodating,' she sniffed, and stood up.

Jonathan looked up at her with innocence. 'Of course,' he said sleepily, 'a ring would be as cheap as one of those hell potions and we haven't seen this carriage yet – *or* the servants. . . .'

'Oh! replied Nell furiously, and swished off in a pet.

But the affair was not so easily settled. The momentous marriage sent a shock through Nell's life whose ripples threatened to overcome her as time passed. For Jonathan's words, though she had disclaimed them, left an uneasy undercurrent in her memory that she could not forget try as she would. Rose bloomed carelessly, like some extravagant plant, flaunting a gaudy ring, of thick engraved gold stuck with stones, around the muddy surrounds of the Coal Yard for the interested and envious gaze of the neighbouring families, and thoughtlessly ordering a succession of luxuries for the adornment of what Rose referred to as her 'boudoir'.

Spindle-legged tables, after the new fashionable French style; embroidered tapestry-stools; one of the new embossed leather carpets now used by the well-to-do; a delicate nest of card tables, backed with Colchester baize; a shimmering chandelier of many glass facets; a large gilt mirror of huge and hideous proportions; a parrot in a cage; and a large collection of brocades and velvets for drapes and curtaining, piled themselves in an unwieldy heap in the stuffy little upper chamber at the Coal Yard. Rose paid a special visit to an upholsterers near the Royal Exchange, to order a special large bed of four posts, with valances and an ornate pluming of ostrich feathers at the corners, with hangings of figured damask.

Mrs Gwynne spent all night in the alehouses in celebration, and all day weeping gin-laden tears into a sentimental grubby kerchief, as she anticipated her daughter's approaching departure from what she liked to refer to as her loving bosom, between deep hiccoughs and sighs.

Life became one long whirl, and though Nell warningly told Rose that she would end up in 'Change Alley, she was relieved and pleased to see the alteration wrought in her sister. The dark shadows under her eyes had disappeared and she had regained her old rough buoyancy and life. Nell breathed silent thanks to the dissolute Cassells wherever he might be. The odd thing was that still Cassells remained at a distance, always one shadow away. He was each night supposed to be coming, but he never did, and though Rose went off every night in a chair to an unknown and secret destination, she never returned with a man whom Mrs Gwynne could crow over as a son and hug to a capacious breast. Nell wondered over the man, but she had other things to occupy her mind.

Ma Ross had started to expand her business and take it into further lecherous, lucrative fields. And her new interest was the Playhouse.

Near to the great Piazza in Convent Garden, one of the fashionable centres of the city, London's citizens had been surprised to see building begin on a huge timbered construction that reached up into the sky; hammering could be heard continuously into the dusk and the wealthy in the Strand had complained to the Lord Mayor about the noise disturbing their repose. Nevertheless, the building had gone on, and, six months before, the players of Master Thomas Killigrew, the King's jester, had moved from their tennis-court theatre in Vere Street and opened grandly a new magnificent theatre in a situation which opened a small timbered fronting on to a narrow alley known as Drury Lane. The players were the King's Servants of the Royal Company of Players, and the King himself came to grace their opening, bearing upon his arm the seductive Castlemaine, together with a bevy of beauties to see the new addition to London's increasing number of pleasures.

Now the theatre opened its doors to rival the Duke's Company of Davenant's in Portugal Row, and it had since become a veritable craze in London and a gold-mine for Killigrew himself.

His good fortune smiled also upon the murky corners of Lewkenor's Lane. Killigrew approached Ma Ross and she agreed to find twenty wenches to put under Killigrew in the theatre as orange girls, to sell the expensive fruit before the appreciative eye of the gallants in the pit, while it was to be understood that they were available later, to any who might fancy, under the hospitable roof in Lewkenor's Lane.

Ma Ross had a further reason to welcome an agreement with Killigrew. A certain gaudy lady by the name of Madam Bennet had set up a rival establishment in Drury Lane and collected a company of fair damsels which bade fair to attract the eye of London's gentlemen, especially those replete with wine and in festive mood returning from the theatre a few yards away.

Ma Ross had been seriously worried, for this was rivalry on home ground, too close for her comfort. There had always been a selection of cheap bawdy houses around Tower Hill and Moorfields, and the whores of Fleet Alley were notorious. But, it seemed, the theatre offered a threat as well as a promise. The old woman was determined that she should benefit from the playhouse and her bargain with Killigrew gave her cause for renewed satisfaction. Again her fingers had found a hold in London pleasures, and once more they would be withdrawn chinking with gold.

She combed London's back alleys and found twelve slatternly wenches, but her eyes still lingered on one girl in particular. Always a trouble to the old woman's mind. Nell had shrugged off a post in which she would have proved profitable, and her very presence cast doubt on the absolute power the thin-lipped old hag was used to command. It was because of Nell's unwelcome presence that she was forced to put up with another unwelcome visitor – Jonathan. So Ma Ross had asked

Nell sweetly if she would like to have the honour of becoming the first of Drury Lane Theatre's orange girls.

Nell had temporized by promising lightly to think about it, but she wished to see Jonathan, and she was uncertain as to her own mind. Ma Ross was impatient; she came up to Nell that same night in Lewkenor's Lane just as Nell was dealing the first cards for the Basset school. She smiled in the way Nell knew so well to mean trouble, laying a bejewelled hand lightly on the girl's arm, and asking for a word.

'Well, Ma'am?' inquired Nell guardedly.

'Nelly . . . child . . . sweetheart . . .,' wheezed Ma Ross gently, 'have you thought on my words yet, sweeting? Or have you perhaps decided against such work as being too menial, since, as we all know, your sister is become a fine lady?'

'What words mean you, Madam?'

'Faith, the wench has a grievous short memory!' laughed Madam Ross. 'Do you not remember what I offered you, a clear sennight ago, concernin' the theatre; you know, Master Killigrew's company in Drury Lane. Ye said ye'd think on't.'

'On what?' asked Nell innocently.

Madam Ross's face turned puce and her chins wobbled aggressively. 'I mean that job . . . that *fine* job I offered ye as an orange girl in the playhouse, wench – you know well what I mean. And I want an answer clear and simple,' she snapped, 'for I've no time to wait further at *your* convenience.'

'I am *still* thinking, Ma'am,' answered Nell kindly.

Madam Ross's eyes glinted. 'You have a slow mind, mistress,' she said tartly. 'Be sure you do not become a lack-wit.' She turned to go back to the counter. 'I shall see you before you go, mistress.'

Nell continued dealing cards with a trembling hand. She had no more than three hours to give an answer. It was not that she was averse to leaving the stuffy confines of Lewkenor's Lane, indeed she had come to hate the smoky, close atmosphere and the innuendoes of the rapacious Madam Ross. But she had neither desire for nor knowledge of the place of her prospective employment. With the rest of London she had seen the theatre being built and wondered at its proportions, but Nell's was a strange life – she worked at night and slept in the day, seldom stirring till past noon. As the theatre had only been open six months, she had not yet been to see a play, though Rose had been squired to the grand opening to see a long tedious epic she had stigmatized as 'one long wind-conkered blow'. And *she* had not been since.

A shrill scream in the corner of the tavern interrupted her thoughts. Nell looked up to see Edith, white and shaken, putting out long, skinny arms to fend off the advances of a workman with an ugly, pock-marked face. Edith retreated behind one of the tables, gibbering with fear, and holding one hand up nervously to her bodice.

''Ods'so! Is that your game?' grunted the low-browed assailant with a chuckle. 'You'll find I can beat down those pretty little defences, my girl. And so I warn you. . . .' He moved suddenly and Edith scampered round the table like a terrified rabbit, to the huge delight of all the company.

'She likes me really,' he informed the tavern at large. 'She's just a *little bit* shy, aren't you, my pretty?'

Edith's eyes looked terrified. She opened her mouth but no sound came out. The workman was loudly complaining.

'She lets me buy 'er a drink, leads me a rare old dance for an hour or more, and then – when I presses for me payment – she turns all shy on me. 'Tis not fair and I won't stand for it, marry and I won't.' He sounded aggrieved and belligerent.

Edith found her tongue. 'Sir . . . please sir . . . I beg of you,' she whispered, 'please sir. . . .'

Nell made her way purposefully through the press of people. She took from one of the tables as she passed an enamelled snuff-box, which she tucked securely into one small hand. Coming up behind the amorous workman and the hapless Edith, she tapped him on the shoulder sharply. He turned and scowled at her.

She smiled brightly. 'Why do you waste your time with those as don't want you, you block-headed rogue? 'Odsbud! There are plenty I dare swear who do. . . .'

His bloodshot eyes narrowed in suspicion. Nell's gaze appeared, to his bemused brain, to be inviting. She was walking slowly backward from him, still smiling.

'Let me tell you, sir,' – she pulled free the ribbon at the top of her stomacher ' – that not all girls have to be persuaded. . . .' She placed one hand on her hip, and looked at him critically over one white shoulder. 'Am I not right, gentlemen all?'

There was an almost unanimous roar of agreement.

'Anyway,' she sniffed, 'who could fear *you*? I dare swear the only woman your whiskery lips have ever touched was your mother – and I feel sorry for 'er, poor old dam.'

The workman grinned at her, his scowl gone. 'Ay, my pretty slut, I'll bet you have a secret or two I could discover – upstairs. . . .'

He came towards her, forgetting Edith. Nell beckoned him with one imperious finger.

'Come to me, my blade, if you want to discover my secrets,' she whispered. The workman lurched towards her, chuckling.

Nell sighed; with desire, the workman thought in anticipation.

'It is always a surprise,' she said slowly, looking up at him with a certain glint in her eye, 'to take a woman. *Some* have more secrets than others. . . .'

Her fingers clicked over something in her right hand. She raised her fingers, as the workman thought, to stroke one rough cheek – then the world erupted in a flash of blinding white light, and his nose felt as though it were being pulled off by red-hot pincers. Nell threw the contents of the open snuff-box straight up into his face, and crowed with laughter as she watched him double up in paroxysms of sneezing coughs and gasps.

She thoughtfully tapped out the last few grains on to his head, as he was bent nearly double in spasms.

'I vow 'is feelings have overcome 'im,' she said thoughtfully.

The whole tavern exploded with raucous mirth.

Benjamin, the huge doorkeeper, came forward and grasped the unfortunate sufferer by the scruff of his neck. 'You come along o' me,' he said good-humouredly, carrying the jerking form to the door. There was a thud as a body landed in the gutter outside.

'That finished 'ee,' nodded Benjamin with satisfaction.

But Ma Ross was not so pleased. Bustling wheezily up to Nell, she shook a fat finger under her nose and boomed in wrath: 'You little slut! How dare you eject all the customers, you interfering jill-flirt. I'll thank you to remember that *I* run this establishment, and when I want your help I'll ask for it.'

'But Ma'am, Edith was. . . .'

'Edith can look after herself,' said Ma Ross flatly, 'without *your* help.' Her eyes glittered balefully. 'And further, since I'm on the subject, mistress. . . .'

But Nell was never to know what Ma Ross had been about to say, for at that instant a panting, dishevelled, fat figure pushed past Benjamin at the door and stood wheezing, clutching at the doorpost, while tears visibly coursed down each cheek. Four men playing cards by the door looked up in surprise. Nell gasped.

'Ma . . . what's the matter?' she asked frantically.

Mrs Gwynne's breaths came in short, sharp gasps as she strove to regain control, shaking her head in reply. The bulk of her heaved up and down.

'It's your sister, Nelly . . .,' moaned her mother.

'What about her?' demanded Nell, grabbing her by the shoulders and shaking her furiously. 'Where is Rose?'

'She'll die of the cold in there,' wailed her mother, 'she'll never see the winter out. Oh, Rose, you wicked girl. . . .'

'What are you talking about, Ma? Where *is* Rose?'

Mrs Gwynne's chest heaved up and down.

'Oh Nell, she's been took off by the constables. She's in Newgate.'

Nell felt as though she had been hit in the face by a douche of cold water, 'No . . .,' she murmured, shaking her head slightly, as though to rid it of some horrible dream. 'What for, Ma, for God's sake?'

'Debt,' said her mother. 'They've took away all that stuff,

parrot and all – confiscation they called it. And she owes more, too.'

'But where is her husband to pay her bills? Where is Cassells?' Nell almost screamed.

'I don't know. Gone,' babbled Mrs Gwynne, and sitting down on a chair, burst into a flood of gusty tears.

CHAPTER III

I never till this day observed that the King
is mighty gray.

The Diary of Samuel Pepys

'I tell you Charles, I won't stand for it!' Barbara Castlemaine's
eyes flashed as her voice rose to a hysterical pitch. Charles
raised a hand to stem the flow of words.

'It's no use screaming at me, Barbara,' he said equably. 'It's
something you will learn to live with. 'Odsfish! I have to, so
why can't you?'

'You? You have to live with it? Faith, you're a damned
rogue, Charles Stuart. I should think that you do have to live
with it and not so uncomfortably either. Stuck between two
women; one the first night, the other the second. How
tiresome for you. . . .' Her voice rasped on his ears. 'The agony
of choice must torture you, my liege. Which one tonight shall
it be?'

'God's body, Barbara, one day you'll try me too far!'
Charles' saturnine face glowered hotly at her. 'Two years ago,
when I married, all the world thought you would be cast off.
Everyone waited for the downfall of my lady Castlemaine.
Instead you stayed, instead I made you a Lady of the Queen's
bedchamber, despite all the trouble which ensued – and now
you ask me to choose between my Queen, who is, may I
remind you, *your* mistress, and yourself. I have a duty to her
and a duty to England. The country needs an heir. My duty as
King is to provide one.'

Barbara watched him slyly. 'Did you ask me to stay because
you felt an obligation, Sire? Or was it perhaps some *other*
feeling which guided you?'

Charles said nothing but looked at the fine limbs and
beautiful figure of his demanding mistress. She pressed home
her advantage.

'There are some who say Catherine of Braganza will never

have children,' she murmured softly. 'Some who know their King have seen that he can beget children without any trouble at all. Such people suggest that the King rid himself of his present wife and take another . . .,' she paused, '. . . who can bear England many sons.'

'Meaning yourself no doubt. I have already acknowledged two of your offspring, Barbara, though I must say the first bore a strong resemblance to your good friend, my lord Chesterfield. In truth, *you* are a fertile woman.'

Barbara seemed unconcerned. She shrugged airily. 'There are some who say –.'

'There are some who had best keep their tongues between their teeth, if they wish to keep their heads on their shoulders. By the Mass, Madam, I will have no word spoken against my wife. She is one of the few virtuous women I know of in this Court.'

'But barren,' slipped in Barbara sweetly.

He turned on her with such an expression on his face that for a second even she felt frightened. The good-humoured light had died out of his eyes, to be overtaken by an unaccustomed look of dark wrath. He spoke with greatly repressed violence.

'My Queen is not barren, and I do not doubt for a second that she can, and will, bear me many sons. The doctors have examined her and pronounced her fit and well. But even if this were not so, even if she *were* barren, she is still my Queen until death. God knows I am not a faithful husband but I will be a steadfast one to her, poor lady.'

Charles' mind turned to Catherine. She was so tiny, so defenceless. She could inspire his pity and his kindness, but she could not give a man such as Charles everything he desired in a woman. He could not love her alone. He looked at Barbara, itching for power and wealth, in open disgust. She picked up dainty nail-scissors, sat down in front of her dressing-table, and began paring her nails gently as she spoke, looking at his reflection in the mirror to see his reaction.

' 'Tis a passing long time since Her Majesty was with child,' she said quietly, ignoring his outburst. 'And last time the Queen nearly died of the miscarriage.' Charles' fists clenched and she saw she had hit home. 'It might be best were she not to attempt to have any more children, for they may be the death of her. I pity her – sacrificed in the cause of the Royal House of Stuart.' Now a brush went back and forth, back and forth, over her tinted nails as she went on. 'The country would not wish to see James's children on the throne – not since he married that frump Anne Hyde.'

'I have countenanced the marriage and there is no more to be said,' snapped Charles – remembering, however, the scandal when his brother had secretly married the Chancellor's daughter.

'Yet Clarendon has many enemies. Our Lord Chancellor is not a popular man. Who would wish one day to be ruled by the children of his daughter, though they be of royal Stuart blood also ?'

'Clarendon is an able man –.'

'But tactless.' Her words fell like ice cold water.

He looked at Barbara's back with smouldering eyes. She was a very dangerous woman. So cruel, but yet how wickedly right she was so many times. She glanced up at his reflection in the mirror, and put down her nail-brush.

'If,' she murmured. 'Her Majesty could be persuaded to go into a nunnery, the country would benefit and so would she. Her health is not good and she is a pious lady. And if she could be removed. . . .'

Charles grabbed hold of her arm and twisted her round so that she faced him, looking up rebelliously into his thunderous face.

'By heaven, Madam, if aught should happen to the Queen, I tell you clearly within the day you would be in the Tower and charged with treason – and I myself should sign the warrant for your arrest.'

She laughed quietly at that, and widened her eyes in innocence. 'I know not what you can mean, Sire. But would you, in very truth, sign away my liberty – I, who have borne your children and given you my all, including my honour.'

'Your honour,' scoffed Charles. ' 'Pon m'soul Barbara, that's rich coming from you.'

A solitary tear trembled on her eyelashes. 'I vow I know not how you can abuse me so. . . .'

But Charles had turned away, sick of these tears that she always used to grind him down. Barbara saw her trick was not working and her temper got the better of her, though she had held it in check so far. She was never one to mince her words. Her voice cut the air like a whip. 'I know well how you hate me, Sire, but still you come back to me, do you not? Do you not? For you like my body. . . .'

Still he did not move. Barbara lost all control.

'May you keep your pox-ridden Queen, then! I swear I care not! And may she die, bearing the son you want and none will mourn less than I, and so I promise you.'

Charles wheeled round. He took from under his shirt the locket in which Barbara knew he kept her picture in miniature, which she had given him years ago. He placed it carefully on the dressing table. Barbara's hands went up to her mouth – too late. Then he stared at her and said coldly, 'I know of your intrigues with Buckingham, my lady. My spies tell me of various little plots; visits to fortune-tellers, experiments with potions to arouse love and . . . extinguish life.' His voice hardened to an inflexible note of quiet anger. 'I tell you this, Madam. I will not tolerate treason within my realm. You play with fire, be sure you do not get burnt. Buckingham is being watched. I have a care to those I love and will know where to look should accidents happen.'

Barbara said nothing. She knew her lover well. When he was moved to adopt such unaccustomed dignity, she retired into silence because his anger, slow to be aroused, was the more terrible when it took control. She pouted sulkily.

Charles turned to leave. 'A little hint of extra warning, Madam. I advise you not to ask me again to choose between the Queen or yourself. For if you do it is quite possible that it would be you, and not she, who leaves the Court.'

She gazed at him in horror. She knew her very survival was now in question.

'Charles, I did not mean –.'

He looked at her with shrewd eyes, knowing that he could never cast her off; she fascinated him too much. But he could frighten her when the need arose.

'I give you good-day, Ma'am.' He slammed the door behind him.

Outside in the corridor Charles sighed and turned to go back to his private apartments. But a small, wheezing figure hurried up towards him, anxiously gasping. Charles doffed his hat in greeting and waited until the small, tubby man stood before him, bowing and clucking with worry. Watching him, Charles' mouth twitched in amusement.

'My lord Clarendon. . . .'

The Lord Chancellor of England looked more harassed than ever. 'The French Embassy, Sire . . . you promised to receive them at two o'clock and 'tis now gone half past. . . . I have left them in the Stone Gallery, admiring His late Majesty's collection of paintings. But time presses, time presses.' His voice grew more flurried than ever.

'Time and tide wait for no man, my lord,' quoted Charles.

The Chancellor looked at the white and gold doors to the Countess of Castlemaine's suite of rooms and his lip curled. 'One can always make time for what one wishes, Sire,' he said in a pointed tone. Charles looked surprised, but then burst out laughing with that easy rumble so often heard in the corridors of Whitehall.

'I see you knew where to find me, my lord Chancellor. 'Oddsfish, my dear sir, I know I am a prodigal rascal and not a proper sovereign at all. Don't prate at me again, I beg. I am a sorry dallier and vow to mend my ways.' He glanced at the Chancellor who still seemed sunk in gloom. '*Allons*, my friend, let us go and find these illustrious Frenchmen and hear yet again what my golden cousin Louis is doing to beautify his court, I hear the power of La Vallière is waning. . . .'

Together they traversed the maze of corridors and doors that led across the rambling Palace of Whitehall to the long Stone Gallery, the focal point of Charles' court, where the gallants ogled all the ladies, and where could be found the awe-inspiring collection King Charles the First had made of the world's best masterpieces. Charles, his son, strode ahead briskly, the small Chancellor struggling to keep up with his long stride. But gliding up a staircase towards them came a small, dark girl with piquante features, a little Roman nose and a mass of fairy curls, who stopped when she saw the King and curtseyed shyly. Lord Clarendon heaved a deep sign and looked up sidelong at his Royal master, who was standing stockstill, with a rapt expression the Chancellor knew only too well.

The girl he recognized; her name was Frances Stuart. She had arrived over six months before, as one of the ladies to Her Majesty's bedchamber and made Castlemaine mad with jealousy. She was the Court's newest beauty. Charles had noticed her on the first day of her appearance at Court and had been pursuing her ever since to no avail. He had named her *La Belle* Stuart and the Court had been only to quick to agree. But though an obedient subject, the little Stuart had shown that, while she held dear the King's favour, she held even dearer the chastity she so zealously guarded. She was not of the stuff that Castlemaine was made – and the two ladies hated one another like poison.

Frances adopted a lofty contempt to the ill-bred manners of Barbara, which she said reminded her of a street-walker, while the Countess sneered at the pose of *La Belle* Stuart, who, she said, had lost her virginity at the age of twelve, as no doubt His Majesty would find out one day.

But, try as he would, Charles could not break down the barriers that Frances put up between them, though she was always polite and ready to smile at him. And perhaps because of this he found her more fascinating, more irresistible. Castlemaine fumed and swore she would scratch out the eyes of the little milksop, but Charles was so infatuated that Barbara never dared mention her, for she was beginning to realize she could not trespass too far on his tolerance. Her position was no longer so steady.

Clarendon looked on Frances with a cynical eye: he did not believe that any of the women of Charles' acquaintance could be called virtuous.

'Your Majesty . . .,' he began urgently, tapping his large pocket watch.

'In a minute, Chancellor. . . .' The King waved an impatient hand at his minister. He bowed as Frances came up to them. 'I give you good day, Madam, whither away?'

She smiled shyly. 'On an errand for Her Majesty, Sire, which cannot wait.'

'Pish!' The King flicked his fingers. 'All things can wait. I have a crowd of rascally Frenchmen waiting to see me, and they can certainly wait a minute or two.'

Clarendon sighed heavily behind them.

Charles spoke over his shoulder. 'Go and tell them I will be with them in five minutes, my lord. . . . No . . . say ten. . . .'

He eyed Frances speculatively and she blushed and dimpled.

Clarendon's voice was fussy. 'Your Majesty, 'tis already. . . .'

'I know, you clock-watcher, gone half past the hour, is it not? Well. . . .' He paused and then smiled. 'Tell them I will be there in seven minutes exactly.'

Clarendon shuffled off, muttering. Charles laughed gaily. Then he looked down at Frances for a long while in silence. She appeared to be embarrassed and gazed at the floor.

'I swear 'tis an age since I last saw you, Frances. Her Majesty must keep you very busy.'

'I have my duties, Sire.'

He smiled. 'You also have your duties to your King, Frances. Though you seem to see him very seldom.'

She did not reply. The King's eyes narrowed.

'Can you have been avoiding me, Frances?'

'Avoiding you, Sire?' Her tone was nervous. Charles took a step nearer. 'You know what I mean, lady how can you pretend you do not? I must be a sorry looking fellow, I swear, for you to dislike me so much. I assure you I do not mean to press attentions where they are not wanted.'

She coloured. 'Sire, it is not . . . I beg of you . . . I do not dislike you, Sire.'

'Could you ever . . . like me, Frances?'

'I am without experience in Court life, Sire. I do not yet know how I should respond. Perhaps one day. . . .'

He caught both her hands in a tight grip. 'Frances,' he pleaded. 'Can you not lower your barriers, not for just one minute? Can you not trust me at all?' His voice was low and intense.

She stared up at him, her eyes wild and full of panic. 'I don't know, I can't tell . . . but that which I have to lose, I wish to lose in a marriage bed, Sire. I know that some people may laugh at me for it, but I cannot help it, indeed I cannot.'

'I do not laugh at you, Frances.' They exchanged a long glance in the quietness of the corridor.

'I know Your Majesty is very kind,' she murmured, and smiled at him shyly. 'But indeed I must be off; Her Majesty awaits my return.' She curtseyed and was gone before Charles could stop her. He watched her go, and, shaking his head, mused on the divergencies of women. He thought of Barbara and Frances. 'One screams and is willing. The other says nothing and is unwilling. Yet both are a sore trouble. 'Odsfish, life becomes complicated!' A clock struck the quarter in the distance over the Banqueting Hall. 'Faith! I'm over a quarter of an hour late now,' said the King.

Catherine of Braganza's slight form took up little space as she perched on the satin stool, with her tiny feet barely touching the ground. She was having her long, dark hair brushed ready for that evening's banquet in honour of the French Ambassador. Frances Stuart took a long-handled ivory brush from the dressing-table and gently began to tease out the flowing mass of hair that rippled down Catherine's thin back. A French boy plucked a lute and sang love-songs in the corner of the apartment, by the window seat. Lady Suffolk, Queen Catherine's Groom of the Stole, laid her gown of shimmering brocade, edged with ermine, carefully over the bed, while two of the Ladies of the Bedchamber, Lady Arlington and Lady Falmouth, gently smoothed *crème d'essence alabastre* on to the Queen's arms and hands.

When she spoke, her voice was heavy with a Portuguese accent. 'Did you give my message to Duchessa Alber-r-marle, Frances?' She enunciated the words with care.

'Yes, Your Majesty. She was sorry you could not come to her card party, but said she quite understood. Perhaps another time.'

'Ah,' nodded Catherine quickly, 'that I should like. . . .'

Frances looked down at the small head in sympathy. Catherine was so small, so tiny, hardly big enough to be a woman let alone a Queen. She was far too naïve and vulnerable in the Court of Whitehall. Hers had been a stormy marriage. But what else could one expect? Was it not inevitable that there should be trouble in this match between an innocent, convent-bred girl from Portugal, and Charles Stuart, King of England, the lusty grandson of Henri the Fourth of France?

In the mirror Frances could see the reflection of the great bed belonging to the Queen. Huge and gilt, with embroidery of silver and crimson velvet, it had curtains of puce brocade and its headboard sparkled with a peacock's array of precious stones. It had been a wedding present from the States of Holland nearly two years before, and had cost over eight thousand pounds in gold. At the top were the arms of England and Portugal, joined by an encircling love-knot. Frances sighed and glanced at the *prie-dieu* and stoop of holy water the Queen always kept by her bed. She was a simple person who, thought Frances, would have given all the jewels on the bedstead that the legend at the top might be true. Her shock had been great when she arrived in England.

She had been too young, too inexperienced, to deal with the situations she found. And then there had been the matter of the list of the Queen's ladies. . . . Charles had been so enamoured of Catherine when they had married. It had looked as though he would settle down and end his peccadilloes. The

Court waited for the casting off of my lady Castlemaine who had tearfully gone to Richmond for the birth of a child, which all the world knew was begotten by Charles – this looking like banishment, for she had sworn to have the baby at Whitehall.

At first Charles had seemed so careful of his Queen. Catherine had not met the lady confined, and Charles and she had appeared to be deep in love. The Court had sniggered at the outdated farthingales worn by Catherine and her Portuguese ladies, and sniffed daintily at the gaggle of priests that she had brought with her. But they did not sniff in public. Charles had persuaded Catherine into an English mode, and his love was so obvious that the young bride found herself on all sides beset with suitors and flattery. She was in fact quite pretty. Though her complexion was a little dark and her teeth protruded slightly, her figure was finely-knit, and, though small, she had a quiet dignity. But trouble was soon to mar their early happiness.

To Barbara was born a son whom Charles swiftly acknowledged, as he always did, never seeking to evade the responsibility that was his. But when he went to see Barbara, so the Court whispered, the embers of his old love were still warm, and my lady Castlemaine, freed from the burden of pregnancy and looking apparently more beautiful than ever, could stir them again to fire. Barbara had a claim on Charles' affections and she did not fail to use it, proffering her son and asking sweetly for a Court appointment to support her in her 'retirement'.

Charles had agreed and put Lady Castlemaine's name at the top of the list for Her Majesty's Ladies of the Bedchamber. But Catherine had heard the whispers, and was told with horror, by her old harridan of a duenna – that hawk-nosed old Duchessa Penalva – that Lady Castlemaine was to come to Court and that she, the Queen, must receive the woman – Charles' mistress and mother of his natural son.

When the list had arrived, Catherine had struck Barbara's name off the list and sent it back to the King covered with tears of a love now blighted, and shocked at his apparent

9   129

cruelty. Charles had reasoned with her and Clarendon had been sent to persuade her – to assure her of His Majesty's love for her and the fact that his passion for Castlemaine was at an end. He merely wished, Clarendon explained, to establish a place for her at Court so that she might not be made the butt of the world's humour.

But Catherine had still been upset and would not listen. Alone in a strange country, too young to understand the vagaries of the husband she now adored passionately, she had reiterated her refusal. She thought that in refusing she could dismiss a rival, whereas, as she later realized, he had only been driven away by her tears and tantrums.

Frances remembered the tale she had been told by my lady Suffolk, of the King standing wroth in his wife's bedchamber while she sobbed hysterically in a corner, surrounded by her priests, refusing to reverse her decision. The old Duchess of Penalva had stood coldly surveying the King with her steel grey eyes and informing him that good Portuguese Catholic ladies did not behave as did the English ladies of Court; they were not used to being treated as harlots. Charles had heard her out and then left the chamber without saying a word.

But two days later, most of Her Majesty's retinue had been ordered to leave the country and Catherine had been left with Penalva, a few ladies, a confessor – and a marriage that seemed in ruins.

Sighing at her thoughts, Frances put down the hair-brush and took the Queen's thick, dark hair, plaiting it skilfully and piling it on her head with the aid of several jewel-studded combs.

Catherine spoke over her shoulder. 'Thank you, Frances. You are indeed a good girl. I do not know how we managed before you came to us.'

'Your Majesty is most kind.'

'No, I but speak the truth. His Majesty told me only yesterday how much he admired the way you worked. He said you were so busy he hardly saw you at Court. I must tell you not to tire yourself out, my dear.'

Frances's cheeks burned, and she dropped her eyes guiltily. The Queen, she thought wryly, was still very innocent.

At the time of the royal quarrel, Charles had been driven back to Castlemaine, and there had been an open scandal when she had been first received at Court in the Queen's presence. Catherine had fainted and been carried out by her ladies. The whispers had spread through the city of London that the King's fidelity was at an end.

But then Catherine had become pregnant. When Frances had arrived to become one of her Majesty's ladies, the Queen was heavy with child and the country waited for its heir. Frances had seen Charles constantly, in his wife's apartments, asking after her health and treating her with great affection and gentle consideration, telling her she could have anything she wished and scolding her for not taking enough rest.

But Catherine miscarried and nearly died of her child. To avert the tragedy, the priests said masses for her soul, all the windows of her apartment were shut and a live cock was cut in half and placed over her fevered brow. All the bleeding had been to no avail and the doctors prophesied her death.

Frances had been in the bedchamber when the King was told of his wife's desperate condition, and all had been shocked at the grief and pain written deep into his face after two sleepless nights of sitting with his wife's tossing, fevered body.

He had taken one look at the musty rooms with the incense heavy on the air, and the chanting priests and gawping Court, and burst into anger. All had been ejected, and only Frances and Lady Arlington had stayed behind, to raise the Queen in her bed to receive one of Charles' own prepared remedies, which he called 'quinine', a brew from the Americas upon which he pinned his hopes.

Catherine had taken it, but it was Frances's own view that it was Charles himself who had made his wife live. Bending over her, with tears streaming down his face, in the quiet bedchamber, he had sworn he could not live without her and implored her to get well. Frances had seen the Queen's eyes slowly open, as she looked wonderingly at the King and asked in a hoarse whisper: 'For . . . you . . . Charles ? You wish me to get well for you ? You love me so much. . . . ? I did not know . . . did not understand. . . .' Tears had rolled down her sunken, sallow cheeks.

Charles kissed her and left her sleeping. And Catherine had got well.

But Catherine of Braganza had learnt her lesson – that the country she had come to was a wild one, just freed from one of the dreariest periods in its history. That its people now wanted to enjoy themselves and that the man she had married was of the same mind. His loyalty she could count on, his kindness she already knew. But if she wanted his love she must be prepared to share it. She must receive her husband's mistress, affect a friendship for her, and attempt to show Charles that she was the better woman. When he thought of her, she resolved, he would think of peace; of warmth, laughter, music – and love. So Catherine had received Barbara at White-hall, and Charles, ever kind and easy-going, had drawn close to her again.

Indeed Catherine had even taken to Castlemaine's own game of wits and beaten her at it. Once when the Countess called and found the Queen dallying over her *toilette*, pushed and pulled by her bevy of ladies, she had sneeringly asked Her Majesty how she had the patience to bear with it. Catherine had looked Barbara up and down and told her plainly in front of the whole Court that she had to be patient over many things and so was used to it.

But as Frances held the cosmetics casket for Catherine, she wondered if the innocent girl who was her mistress had yet learnt how to deal with the intrigues of Court life and withstand the jealousies of such as Barbara, Countess of Castlemaine.

Now Catherine stood up in the centre of the apartment in her shift, and her ladies gathered around her and lowered her gown over her head. She selected some trinkets from the jewel-box Frances proffered, and placed on her finger the ring containing one huge blood-ruby that Charles had given her at Christmas.

There was a knock at the door of the apartment and behind several backward-bowing footmen there appeared in the doorway – alone and without any gentlemen – the King himself, sparkling with the Order of the Garter, and dressed magnificently in a suit of old gold slashed with scarlet, set off by a dark periwig and scarlet ribbons.

The ladies curtseyed low.

Charles approached his Queen, who stood small and defence-less in the middle of the apartment. Frances watched as he drew near, but he gave no one but his wife so much as a glance. As he lifted her hand to kiss in greeting, he saw the solitary ring and noticed its contrast with the usual profusion worn by the glittering, gorgeous Barbara. Catherine seemed tremulous and anxious. Charles' eyes looked down from under hooded lids and the harsh lines of his swarthy face softened. He knew the seductive spectre of Barbara could not be banished entirely; he knew himself too well for that. Yet resolutely he thrust her into the background.

'My wife,' he whispered. 'Married, as I know, to a curs'd rogue of a husband – inconstant and profligate. But yet, believe me, always steadfast.'

CHAPTER IV

Oh Liberty, thou goddess heav'nly bright,
Profuse of bliss and pregnant with delight.
Eternal pleasures in thy presence reign,
And smiling Plenty leads thy wanton train.

Addison

The turnkey opened one lethargic eye, grunted – and closed it again. A renewed banging on the great and ancient door insisted on disturbing him, and he shifted in his seat and spoke.

'Dem it,' he yawned, 'can't a man 'ave a whisper of peace? Ooh. . . .' He pressed a large hand on a reluctant knee joint as he got up, and, sniffing, grabbed a lantern to light the way from his small office to the great gate with its peep-hole window. He pushed the shutter back, peered out, and blinked.

A slight figure stood outside on the cobbles, one hand clutching the huge, rusty, iron knocker and banging it frenziedly up and down.

' 'Ere, 'ere,' he murmured weakly, 'stop that, can't you, you'll have the whole street up and abaht. What d'ye want at this hour, 'tis gone two o' the clock. What are you doing abaht the streets at this hour anyhow – you got a touch of the moon madness?'

'I had to come,' gasped the girl. 'I want to get inside.'

The turnkey rubbed his nose with one puzzled finger. 'That's a new one,' he ruminated slowly. 'I don't think I've ever bin asked that afore. I swear I 'aven't. Most of them as I know want to get *out*.'

'I want to visit someone,' pleaded Nell. 'Please. . . .' A pair of almond shaped eyes sparkled winningly up at him.

The turnkey shook his head. ' 'Tis very late –,' he began ponderously, but the clink of a coin on the courtyard between his feet cut short his excuses.

'*Please,*' said the voice, and the turnkey looked through the

134

rusty bars at the most beautiful face he thought he had ever seen, reflected by the light of the lantern. He rumpled his wiry hair in bewilderment.

'What was your business about, Miss?'

'It's my sister. She was brought in today – took off by the constables. I *must* see her. Please.'

'I don't rightly know as it's by the rules like, Miss. Where was your sister put in the prison here?'

'I don't know,' fumbled Nell. 'She hadn't paid her bills, you see, and they said she. . . .'

'Ah,' responded the turnkey in gloomy relish, 'it'll be the Debtors' Ward.'

'Yes, yes, I suppose so.'

The turnkey smiled back at the troubled young face behind the bars.

'Then you 'ave a ray o' hope, Miss. Jest a ray, yer might say. Nah the debtors, they ain't locked up same as the other prisoners what we got in 'ere, cost they ain't crim'nals, quite, if you follow. Leastways, not till they're tried they ain't – and your sister were only brought in today so she ain't bin tried yet an' so I promise you. 'Sides, she'd only get the old jaw and curtains.'

The girl's face showed white and strained behind the bars.

'Could . . . could I see her?'

'Well, not really,' said the turnkey crushingly. 'Not at this time o' night. 'Cept I 'appens to know the wardress of the female Debtors' Ward – by name of Mrs Judkin, luverly woman, you know – been a widow these past five years and that lonely. . . . Well as I was saying, I do know Mrs Judkin and p'raps we could come to an agreement. But she'll need persuadin'.'

A slim white arm pushed through the bars and pressed a coin into the turnkey's hand. He watched its withdrawal with a barely suppressed sigh of pleasure and then looked down to see a glint of gold in his hand. 'Yes, well . . . I'll go and wake 'er up – I sometimes go for a chat with 'er round abaht now if I can't sleep. If you'll just wait 'ere. . . .' He shuffled off into the distance with his lantern, and his footsteps died away in the distance as the dark mass of Newgate prison swallowed him up.

Nell paced up and down the wet cobbles in impatience. The December night was cloudy and iron cold so that the air hurt the lungs. It seemed an age until the turnkey returned, and she did not catch his footsteps, only hearing him when a slightly slurred voice said jovially through the shutter, 'It's horl right, Miss. Come along in . . . and think yourself lucky you're not stayin' – for it's mortal cold, mortal cold.'

Nell wrapped her cloak around her and waited while there was a deal of fumbling with keys and pulling of rusty bolts, until a small door in the centre of the vast arched gate creaked open and she hastily stepped through into the courtyard. The gate banged behind her with a heavy thud, and she shivered – realizing for the first time where she was. The atmosphere was still and airless; oppressive in its gloom and Nell's knowledge that all around lay the sleeping bodies of men, women, and children, condemned to a grim period within these walls. Where, she wondered, looking around in the dark, was Rose incarcerated, and was she, too, asleep? Nell doubted it.

Following the turnkey's footsteps she went across the courtyard, around the corner along a paved alley between walls that loomed blackly above. Nell felt the icy night air blow down the passage against her cheeks. The low bulk of the hunched figure of the gaoler stopped at a door on the left, set in the wall. Nell followed the dim light, stooping under the lintels, then for a long time she climbed. Bare steps went up and up in a spiral, Nell slipping on the damp stone and gasping as she followed the bobbing, uncertain, light of the lantern in musty darkness. Their footsteps echoed eerily. Then, as the lantern cast light into a passage, Nell saw a sharp-featured woman in a drab gown with a bunch of keys hanging from a chain at her waist.

She raked Nell up and down with a cold pair of eyes and her thin lips closed even tighter. She glanced at the turnkey, who said, 'I told m' good friend Mrs Judkin 'ere that you're desirin' to see your sister. What's 'er name?'

'Gwynne . . . no . . . Cassells, Mrs Cassells. . . . She just got married, you see, and. . . .'

'She was the pregnant girl brought in this mornin', right?' Mrs Judkin replied briskly, nodding in understanding as she tucked a strand of hair of an unlikely looking shade of copper into an old mob-cap. 'I recollect 'er now – fine looking, well set-up girl with long dark hair if me memory don't mistake, eh?'

Nell nodded dumbly.

' 'Ad a bit of the clinkers with 'er, I recall, which is more than most of them 'ave. Some 'ave to sell the rags off their back, you know – this is a prison, not a hostelry. Anything you wants – food, bedding, wine – you pays for, *'andsome*. No, your sister was lucky, and she didn't like the idea of going down the Common Hold, so I got 'er to pay for a room sep'rate and right glad she was to have it, and so I promise you. Do you recognize this?'

She pulled back her shawl to reveal a string of milky pearls clasped about a thin neck against an alien background of grey serge. Nell's hand shot out to pick at it.

' 'Ands off,' barked Mrs Judkin. 'She gave 'em up to me. I told 'er – in the Common Hold she'd be dead of the gaol fever within six months, so she saw there was no choice and she paid up with the gawdies 'ere for 'er perks.'

Nell's eyes narrowed in anger like a cat's. 'Six months, Ma'am?' she inquired softly. 'What about Rose's trial?'

Mrs Judkin chuckled. 'Lor', dearie, where've you been living – under the lovers' star all your life? There's more 'n a score waiting for trial up in the cells and God knows how many we've got down the Pit – and they're just the debtors. Your sister'll be lucky to find a hearing before March, sweet-heart.'

Nell was horror-stricken. 'But she can't stay in prison all that long,' she burst out.

Mrs Judkin pointed to the floor. 'Down there,' she said with slow emphasis, 'lies at least two hundred people. Some of them 'ave been 'ere for two, three, five years. Can your sister pay 'er debts?'

137

'No . . . I don't know . . . we can't guess at what she owes.'

'Then a trial won't do her any good anyway,' shrugged Mrs Judkin. 'She'll only be condemned to stay in Newgate till she's paid.'

'But she might never be able to pay –.'

'She'll have to stay in that case, till she's carried out in 'er coffin.' Unconcerned, Mrs Judkin fingered her keys.

'Will you come with me then, Miss? I've got no time to waste. It's very late.' She glanced at the turnkey. 'And I've got me bed to think of.'

'Of course, Ma'am,' said Nell, trying to infuse some warmth into her voice, knowing that upon this unscrupulous woman's shoulders lay the question of Rose's future and welfare, though she found herself loathing her cold, business-like methods. She pitied the wretches under her greedy hands, but realized that to make an enemy would be foolhardy and dangerous. So she smiled at Mrs Judkin and replied lightly, 'I would not for the world keep you from your rest, Ma'am. Lead on, I beg.'

Smiling tightly, Mrs Judkin led the way down a steep flight of steps and along a dim corridor lit only at the corners by inadequate rush-lights. She paused by a length of grimy iron railings which served to make a balcony of the corridor along which they were passing and gaped out on to a void of gloomy blackness. Mrs Judkin paused momentarily, one hand on the rail, and looked down into the pit. Out of the darkness rose up towards them a long moaning cry as if of pain. There was a pause and then it was repeated, bringing with it this time an accompanying noise of low moans and an unnerving wail of hysterical crying.

'Some of 'em never sleep,' she said. 'They keep it up like this all night till they get the buckets thrown over 'em. Some's bosky, some's touched.' She put one finger to her forehead. 'We allus get 'em in 'ere till we can get 'em shifted to Bedlam, o' course.' A repeated wail reached out to them. 'Follow me,' sniffed Mrs Judkin. Further along the gallery, she pointed down at a massive iron grating set in the stone.

'Yonder's the Common Hold,' she said matter of factly. Nell

waited for her to say more, but Mrs Judkin apparently deemed herself to have said enough. And as a smell of sweat, excrement and stale, close-packed, humanity rose up fetidly to Nell's nostrils, she felt inclined to agree. She raised her handkerchief to her nose in disgust. This was worse than the Coal Yard.

Mrs Judkin noticed her action with faint amusement and laughed in a crackled chuckle that set Nell's nerves on edge.

'Ye get used to that smell when you're in 'ere for long.' Her tone was flat and unemotional.

She clutched her shawl about her and shivered. 'Fierce, this cold,' she said over her shoulder to the girl behind. 'Enough to freeze the life out of your bones and the passions from your heart. Coldest winter I've known this past ten year, but Old Rowley manages to enjoy 'imself despite all, from what I'm told. He's still supposed to be mad over that Frances Stuart fit to turn his head, for all she's held 'im off for six months or more; daft as a mooncalf 'e is over 'er. I 'eard as how he's made 'er model for 'is Britannia on the next year's coins.' She chuckled. 'That'll turn a few men's heads, that will – my lady Stuart revealed on the backside of every flunkey's groat.'

Nell hurried after until the woman stopped in front of a dingy door and inserted a key. Above it the number 157 was carved.

' 'Ere's your sister,' she said in her business-like way, and the door swung gently inward, creaking. As Nell went in, the door clanged to behind her. The floor under her shoe was of pulpy straw. Even as she stood at the entrance, a dark figure rose from a motionless sitting position on the pallet by the wall and ran into her arms sobbing hysterically. Nell held her sister close.

For a full five minutes, Rose buried her face in Nell's small shoulder and cried out the whole sorry tale. But her state was such that Nell could not understand a word. She held her sister tight, letting her release the pent up fear and misery that welled up inside her. Gently, Nell guided her to the bed and sat down holding her in a reassuring embrace.

As her eyes became accustomed to the gloom, Nell could

make out the furnishings – if so they could be called – of the cell occupied by Rose. The cell was long and narrow, and its atmosphere was chill. The sodden matted mass of straw underfoot obviously had not been changed for years. Nell sat on a low pallet bed with no blankets, with her trembling sister beside her.

After some time, Rose, regaining control, moved off the bed to fumble in a corner. There was a momentary spark and then the flickering light from a solitary candle on the table threw into relief the spectacle of one of the better rooms in Newgate prison. High up in the wall of bare, filthy stone, was an opening, barred with stark rods of iron.

The December winds of night drifted upward with the mist, fluttering the flame of the candle in the corner on its rickety table.

Rose was in a bad way. Her hair was snarled and tangled, her eyes sunken in her face like two gouged pits of weariness, her gaze abstracted as she plucked nervously at the cloak she had wrapped around her against the chill of the cell. Her voice was edgy with panic.

'Nelly, what am I to do? What will become of me? They tell me I owe close on five hundred guineas. 'Tis impossible, I swear it; but they tell me it's true.' Her voice choked on a sob.

'Rose, where's Jack, where's your money all gone?'

'Gone, gone . . . gone,' wailed Rose, sitting on the bed and swaying rhythmically. 'I went to see Jack but he never turned up at the Maypole. Anyway, I came home early and decided to go to bed. Halfway up the stairs, I was stopped by a thund'rous banging on the door – I thought it was Ma in one of 'er happy moods. But it wasn't.' She bit her lip, close to tears again. 'There were three men outside. 'Oons! I thought they were footpads come to ransack the house, but when the smallest on 'em, a little beetle-arsed tweeter, started talking, I knew why they'd come. I remembered 'is voice from before, only then it had a different tune . . . "Oh Madam Cassells, 'tis the vogue, Madam Cassells . . . it becomes you vastly." Filthy little worm.' She spat on the floor in disgust.

'He'd sold you goods on credit?'

'Aye, they were duns, and they'd come for their money. Jack always said I could give the bills to him and 'e'd settle them. Anyhow, it seems they all know each other and met in Change Alley as usual – one of the new coffee-houses I collect – discussing their accounts, and all found they had a common outstanding debtor. Me. The payments are long overdue. Some things I've had for close on a twelvemonth, thinking they had been paid for. But now they come round for their money, rubbing their greasy hands.'

'After all, Rose,' said Nell, 'shopmen have to live – same as us. . . .'

Rose scowled. 'They've got plenty! I told 'em I'd a banker friend, a *cher ami* who'd give me the cash. And off they went. So I ran upstairs, packed a valise, and hunted under the floorboards where I keep me valuables, you know.'

Nell nodded.

'I'd got my cloak on and my valise with a few gew-gaws in my hand, and I was just tiptoeing down the stairs again, when there was another lot of banging on the door. I thought it might be Jack and I was so relieved I didn't think. I flung it open. But who should be standing there but old beetle-arse, and his mates – and a Constable. Of course, there I was with my cloak and luggage, ready to flit. And then one of 'em – right little worm he was – smiled and said "Going to see your banker, Madam Cassells?"'

'Oh, no,' muttered Nell.

'Oh yes. Now you know how I came here. Lord, Nell, this place, this filthy rotten place – it's like hell on earth. Half those wretches in the Common Hold won't ever get to trial – most of 'em die of gaol fever within the month; no wonder they fling brine in on top of the prisoners to prevent the filthy humours reaching the rest of the prison.' A faint cry sounded down the passage outside. 'They can't sleep for long down there in that festering pit. You can hear them screaming and shouting like wild animals – and the chains clanking and rattling as they bang them on the bars trying to get out.'

Nell felt sick with horror.

Her sister sighed and shrugged: 'That old hag Mrs Judkin is doing a roaring trade. Everything costs money. My jewels won't last long.' She looked down at her wedding ring. 'And when my money runs out. . . .'

Nell gripped her sister's shoulders. 'We must get you out of here,' she muttered.

Rose turned hopeless eyes upon her. 'Have *you* got five hundred guineas?'

Nell shook her head dumbly.

'Oh I shall rot here I know it, I shall never get out of here, never!' Her sister's voice rose to a shrill wail.

'Rose, give me the necklace and any other jewels, and I'll go and pawn them to buy you off,' urged Nell urgently. 'At least it will get you out of prison.'

Rose shook her head. 'Can't be done, Nelly. I've already pawned the necklace to that slut who holds the keys, for a miserly month's board. Take it or leave it, she said – so I took it. Besides, I owe money all over London – leastways if Jack hasn't paid any of the bills I must, and you know what duns are. When the word flits across 'Change, I doubt not I'll be sued for every stitch off my back and my body and all. They'll all join in and they'll leach until I'm – sucked dry.'

She turned brimming eyes on her sister.

'Nell, find that misbegotten husband of mine and tell him to get me out of this. That's my only hope – I'll give you his direction.'

She searched in a bundle of possessions for the scrap of paper.

Nell watched her hopelessly. There seemed little chance that a man who had lied to his wife and landed her in prison for debt would suddenly be able to find the huge sum required to get her out, or care much for that matter.

Rose found a crumpled slip of paper and turned with the light in her eyes of a feverish hope. Her face was tense and drawn as she gave it to Nell.

'Find Jack, Nelly. For the love of God, find 'im!'

CHAPTER V

Farewell ungrateful traitor,
Farewell my perjured swain,
Let never injured creature
Believe a Man again.

Dryden

Down beside the Thames, within the warren of alleys that lay between Thames Street and the river, lay the worst district of London's slums. The tall, rotting houses touched at the gutters above, leaning until they eventually gave up the struggle and crumpled into the passage-way below. Hardly any light filtered through from above, but the mist from the river drove its way along the alleys, bringing with it the stench of the Thames: the odours of sewage and rotten vegetation.

Here could be found the most miserable of London's poor – and the most vicious. No sensible citizen ventured down these dark passages, and any unwary visitor was likely never to be seen again – except as a swollen corpse floating in with the tide by Tower Wharf two days later.

Off a narrow, winding, street, where rats ran freely about in the gutter, Nell turned under a low stone archway which led into the aptly named Purgatory Row. Compared with this even the Coal Yard looked palatial. The smell was indescribable; the hovels were collapsing where they stood; a few urchins played in refuse scattered across the cobbled alley. Nell felt she would like to give one of the grubby children a groat, but she did not dare. The glance they gave her was not a friendly one and the sight of a coin would endanger her, for she knew she was being watched.

Nell stopped by an old crone who sat knitting by her shabby dwelling, to ask the way to the Cat's Paw.

As the woman looked up, Nell saw in horror that one eye was missing. A thin, stitched, lid was all that remained, screwed up in the empty socket, while the other regarded her with suspicion.

'For why do ye want to know, sweetheart?'

Nell stammered, 'I . . . I seek Master Cassells, Master John Cassells, Ma'am. If you would be so good. . . .'

The old crone laughed. Her cackling grated on the girl's ear. 'Ho, Tyburn Jack, is it? I warrant he'll be glad to see you, my lovely – for there's naught like you around here, ye know. Leastways, apart from me there ain't, and that ain't saying much, is it?' She wheezed to her feet. 'Follow me, child.'

Holding a kerchief firmly to her nose, and inwardly quaking, Nell did so. Picking their way up the alley, they walked for some minutes until they entered a tiny cobbled courtyard of four houses, propped against each other at a drunken angle. A wooden sign swayed aloft from a chain above their heads. The old woman squinted at it with her one eye.

' 'Ere we are, dearie.'

Casting a furtive look round, Nell pressed a groat into her hand, and, ignoring her thanks, pushed open the door nervously. The tavern was empty. A few stools lay upturned about the floor, round barrels obviously used as tables, and a broken gin bottle scraped against Nell's foot as she trod softly across the room to a narrow staircase that went up behind the counter. She followed it up.

Pushing open the door at the top of the stairs, she came into a chamber, low and dark. But the room was empty. Its owner had obviously been hasty to vacate it, for rumpled clothes lay across the floor, tumbled linen still hung out of the drawers pulled open and left, and the bedclothes were flung back as though someone had just got up. Nell stepped across to feel if it were still warm, but as her hand stretched out to touch the sheet, a voice spoke sharply behind her.

'Was ye wanting sommat?'

Nell spun around in alarm. Leaning against the doorpost, eating an apple, lounged a frowsy-looking girl wrapped in what looked like an old bed curtain.

'I said, did ye want sommat?'

'I seek Master Jack Cassells,' announced Nell. 'Tyburn Jack I think you call 'im. 'Tis most urgent and I *must* find 'im.'

The girl shrugged in a bored fashion and took another bite of her apple. ' 'E's gorn and good riddance,' she grunted.

'But where? When did 'e go?'

The girl spat out a piece on to the floor and grimaced.

'I don't know, least I wasn't with 'im when 'e left.' She glanced at the bed. 'He don't favour me no more since he took up with that fancy-piece, he's supposed to be bedding; a fine lady with a place at Court, so I'm told. He reckoned he'd just married her a month back. But he still stopped here, so I doubt not it's but another of his tales.'

'He's married to my sister, and she's no fine lady, for all the airs she gives herself,' said Nell furiously. 'When did Cassells go?'

'Early this morning, I think. 'E said nothing and left quick-like after he got a message from 'is friend, old Thumbscrew.'

'Old Thumbscrew?'

'That's the name 'e's called on account of 'is job. He's a warder at Bridewell . . . no, Newgate it is, I reckon. Sent a warning, see. P'raps the warrant's out.'

'No,' said Nell sadly. 'Just 'is wife.'

'Comes to the same thing, don't it,' jeered the girl, and tossed the core on to the unmade bed.

Nell groaned. It was obvious to her what had happened. Cassells had got wind of Rose's arrest and got out while the going was good. Rose could look in vain for him to get her out – and if he did not, she could stay there till the end of her days.

Sarah was intent, painting her nails with a bright crimson varnish from a small crystal bottle on the table. Her hand was splayed out on its surface and she dabbed at it briskly as she listened to Nell's miserable tale of the plight of her sister, with one eye on her cosmetics and one ear on Nell's story.

'Gone off has 'e, and left 'er? Well it happens all the time, don't it. Soon as you're breeding, they're off like a Puritan in a theatre.' She glanced sympathetically at Nell. 'Not that it helps *you* much, sweetheart, I know. 'Faith, I wish you were here, Master fancy Cassells, and I warrant I'd have a few words to say to you and a lot more besides.' She slewed around in her chair and frowned.

'If Rose is in Newgate you can give up hope of a release, Nelly – I know someone whose mother stayed in there for thirty years, and she only left in 'er box, poor dam. Sorry, but there it is – there's no release without you pay, and if you *could* pay you wouldn't be in there – stands to reason.' She snorted. 'Devilish system, ain't it? Now if she were in Bridewell I might be able to help; I know a turnkey there. . . . But she's in Newgate, so it don't signify. 'Ow much does she owe?'

'Close on five hundred guineas,' whispered Nell.

'Lor',' murmured Sarah, impressed. 'What's she been doing, *eating* the stuff?'

'No, but those leaching duns have added everything up, and added a few things here and there. They mean to have every last penny-groat.' Sarah examined her hand against the light with a critical eye. 'Well, there's only one thing for it,' she said at last, and turned round to wink at Nell. 'She'll have to bed every squinting turnkey in the whole curs'd prison.'

Despite herself Nell burst out laughing.

But depression soon reasserted itself as even Nell's spirits drooped. How was Rose to solve her debts when she could not even be let loose from prison to attempt to do so? Even her body, her chief source of income, failed her in this instance.

Nell looked down at her own slim form in its tight-bodiced woollen gown, and ran her hands down over her breasts, feeling her slender waist. Would men pay, she wondered, five hundred guineas for such a body? How many times would she have to endure it? How many panting, middle-aged men . . . ?

She hugged her arms around her body to protect it from the thought. Yet, if it were not for Rose, she might not even have such a body to offer. If her sister had not cared, that slender

146

frame she now held might have perished through lack of food. If it were the only way. . . . The thought hung over her like an ominous hand beckoning her on to an inevitable doom.

But after she arrived that evening at Lewkenor's Lane, her drink-sodden mother sobbing about cold, rats, and agues, Edith met her with good news. Her eyes shining in her pale face, she drew Nell into a corner, and before the girl knew what was happening, poured five gold broad pieces into her hand. Nell opened her mouth to protest but Edith closed her hand over the money, cutting in, 'No, take it – 'tis for your sister, not for yourself, and I would that you have it. 'Tis not much I know, but it's all I have, you understand, and it might help. I pray that she be released soon.'

Nell hugged Edith and thanked her with tears in her eyes. Edith smiled. 'You have a good heart, Nelly,' she whispered. 'I will pray for thy sister's future with all my heart.'

Feeling slightly embarrassed at being addressed in such Quaker terms, Nell smiled tremulously. But better was to follow. For before any of the customers arrived that night, a tall, thin, figure pushed past Benjamin into the tavern and glanced around. Ma Ross was nowhere to be seen, but in the corner a small figure was busy lacing up a dress with one hand striving to reach around her back.

'Can I help you, mistress?'

The figure turned, looked up in surprise and saw the man.

'Jonathan,' she cried – and burst into tears.

Much later, sitting in the high-backed settle in the corner, Jonathan nodded morosely at Nell's lamentations. He agreed with her brusquely that escape was impossible.

'In sooth, 'tis as easy to get to heaven as winkle a hole in Newgate's walls, I know.'

'Then Rose will stay in Newgate till she rots,' murmured Nell.

They sat in silence a while. Jonathan stared at his brandy glass, then murmured, 'Rose has many friends, as I remember – or at least she had. My dear, she was the veriest bawd of

147

London in those first days when our beloved Black Boy returned to rule us. She knew people who mattered – people at Court.'

'I remember her once saying she had sat next to his Grace of Buckingham at the play, and how the Duke and Duchess of York had the opposite box. But the King often goes to the theatre like that with no ceremony,' Nell remarked. 'How can that help?'

'Rank does not stop a man from noticing a pretty face, my dear, or a fine-turned ankle. You would do well always to remember that. Rose had, as her beaux, many of our foppish gallants at Court. She rubbed shoulders with the Duke of York's set, and even *he* – I happen to know – before he married that poor frump Anne Hyde, cast a speculative eye on her. However, that is by the way. Rose had one friend in particular. His name was Killigrew. Does that name arouse your interest?'

'Master Thomas Killigrew owns the new Theatre Royal in Drury Lane, Jonathan, everyone knows that! Was it 'im that Rose knew?'

Jonathan smiled as he swilled the brandy in the glass around and around.

'Aye, he knew her. And his young scoundrel of a son was mightily smitten by Rose Gwynne. He could not take his eyes – nor his hands – from her.'

'But what . . . what happened Jonathan?'

'She met *me*,' remarked Jonathan easily, 'which was undoubtedly a good thing since it stopped the boy making a fool of himself over her, and relieved his father of having to provide for several bastards.'

Nell looked up sharply, then caught the glint in Jonathan's eye and smiled reluctantly.

'Harry Killigrew – that is the boy's name – ever had a soft memory of Rose. And he is still at Court, as groom of the bedchamber to the Duke of York. Nell, you must see this fine friend from the past and pour the tale of Rose's woes into his ears. I warrant he'll listen.'

'But, Jonathan,' she protested, 'how could *I* get into the

Palace of Whitehall to see such as he? They would never let me past the gate.'

'If you wish to see Killigrew, go and see his father at the Theatre. I hear that now they're beginning to employ girls instead of boys to play female roles, a lot of young men have suddenly discovered a taste for the play – His Majesty included. I doubt not young Killigrew will be down there many times o' the week.'

'How do you know so much about the Court and the Duke of York and all?' demanded Nell suddenly.

Jonathan flicked her nose with his finger. 'Don't ask questions, my child, and you will be told no lies.'

Nell punched him on the arm with a small fist. 'Ogre,' she scolded. 'But, despite all, thank you truly for your aid. I always knew you had kept a fondness for Rose within that cold heart.'

'I have no fondness for Rose at all,' said Jonathan. 'Do not delude yourself, Nell. My memory and my affections do not last so long.' He stared down at his clasped hands. Nell was puzzled.

'Then why do you help me? Is it . . . to spite Cassells?' she hazarded in disgust.

'No, Nell,' answered Jonathan simply. 'It is for you.'

Thomas Killigrew tore his sandy-coloured wig from his head and threw it to the ground before him with an oath.

'Body o' me, you insensate bitch, can't you understand a word that's said to you? When I say speak forcefully, I don't mean scream at Master Kynaston like a demned fishwife. You're at the King's House, my girl, not the Royal Exchange!'

Above him on the stage, at the level of his forehead, a somewhat plump girl pouted and began to protest shrilly, while the actor clasping her in his arms cast a pained look down at Killigrew.

Tears dripped down the girl's face. 'We've been on this curs'd stage for close on four hours, and I tell you plainly I'm cold, I'm tired, and I'm miserable. I vow and swear I've done nothing but parade about here at your beck and call all morning long and I'm frozen to the marrow. Pox take you, 'tis nothing less than sheer cruelty to use me so.'

Pushing off the dark actor holding her about her ample hips, she flounced off the stage. The young man clapped his hand to his forehead, uttered a string of oaths, and stalked off the other side.

Thomas Killigrew sighed and sat down, stretching out his long, thin, form upon one of the matting-covered benches in the pit of the theatre. He watched unmoved as a rat scuttled past him and disappeared down a crack in the boards of the apron.

It was always thus, he ruminated sadly, with Ann Marshall; unless he agreed with everything she did, she took a pet and refused to act at all. Killigrew was tired of the feminine wiles that had crept into the theatre. She had been his first actress, of course, and it had been she that had graced the stage of Drury Lane at its opening in May, playing Celia in *The Humorous Lieutenant* – she, the first actress on the stage of London.

It had turned her head, of course – since then there had been no doing anything with her. Though other actresses joined her in the women's shift, the tiring-room behind the stage, she retorted grandly that she had been presented to the King and imagined herself as good an actor as Charles Hart himself.

Killigrew smiled, as he remembered presenting his company of King's Servants to his royal master in the Grand Box, surrounded by his courtiers. He had eyed Mrs Marshall's well-endowed figure with a shrewd smile and then turned to Killigrew, his dark eyes glowing with amusement. 'Well, Tom, 'tis better, I own, than last time I came to the play and had to wait for the heroine to be shaved! I see now there is no such problem.'

The courtiers had tittered and Ann Marshall had dimpled and blushed. But Killigrew had been emboldened to retort. 'Nay, Sire, never let it be said *I* was an aid to furthering your delights – I doubt if the country can afford more.'

Lady Castlemaine, glittering with diamonds as usual, had turned noticeably pink with suppressed fury. But Charles remained easy and unruffled.

'Fie on you, Tom,' he remarked genially, 'for you, who shared my exile and saw my miserable pinch-penny existence, to begrudge me my pleasure now I have returned from my travels! For shame, Tom! God will not damn a man for a little pleasure out of the way – always remember that.'

The theatre had returned to popularity; everyone flocked in, so that Killigrew had no cause for complaint in that direction. Yet things were not easy. It was difficult to find women suitable for the boards. Acting took a lifetime's training and there were no women who had been acting long enough to match the feeling of Charles Hart or the sensitivity of Michael Mohun, his two leading actors. He had established his own 'nursery' for the King's House, but it had hardly yet borne fruit. He had to choose, it seemed, between the stiff, affected style of Mrs Marshall, and the vivacity of little Beck Marshall, Ann's sister, whose gamine wit was admirable for the farce but could hardly be fitted into the tragedy of Shakespeare.

Shaking his head, Killigrew got to his feet, and putting on his wig, made up his mind to go and pacify Mrs Marshall. He must, he reminded himself, be more wary of hasty words – they wasted too much time that could be better used for rehearsal. Perhaps it would be easier to return to the good old days of Hart's great-uncle, William Shakespeare, when boys had taken the girls' parts and he could cuff them into order, without going cap in hand to offended matriarchs, ensconced in scented dressing-rooms. Times had changed, and so had the theatre, though whether for better or worse was a question best left unanswered.

More people came to see the plays, even tragedies, when it was known that a beauty was taking the leading role – and the farce now impelled many to come, who wouldn't before. The sprightly Beck Marshall saw to that.

Yet the old-fashioned Killigrew felt the drama was not what it had been – there was no life in the theatre any more, he decided as he turned the corner of the stage. In the passage leading to the dressing rooms, he collided with two brawling figures, one large and one small. He recognized the larger as Mrs Meggs, the woman who looked after the orange girls who had just started plying their trade in the pit. The smaller was a young girl with coppery hair, pulled loose by her exertions, who kicked at Mrs Meggs' legs and endeavoured to loose herself from the iron grip on her collar exerted by that redoubtable lady.

Killigrew paused. 'How now, Mrs Meggs, what have we here? A visitor?'

'Nay, sir,' replied Orange Moll, as she was known from her profession. ' 'Tis but another of Ma Ross's whores, come for a job, I doubt not.'

'I am *not* a whore, you filthy cow, and let me ... *go*!' gasped Nell furiously, wrenching herself free of Orange Moll's clutches and facing Killigrew, panting.

His first impression was of her size. Small and finely made, with tiny hands and feet, she stood gazing fiercely up at him with bright hazel eyes blazing. The second memory he always had of her was those eyes. Almond shaped and translucent, they glowed with a fire at once bewitching and compelling. He had to know more of her.

'Are you one of the young ladies in Madam Ross's employ, my dear?' he enquired equably.

Nell tossed her head. 'If I am, it does not signify. I come to see you on other business – urgent business, sir, if you please. And I *would* have reached you, if that malapert slut, that cunning bitch. . . .'

'I think we will leave your analysis of Mrs Meggs out of your account if we may.' Killigrew glanced at her face and saw anxiety as well as spirit in those eyes. 'What is your name, child?'

'Gwynne, sir, Nelly Gwynne.'

'Well, Nelly Gwynne, you must come to my office if you must see me so urgently. Mrs Meggs, you may go – thank you for your vigilance.'

Orange Moll strode off, muttering about small girls that needed a whip taking to their shoulders, and Nell's fate should they ever meet again.'

'You have made an enemy, I fear,' murmured Killigrew.

'I care not,' retorted Nell. 'I *had* to see you.'

'Ah,' muttered Killigrew querulously, and stepped across the recess usually occupied by his small orchestra in front of the stage. Here he disappeared through a door which led into a large room stacked with odd rails of costumes, pieces of wood lying in a heap in a corner, and a dusty selection of stage furniture and fading backcloths. Nell gazed in wonder, as she sniffed at the smell of wood shavings and stuffiness that she had never smelt before. Stopping at a neat green door leading out of this chamber into the passage, Thomas Killigrew beckoned Nell in.

'I will give you five minutes and not a second more,' he warned, as he let Nell into his small office. 'So say on, Nelly Gwynne, and let me hear this troublesome business that concerns us.'

Nell looked up from staring at her lap only when she had finished her story. She had not taken the courage to look at Killigrew while she spoke. Perhaps if she had, Nell would have given up before, for Killigrew heard her out in growing scepticism, an expression of controlled amusement on his face.

The tale Nell told appeared to him to be sordid and not even to possess originality. Such stories were common about the London which Killigrew knew. The story of his son's liaison with Rose Gwynne, he doubted. Harry had too many girls for his father to remember one in particular – and most affairs were conducted away from his father's eye. Killigrew felt, however, that it was his duty to protect his son from any designing woman who claimed any hold on him that might prove expensive. He had expected Nell to claim Rose had borne Harry's bastard. When she did not, he lost interest, save that of saving his son from the results of his indiscretions.

He prided himself he was too old to be floored by a pair of pretty eyes or the glimpse of a slim ankle. The girl's story came down to one thing, it seemed to Killigrew – she wanted money. Her sister was undoubtedly a bawd who had run herself into deep water and now sent her pretty sister to beguile unwary men to pull her out of it. The girl herself, he remembered, from Orange Moll's self-righteous voice, came from that notorious tavern kept by Madam Ross down Lewkenor's Lane. Killigrew ran a theatre and he knew the dirtier side of life too intimately to be easily taken in. And he had no intention of parting with a groat.

'My dear young lady,' he murmured politely. 'I am sorry but I fail to see how I can help your unfortunate sister.'

'But . . . but . . . if your son could take up her cause, sir. . . .'

Killigrew permitted himself the ghost of a smile. 'I think Harry is less in a position than I, if I do not mistake, to find a large sum to free your sister. Five hundred guineas did you say?' he inquired gently.

'But if I could see Master Killigrew . . . your son . . . .' stammered Nell.

'I regret that is impossible,' answered Killigrew, imperturbably polite, and making a mental note to tell Harry to stay away from the theatre for a while at least. He rose from his chair, as if to signify that the interview was at an end.

Nell faced him squarely and her voice was low.

'My sister needs help.'

'But not from me or my son.'

'From anybody.'

Killigrew sighed. 'It is not in my power.'

'It *is* in your power, an' you wished it.'

'I am sorry there is nothing I can do. Now if you will excuse me, I have a good deal of work to attend to and. . . .'

A cold voice of contempt rasped on his ears. 'May you rot in hell, you smug, thick-skulled fop! Go back to your whoring women and your painted men, you greasy pimp!'

Killigrew looked up, shocked, to see a small virago before him, with a pair of furious, flashing eyes, afire with rage. The small breast heaved uncontrollably with a pent-up passion. Her chair lay behind her upturned, but she did not notice.

Nell's eyes travelled over him in a way Killigrew found singularly disconcerting, as she raked him with her scorn. Her lip curled and the words spat from her.

'You, you little god, sitting there listening to me so polite. I thank you not a whit, for your precious time, you scrawny coxcomb. "I regret I cannot help . . . six hundred guineas, was it not, my dear?" ' Nell's voice mimicked Killigrew's precise accents. 'You can keep your filthy money, every penny groat, and I'm sure I care not! My sister is in prison; she's been deserted by her spendthrift husband – and if I ever catch 'im I'll tear out his innards with my nails, if I have to – and all you can do is sit and squawk like a curs'd jackdaw!'

'Nelly . . .,' mutter Killigrew weakly. 'Mrs Gwynne. . . .'

'*My* sister,' pursued Nell ruthlessly, 'can stay in that filthy prison till she rots, and you care no more than if she were a fly. I didn't come to ask you for charity – a good thing, since it seems you have none – but merely to ask your son if he can secure justice for 'er, for all she's the selfishest bitch I know. Oh, what's the use. . . .' Nell burst into tears.

'Bravo!' said a genial voice behind her. 'And when are you going to take on this new actress, father, may I ask?'

Nell looked up to see a thin gentleman in periwig and blue brocade stroll nonchalantly into the room. His eyes were alight with amusement.

'Oh God!' moaned Killigrew, and slumped back in his chair. 'Harry, you fool, why do you have such a knack of appearing when you're wanted least?'

CHAPTER VI

Can life be a blessing,
Or worth the possessing,
Can life be a blessing if
Love were away?
Sir Charles Sedley

'She is just the same, truly she has not changed,' murmured Henry Killigrew in delight as he opened the rusty postern door of Newgate so that Nell could go out. The turnkey winked a watery eye at Nell as he closed the door, then the iron bolts of Newgate shot to behind them. At once they were again in the land of the living; Nell sniffed at the air of the London street and gazed at a knot of urchins in the gutter with interest – any scene of the city was a relief after the gloom and sheer isolation of the confined, within the walls of Newgate. She wondered at Harry Killigrew's face as he gazed at his manure-splattered boots, until she realized that he was still back in the prison – back with Rose.

'She is just the same as I remember her, with that flame of life in her, and those eyes fit to turn a man to the Devil himself, I doubt not. Ah, there are few like her.' Killigrew shook his head as he remembered.

Nell regarded him shrewdly. Rose had certainly worked her magic, she thought, as she looked at the bemused result of her sister's charm. She wondered what Rose had said as she, Nell, had waited outside the cell for an hour or more. More to the point, what had she done?

As for Killigrew, his mind could still see the luminous, dark eyes of Rose as they shone in the candlelight of the gloomy cell. He could still see her raven hair, tossed on to her white shoulders and down her smooth, naked, back, still smell the perfume of her as she pulled him to her, pressing soft kisses against his mouth as she murmured, 'Come to me, my love, give me the only joy I have had since I came here and

156

stopped living. Oh . . . my love of the past, my love. . . .'

Killigrew loosened his cravat and coughed, feeling again her body below his, yielding, soft, and yet intense with passion, and those eyes . . . those black, black eyes. . . .

Nell broke in on his memories.

'What did m'sister say, sir ?'

Harry flushed. 'She told me of her plight, how she had not the means to pay for her cell for ever – and no chance at all of paying her debts that she could see.'

'But she cannot go in the Common Hold, sir, she cannot!' cried Nell.

'No, indeed,' answered Killigrew heavily. 'God forbid. If there were only a way. . . .'

He racked his brains for a means to free Rose, to save her from that death by slow degrees that awaited her, chained to a wall in the pit of Newgate's damned. He couldn't pay her debts, he knew that; indeed, his father had forbidden him to try, even while he agreed to the visit being made. Yet how else could she be freed ?

Rose's words rang through his brain with increasing intensity. When he had asked about her husband, she dismissed him in a string of words more fitting to a Thames waterman than a woman, yet this did not dim her glamour in Killigrew's eyes, for her next words had sent the blood pulsing in his veins.

'Perhaps one day I shall escape this prison, Harry. Then Harry,' her lips brushed his cheek, 'I shall be truly free. Free for you, Harry . . . my love. . . .' Her breath had warmed his eager ear, her flesh lay beneath him, soft and inviting. Some day . . . some day. . . .

His fists clenched as he remembered. Then an idea struck him.

'Nelly, I have to see someone. Someone at Court who might help Rose.'

Killigrew remembered Edward Browne, and his way with women. Better to lose Rose for a night than for ever. He forced his jealousy down with an effort.

'Could you take this . . . gentleman into the prison also, as you have me, if I can arrange it with him?' he asked urgently.

Nell's eyes betrayed her surprise.

'Yes, I suppose so, sir, but what about Rose? Can you not help her?'

Harry Killigrew took her face in his hands and smiled.

'I hope so, Nelly, and better this way than any other. If Rose pleases my friend, it is not improbable that he could get her out of prison.'

Keeping a tight hand on her purse, Nell wove her way through the sweating, pressing, mass of people thronging around the stalls in Newgate market. By her side was the now familiar clomp, clomp, of Hobey's crutch.

Though she had no real need of him, the old man had insisted on coming with her, declaring that he had known Rose from the time when she was a 'snotty tot' as he called her, and he wanted to help Nell 'bait the trap'. The steady thud of the crutch on the cobbles helped to calm her – it was the sound of her childhood, reassuring and safe. Time rolled back, and she felt again as if she were the thin, scared, child being guided home in the dark by the old man's friendly lantern, after a long day's skivvying for Ma Ross. Yet things had changed so much; now it was Hobey who followed *her*, to the prison where the sister of her childhood days and her childhood fears now lay, relying on Nell to procure her release.

Around them bawled the shouts of the stall-holders, seeking to outbid each other until the noise threatened to deafen the stolid citizens' wives inspecting their wares. Mumbling, Hobey followed her round the corner to where the high, grim, stone of Newgate's dank wall cast a chill over the whole street. They could still vaguely hear the noises of the market behind them, but there was an eerie silence as they came under the shadow of the prison.

As they came to the high, spiked, gate, with its peep-hole door in one corner, both of them saw a dark camelott-clad figure turn towards them and bow stiffly. His hat was pulled low over his head, but his black periwig brushed Nell's arm, as he kissed her hand without emotion.

'Mrs Nelly Gwynne, I believe. . . . ?'

'The same, sir,' answered Nelly, bobbing a curtsey, and speculating that his courtesy was slightly out of place in the muddy street outside Newgate prison.

'I am truly glad to see you here.'

The man grunted and looked suspiciously at Nell's companion. Hobey sniffed noisily and spat on the cobbles. Nell ignored him.

'Might I enquire who you are, sir?' she ventured softly.

'The name's Browne, that's all you need to know,' he returned shortly.

'It is your sister I have come to see.' He jerked his head at the door.

'Shall we go in?'

Hobey looked at the high walls in fear. 'If I went in, 'tis likely the likes o' me would never see the street again. Plenty like me never come out again, save to Tyburn.'

Nell stared at him with horror in her eyes.

'Lord, I'm sorry, child,' murmured Hobey in apology.

'I'd no wish to put the jerks up you. But the place gives me the grims. I won't come in, but say 'ello to Rosie for me, will you, Nelly. Tell her . . . I don't know . . . tell her I miss her. . . .' He smiled tremulously as he turned away.

'Mrs Gwynne?' said Mr Browne.

'Sir, at your service.' Nell turned back to the business of saving her sister's life.

As she bent her head under the low lintel of the door into the courtyard, the warder – now friendly, due to Nell's monetary gifts – whispered at her, 'I give your sister the message, me dear. And I reckon she'll be ready for yon fine gentleman. She said to meet you by the prison taproom.' He gazed impassively at the stranger's back, and winked at Nell. 'Let's hope he finds her worth a plunge or two.'

Mentally saying 'amen' to that, Nell followed the gentleman into the labyrinth of Newgate Prison.

A woman carrying a slop pail down the steep stairs from the Female Ward watched with interest as the two figures entered the huge vaulted chamber of the prison. Prisoners wandered about vaguely, in sweating inertia, for although Newgate kept all prisoners under close guard, during the day all inside doors were opened, so that within its smelly confines felons were free to go as they pleased; to the taproom to drown their sorrows, or to the chapel to pray for release from their misery. Or, merely to wander, free for a few hours short though they were, from the wretchedness of a tiny cell and the stench of the latrines. There was a sorry clink of shackles about the wrists and ankles of those prisoners too poor to pay for their removal.

Striding forward arrogantly, he ignored the thronging mass of prisoners and their murmured pleas for alms as though they did not exist. He took a perfumed pomander from his pocket and held it close under one nostril, comparing the smells around him to those of the City's sewers and prophesying epidemics of the plague.

'Where's your sister, mistress?' he said sharply to Nell. 'I'll not wait till Doomsday to meet a paragon of Killigrew's who as like as not is a figment of his imagination.'

'I think you were wanting me, sir.' There was a cool voice from the stairs.

At the top of the staircase stood Rose, one hand resting delicately on the iron banister as she stood silently, her face an enigmatic mask. She was dressed in a gown of wool which Nell had never seen before. It was plain, stark, black, and fitted tight around her. Nell wondered how she contrived to look so small, carrying a child, though Rose had always had a tiny waist. Aloof and fragile, she seemed like a misty figure, even witch-like in her distant intensity. Her whole being breathed a strength of purpose. Above a white brow, her hair was pulled straight back and flowed in glossy ringlets down her back, with a curl of black over one rounded shoulder. She wore no jewels, for she had none, and she carried no ornament save a plain white kerchief in one slim hand. Severe and simple, she looked older, and yet with those large, lustrous black eyes, and her fine white skin, she was beautiful. And she smiled.

As she came down the steps, her gown trailing behind her, her eyes never left Browne's face. She was playing her part so well, thought Nell in amazement – this was a Rose she had never seen. For Browne's eyes never left her either.

She came up to him and held out two hands, more like a queen greeting a servant than a prisoner for debt. Like the courtier he was, Browne bent and brushed her fingers with his lips.

'Your servant, ma'am!'

Rose's eyes looked deep into his and her expression was troubled. 'Can you help me, sir?' she asked quietly. 'For indeed I have no other to ask.' She looked down demurely for a moment, and then looked up quizzically.

He put one hand on her shoulder, and gently pushing the material back, slid his hand over her flesh. She came closer, resting her hand over his. He saw her eyes glowing and felt her glide smoothly into his arms. His senses reeling, he heard himself say, 'Anything, anything within my power, ma'am, I would be most happy. . . .' He led her out of the press of prisoners crowding around and took her into one corner.

Nell followed them, watching closely. As Rose sat down, Browne's glances grew more intimate. 'Faith,' Nell heard him murmur, 'this time Killigrew did not lie.'

Rose was gazing at him with the same troubled expression, so alien to her usual happy, careless mirth.

'I am in grave trouble, sir. Indeed I fear my cause is hopeless. I have debts I cannot begin to pay.'

' 'Odsfish, so have we all,' replied Browne. 'Your case is hardly singular, ma'am.'

'But I must stay here until I have paid,' returned Rose mournfully. 'And that I cannot do. I must remain in this prison until I die.' She looked down, twisting her kerchief between her fingers – a picture of fragile agitation. 'I know I have no chance of freedom without help of some sort – or a word to procure justice for me. My father fought for the King . . . our family lost all in his service . . . like so many.'

Nell looked at her sister in amazement, but stayed in the background.

'He lost his life for His sacred Majesty, may God bless his martyred soul. Can his son help the children of a father long dead in some forgotten battle?' Rose's voice grew quieter. 'I have writ a letter asking to be freed from this woeful place of torment and begging excuse for my debts as my family lost *all* for the Crown. Sir,' – she pulled a billet from her sleeve – 'will you deliver this to a gentleman at Court who –.'

Browne frowned. ' 'Tis no use writing to anyone, sweetheart, all letters get lost – some on purpose. There's such a curs'd lot of them.' He tapped nervously on the wall and looked thoughtful as he ran his eyes over her.

Rose stood up and put one hand softly on his arm.

'May I offer you such poor welcome as I have in my room, sir? I have procured some Rhenish and we may . . . talk over my misery.'

Browne felt her breasts against his body, her hand sliding slowly up his sleeve. 'Thank you indeed, ma'am. And I promise you, if necessary, I will talk to the Duke – that is to say, to someone . . . myself . . . to obtain justice for your unhappy family.'

Forgetting Nell, and deep in conversation, Rose and Browne walked away up the stairs arm in arm.

Walking out, Nell stopped at the gate and dropped Edith's five guineas thoughtfully into the poor box, watched by an astonished turnkey. Then silently she bent under the low lintel and the door banged behind her.

Mr Samuel Pepys was busy making his way down Featherbed Lane, looking around guiltily as he did so. He pulled his hat, garnished with a magnificent ostrich feather, further down over his glossy periwig, remembering the flattering remarks made by the Duke of York upon it, and His Highness's assumption of the fashion soon after.

The thought comforted Mr Pepys as he reviewed his life as Clerk of the Acts to His Majesty's Navy – in direct contact with the Duke of York, Lord High Admiral of England. Truly his days revolved around the great, he thought complacently, as he flicked an imaginary speck of dust from his mulberry sleeve. Even His Majesty had nodded to him in Hyde Park but the week before. The remembrance was gratifying, and Mr Pepys savoured his new-won prestige as he sauntered elegantly along.

A passer-by stumbled against him and with an oath Mr Pepys jostled him roughly into the gutter. Really it was too much! He must get himself a carriage, he told himself, now that his position was so altered. His wife had told him so for months past. Why, his friend and neighbour, Sir William Penn, had procured one ages ago, and he was only on the Navy Board like himself. Mr Pepys had dreams of a carriage upholstered all in yellow satin, such as that owned by my Lady Castlemaine, but he was afraid his wife might guess his reason for wanting it.

At this moment, however, a carriage was out of the question, as Mr Pepys wished to be as inconspicuous as possible. He was returning from an illicit afternoon watching the cock-fighting at Shoe Lane – a favourite pleasure. A new pit had just been opened; he didn't see why he should resist the temptation offered him, but he was nervous that he might be missed at the Navy Office. In fact he had left a message with his secretary, Will Hewer, that if his cousin the Earl of Sandwich or any other gentleman should ask for him, he must say he had gone home with a sick headache. It would be somewhat embarrassing, if someone should see him in the street just at the moment.

Nevertheless he did not feel guilty. He had tried to cut down on his drinking – a great strain – and he did not wish to forgo *all* his pleasure. Besides, he comforted himself, everyone enjoyed a cock-fight. There had been an amazing variety of men there, from an old Parliament supporter by the name of Wilde, whom Mr Pepys remembered having been Deputy Governor of the Tower, when Cromwell was alive, to a motley lot of 'prentices, bakers, brewers, butchers, draymen, and all sorts. His wife would not approve of his consorting with such low company, he knew. She would tartly tell him he was as bad as her lazy, good-for-nothing brother Balthazar, as she always did on such occasions.

Mr Pepys shook his head as he remembered how the poorest-looking men had scrambled to put ten pounds or more on a fight! Perhaps they were richer than they seemed. A topsy-turvy world. . . .

Keeping his eye open for a plain hackney he could hail quietly, Samuel turned his mind back to the alluring Lady Castlemaine. He had seen her with the rest of the Court around the King, as they walked the Matted Gallery at Whitehall or sat in a box in the theatre; and he could not repress his admiration, nor his fervent attraction to the lady. Though he sternly tried to tell himself that the Court was pleasure-loving, and condemned its licentious abandon, when he saw Lady Castlemaine's shifts and stockings fluttering in the breeze of the morning in her garden at Whitehall, he could not help but sigh, as he imagined the limbs they enclosed.

Yet again someone jostled him. He nudged back fiercely and a girl's figure stumbled into the gutter.

'Indeed, sir . . . I am sorry,' murmured a voice, 'I beg pardon for bumping into you.' A white face glanced quickly at him, then she stumbled again and moaned slightly with pain.

Mr Pepys put his hand under one elbow and stopped her from falling.

'Here, Madam, may I help you?' he asked solicitously. 'You seem somewhat ill. . . .'

She tried to shake him off. 'No . . . truly, sir, I shall be well in a trice. 'Tis naught but a gripe or two and will pass, I doubt not. . . .' She pushed her hair back from her face in agitation and for a second Mr Pepys thought it was Lady Castlemaine's face at which he looked – so beautiful was she. But he saw the girl was seriously ill.

All of a sudden, she toppled against Mr Pepys and would have fallen had he not caught her in a strong grasp, careless of his coat for once. Sharply he called a hackney and then turned to the sagging figure beside him.

'What is the matter, my dear?' he asked softly.

The girl shook her head wearily, and Mr Pepys wondered what it was until he saw the tell-tale stains of blood. Then he knew. As the hackney drew up, he looked down at the half-fainting form and asked her direction and her name. A pair of large black eyes fluttered slightly as she murmured, 'I live near Drury Lane, at the Coal Yard. My . . . my name is Rose Gwynne.'

Mr Pepys settled the trembling figure in the corner of the coach and then, sitting down, leant back against the squabs, eyeing the pallid face opposite in trepidation lest it fall forward in a dead faint. Brushing her snarled hair back from her face with one weary hand, the girl roused herself to speak.

'I feel you should know, sir,' she began slowly, 'what sort of a passenger you are helping. I am not a respectable citizen's wife, took with the colique. My illness fits my character, you will no doubt agree.' Her lip curled slightly as she said it.

If Mr Pepys was shocked he did not show it. 'Aye,' he remarked easily. 'But there, 'twould fit most people an' I make no mistake.'

'I am but newly come out of Newgate prison.' Her chin tilted up defiantly.

'That would account for some slight dishevelment in your appearance,' agreed Mr Pepys, unruffled. 'Demned hellish places, these prisons, so I'm led to believe. 'Tis coming to be quite fashionable – I swear there are more debtors from White-hall than anywhere else. Lord knows, my Lady Castlemaine would have been took off long ago, did His Majesty not pay her debts so kindly as he does. Always seems to me 'tis the wrong people who are took off and the wrong people stay free. But more important – what do you, wandering about the streets like this, and in such disarray?'

'I was released this morning,' replied Rose baldly. 'Someone called with a warrant or something, and I was told I could go, just like that. I haven't even been tried yet, you know, so my luck was in, I doubt not. Faith, who'd have thought one piece of paper would make that much difference between life or death. I'd have been in the Common Hold come a sennight, and that's for certain.'

Mr Pepys frowned, not understanding half of what she said. 'But that does not explain your present plight. Had you no friend to meet you?' Rose shrugged.

' 'Odsfish, I came out with Master Wickham – that was the young man's name – and as soon as we came to the fish market on the corner 'e left me. Perhaps it was the smell of the 'errings as much as myself.' She tried to shake the wisps of straw from her cloak. 'Lord, 'tis hardly surprising, sir. I am not a pretty sight, I know it only too well. Yet. . . .' Her eyes closed as she sank back in the corner, sighing. 'I was pretty for long enough, just long enough to matter.'

Mr Pepys waited silently as the voice stopped, wondering if she had fainted. He heard the rumble of the wheels of the coach bumping loudly over the uneven cobbles, with no interruption. The coach crawled down Bread Street and turned sharply into Long Acre. Its wheel caught the wooden post on the corner and it lurched suddenly to one side.

Mr Pepys sprang forward to catch the girl as she fell from her seat. Coughing slightly, she caught herself in time and grabbed Mr Pepys's arm, thanking him. Something in her gesture, the resolute way she held her chin, touched some forgotten chord in Sam's memory. He was endeavouring to recapture it, when she looked up at him with a set face. A slight beading of sweat on her brow showed signs of fever and her eyes were bright.

'You know what's happened to me, don't you,' she said evenly. 'You knew when you saw me.'

' 'Tis none of my business, mistress,' murmured Sam in embarrassment. 'You were but ill, that is all that matters. . . .'

'Nay, but it is not, sir,' declared Rose weakly. She thrust out a grubby hand. On one splayed-out finger Sam saw a ring. It was tarnished and looked cheap. Looking at it, Sam suddenly felt unutterably sad, though he didn't know why.

'I was an honest woman, did you know – an honest woman. When he slipped this ring on, I thought I was safe – from the sneers of people, and the constable's hands, and all. Madam Cassells,' she smiled mirthlessly. 'It sounds well; so respectable. I swear I fancied myself as upright as any Cheapside goodwife. 'Twas Newgate showed me I was but a Fleet Alley whore. I went into prison because of my husband, I stayed in prison because of my husband. When I sold my jewels to buy food, I kept his ring until last. God's death, I'm a fool! I knew it then, but still I kept it. And do you know, I needn't have bothered. . . .' She laughed tremulously as tears started in each eye. Her voice broke.

'When I came to sell it, they wouldn't buy. It's not even gold – 'tis but a painted lead tawdry from Bartholomew Fair. A base ring, from a base rogue! Don't you think that's fu-funny, sir? Worthless through and through . . . and I . . . believed his lies. All . . . the time I took his lies like a wetgoose for truth o' Scripture. My Lord! To believe *him* . . . Jack . . . Jack. . . .'

Mr Pepys started forward but this time too late. The girl slid down in a collapse.

When the hackney rumbled under the low archway into the smelly court of houses, Mr Pepys was shocked. He looked at the line of grubby washing hanging across from one wall to the other, and the grass growing up through the uneven paving slabs, and recognized the usual sight of London's slums. The Coal Yard was no different from any other district of the sort on Ludgate Hill, Thames Street or the Fleet – the smell was the same, the poignant odour of poverty.

From the open doorway of the house opposite came a girl's voice raised in fury. 'Marry and Amen, ma, I swear I'll stand it no longer! 'Tis bad enough when you come home every night as skinned as a newt. But when you start rampaging about till the place is a shambles, you can clear it up yourself when morning comes – and I hope your head *does* split open!'

Mr Pepys picked up the unconscious girl in his arms and strode towards the doorway, a tiny smile playing about his mouth. He was met by a slight figure of a girl, standing with her back to him, her tawny hair tumbled slightly by the breeze as she shouted to someone indoors, 'Aye go to sleep an' you will, you sot, but you'll clear your own mess when you wake. If it is a slave you want, you can look elsewhere. Go get a blackamoor from Pannier Alley. I've finished, and so I tell you!'

Mr Pepys coughed. 'Mistress, can you tell me the direction of the Gwynne family?'

The girl whipped around. 'Sir, I beg –.' She broke off as she saw whom he held in his arms. 'Rose!'

She rushed forward and caught hold of one of Rose's trailing hands, pressing it, looking anxiously at her sister's face. 'Is she – ?' she began softly.

'No, no,' answered Mr Pepys. 'She has but fainted. However, she is very ill. I expect you know why?'

'No . . . that is. . . .'

'This girl was expecting a child, if I do not mistake.' He looked down at the still figure of Rose. 'She is expecting one no longer. But I believe she will live. Who is she?'

'My . . . my sister,' gabbled Nell. 'Bring her in, upstairs here, will you, sir? I must go to the apothecary's, though it will take more than horseradish ale or turpentine pills to restore her to health, I see full well.'

Mr Pepys followed Nell up the steep stairs and laid Rose down gently on the bed in the cramped little bedchamber. Nell went to the tiny window and shut it firmly.

'There's nothing so cruel to health as air,' she informed Mr Pepys briskly. 'And God knows the stench from the alley is enough to keel over a saint. Oh, Rose, Rose!'

Running over to the bed, she leant over her sister, smoothing the hair back from her forehead and chafing her hand. 'How did you find her, sir?'

'I was making my way home down Featherbed Lane, mistress. Your sister tells me she has been released from Newgate Prison only this morning – I gather she was pardoned by a Royal Warrant.' He raised his brows slightly. 'Brought by a young man your sister described, an equerry, I think, of the Duke of York.'

'The Duke . . . ?'

' 'Twas a messenger from His Royal Highness who called at the prison, I deduce, to obtain your sister's release. Doubtless strings have been pulled in high places. The Duke himself must have signed the warrant, for no other can, save the King himself. Is your sister a friend of his ?' Mr Pepys looked down at Rose and then up at Nell.

In her mind's eye Nell could see three images; the red, excited face of Harry Killigrew vowing Rose's liberty; the silent and haughty figure of Browne; and Rose moving slowly down the stairs at Newgate, acting her part in the drama upon which her life depended. And, between them, they had secured Rose's release. The Duke himself had been induced to sign a pardon. Nell was dizzy with exultation, Rose was free, Rose would live.

But she stared straight back at Mr Pepys, resenting his suggestion. 'If you mean, is this the Duke's child she has just miscarried, then the answer is no, sir.' She shook her head wearily. 'Though if it had been a Stuart bastard, my sister would have done better than she did as wife to the veriest filth ever I came across.'

Together they went down the stairs.

She stood in the doorway to see him out, her chestnut hair with the hint of red in it blowing slightly in the wind. Mr Pepys admired her – from her tiny hands and slim arms, revealed in her turned up sleeves, to the liquid, hazel, eyes that regarded him with a pleasing warmth. She was small and fragile, but Mr Pepys recognized the courage that showed itself in her. Unaccountably he felt embarrassed as she thanked him and protested it was no great matter. She shook her head decisively.

'I beg to disagree, sir. This is not the first time you have helped me; you have done so twice before. You do not remember.' She smiled at Mr Pepys's blank look of surprise.

'*I* remember, sir. And I thank you from the bottom of my heart. Perhaps when I see you next time, I might remind you of the last time we met.'

She stood on tiptoe and kissed Sam on the cheek. His fine, curled wig brushed her nose as she rested one small hand on his velvet shoulder.

'Thank you, Mr Pepys. You deserve your good fortune.'

Mr Pepys climbed back into the hackney and Nell waved him off. As the coach turned the corner into Drury Lane, he still could not remember where before he had seen those liquid eyes, that tiny figure, and that resolute chin.

But he vowed he would see them again.

CHAPTER VII

... I think there's no hell
Like loving too well.
Charles II

Time passed. Winter's cold thawed and found London under a grey sky, huddled and frozen on the banks of the river, eager to welcome the new breath of spring. The trees lining the squares of Saint James's took new leaf, and the courts and alleys of Tower Hill took on new odours – both testimonies to the arrival of warmer weather.

His Majesty the King continued to hanker after the elusive and beautiful Frances Stuart, and it was common knowledge that the Queen knew of it and wept privately in her chamber for his infidelity.

Living was taken up anew in the city. A merchant was struck down in Lyme Street and robbed of four thousand pounds in gold and jewels. The Duke's Theatre mounted a new and sumptuous production of *Henry VIII* which the new Theatre Royal could not match with its paltry play by Edward Howard – though Charles Hart drew the crowds. In the East Indies, the Dutch arrogantly set their flag above the ensign of St George and claimed dominion over the South Seas. His Highness of York spoke darkly of war and the Duke of Buckingham cast off his whore.

For Madam Ross in her bawdy-house, life was satisfying. An unending stream of gentlemen came every night to Lewkenor's Lane and the establishment was profiting as never before. She drew the huge profits from the gambling school set up under her auspices, and the passion for cards grew, while several young men's faces grew whiter in the glare of the candles around the Basset tables as the long evenings followed one another in quick succession.

She fanned herself, wheezing with satisfaction, in the hot, crowded tavern, remembering her interview that morning with

Thomas Killigrew over a bottle of her best brandy. She had agreed to supply a constant string of twenty girls to the Theatre Royal; Killigrew had handed her a large, leather bag that clinked heavily as it landed on the table and they had drunk to their mutual good fortune.

The business was expanding and Ma Ross's podgy hands now glinted with rubies and emeralds where before they had shone with the false glitter of glass and tawdry. Certainly, she congratulated herself, as she walked through the throng of people, she had eclipsed that designing harpy Madam Bennet, whose new establishment had once threatened her. She could take the left-overs – the draymen, 'prentices and water-carriers – an' it pleased her.

She had taken up watch by the door, nodding to Benjamin as she looked at the dark street. The entrance to the bawdy-house was now illuminated by two ornamental lanterns that bathed the portals in an arc of light.

She saw two bobbing lights drawing nearer and nearer, and the sounds of jingling harness. Then two footmen came running down the street, bearing lighted flambeaux as they ran ahead of a light wickerwork carriage.

'What fool could be out at night in a racing chariot?' said Ma Ross, sidelong, to Benjamin. Then she gave a gasp of surprise as the footmen, dressed in cloth of silver, stopped at the entrance to the bawdy-house and ranged themselves either side of the door, breathing heavily as they held up their flaming torches. They ignored Ma Ross, staring straight ahead. With a crunch of wheels, the light carriage whirled up behind and came to rest with a slight jerk. Ma Ross took one glimpse at the fat, bewigged, gentleman regally descending and gave vent to a gasp of amazement.

'God's death!' she murmured.

The Duke of Buckingham was followed by a company of three gentlemen Ma Ross had no difficulty in identifying as Sir Charles Sedley, Lord Buckhurst and Henry Jermyn. She dropped a low curtsey, expressing her delight, her surprise.

''Evening, Ross, you old whore,' responded his Grace

affably. 'How runs the world? We have heard interesting scraps of news concerning you, and the company of lovelies you've got battened down under your rotten hatches. Your fame – or should I say notoriety – is spreading.'

'Your Grace is too kind,' wheezed Ma Ross, watching warily.

'Aye, perhaps, perhaps. I tell you this though, Ross, we've even heard about you and your gaming in Whitehall.' He shrugged. ' 'Tis not surprising, the place is the veriest bawdy-house of all – eh! Am I not right. Charles ?'

The gentlemen behind bowed. The Duke looked around him, seeming pleased by what he saw.

'You'll have Old Rowley down here afore long, Ross. Lord knows all the whores in the Palace were exhausted long since. My little Barbara looks like the ghost of Hamlet's father, I swear. It needs more than a bucket-load of pomatum essence to restore her, I fancy. Desperation will get His Majesty before the year is out, mark my words.'

'His . . . His . . . Majesty would be most welcome,' gasped Madam Ross, wondering whether to believe a word. 'In-cognito, I suppose,' she added.

'Of course incognito,' snapped Buckingham. 'You hardly expect him to announce himself in this flea-pit with a flourish of trumpets and that damned stupid herald of his, do you ?' He appeared to lose interest in Ma Ross and pushed past her, calling for a table and demanding service. Madam Ross watched as he and his friends arranged themselves around a table; then she edged over to the gaggle of girls she saw in the corner.

'You, and you,' she whispered, pointing to Sarah and Edith. 'Go and make yourselves pleasant to yon fine gallants. See if you can get them interested in the Basset after a brandy or two – and I doubt not we'll all make our fortunes.'

She grasped Sarah by the wrist as she passed. 'Make sure you find out first which one is the lady seeker. Either my lord Buckingham or my lord Buckhurst has a mind to a new whore – which one I can't recall. It may be worth your while to find out.'

Sarah bobbed. 'Trust me, Madam,' she said, and went forward to tip Sir Charles Sedley's hat over his nose and lean across, twining her arms around his shoulders.

Nell saw Buckingham roar with laughter and pull Sarah on to his lap. She turned away. She had seen it all before.

Nell went as if to pass her, but Ma Ross stood firm.

'I had a talk with a friend of yours today. Master Killigrew. I believe you know 'im.'

Nell avoided her gaze.

'Wasn't he the one who got your sister out of prison?' queried Ma Ross knowledgeably. 'I heard t'was he and his son and the cup-bearer to the Duke of York who got her released. At a price, I doubt not. You have friends in high places.'

'Not really, Madam, I. . . .'

'Yes, I know your sister parted from Harry Killigrew a sennight past. Both wanted new sport, so I'm told. Ah, well, Master Killigrew, his father, remembers you. In truth, he said he remembered your tongue more than anything else. We had quite a talk about you, child. He said that you were – *memorable*.'

'Master Killigrew is most kind.'

'God's death, you silly slut, don't be so provoking. You know what I'm hinting at, you're not a thick-skull. Killigrew owns the theatre – he needs girls to sell his oranges. He likes you. Well?'

'I have already said I don't want –.'

'Yes, we know, mistress,' sneered Madam Ross. 'But last time I asked, things were different, an' I remember aright. Your sister was but new-married – you looked to be set fair. Now she's a widow, or nearly – for I'm right in saying that her husband's not been seen since your sister was took off by the constables. Is it not so? And,' she continued swiftly, 'now that she's only just recovered from 'er illness – a tertian ague I believe you said, of a particularly *long lasting* type – you need the money. It will take some time before Rose finds few of 'er old friends again; I doubt not she will have to search a bit in the Fleet Alley to start to earn a living.'

Nell's eyes glinted. 'Madam. . . ,' she said softly.

'Aye. So fine and hoighty-toighty, mistress, are we not, are we not? I tell you plain I have stood enough.' She stopped for breath and her lips twisted as she looked over Nell's shoulder. 'So your gilded knight has arrived.'

Nell turned and saw Jonathan standing on the threshold, scanning the crowd for her.

Madam Ross dug her nails in the girl's arm. 'I want you out, mistress. Do you understand? I am sick of you. You bring me no custom; you won't bed a man for me as Sarah or the other girls do. Ah, I know! You think that your fine friend can protect you. But I have had enough. You're of no use to me. You may tell him that I, too, have friends, and gold enough to buy more. I fear him not at all. Take care your gilded knight does not become a gelded one, my fine lady. For odd things can happen o' nights on the way home.'

Jonathan began to make his way across the room towards them. Ma Ross ended her tirade swiftly. 'Take your choice, my little innocent. Leave here and join the theatre, or leave and starve – I care not! But leave!' She turned and disappeared to find her orchestra.

Jonathan approached and bowed, examining her troubled face. 'Is she chafing again?' he demanded, nodding in the direction of Ma Ross's broad back. Nell nodded, then explained. He whistled in disbelief. ' 'Struth, the acid-tongued old harridan, does she fancy herself so secure now? Faith, the patronage of the Court has given her ideas she never used to entertain – Madam Ross, Procuress to His Majesty. By appointment, I make no doubt.'

He looked across to Buckingham and his friends, and smiled mirthlessly. 'If she thinks to frighten me off with such tales to tell children, she can think again.'

'I shall have to go, Jonathan,' she said in a low voice.

'Why?' He was startled. ' 'Odsbud, child, you needn't take so much notice of Ross's distempers; she's always had 'em as long as I can remember. If she wishes she can cross swords with me – *if* she wishes.'

'No!' Nell's voice was resolute and Jonathan looked down,

shocked at the violence in her tone. He squeezed her shoulder.

'What's the matter, Nelly?' he asked softly.

'I can't stand it here any more, Jonathan, it's driving me crazy – the pox'd virgin among the thorns, 'tis all I am and all I'm like to be. I neither become an honest whore nor –.'

'There's no such thing as an honest whore, child.'

'Has life made you so bitter, Jonathan, that you just despise us because we have to become whores? Because there's no way out, because 'tis all that life offers us – to sell what we have while we still have something to sell. I begin to feel like a moneylender, hoarding up what I fear to spend and keeping it till it turns useless.'

'Nelly, I do not want you to –.'

'You?' she demanded. 'You do not want? What, pray, has it to do with you, sir? Can you offer another life – do you suggest anything different? If so – tell me and be sure I will be grateful. I don't wish to stay with old Ross – but 'ods my life, the old cow has put up with me long enough. No more do I need your help, an' I thank you. Master Killigrew has asked for me – I shall go to Drury Lane, to the Theatre Royal, tomorrow.'

'Nell –.'

'Aye, I know, sir. You don't wish it – no more do I. An orange girl sells more fruit than sits in her basket, and 'tis not only the fruit that is felt by certain fingers. But I, unlike you, have faced the fact. You will have to accept!' She stared at him with a white, set face. 'There is no choice. I am a whore. I was a whore when I was born, it was written in the gutter-mud I come from. What else is there? And a whore I shall have to be – a Fleet Alley *bitch* – till the end o' my days.'

His voice was cold. 'Do you really wish it? Do you want to become like Rose, your sister – no sooner out of prison than on the town – last time I heard, she had caught the pox from a sixty-year whoreson, who tipped her a ten-guinea.'

'That's not true!'

'No? But she lays a few, does she not?'

Nell's eyes bored into his. 'What if she does? Since you saw fit to honour me with your company, that's always been your problem, hasn't it? To consort with such as me, is to ditch-crawl. Well, *sir*, be ready and make no mistake, for I have no wish to pretend to be other than I am. I come from *nothing* – do you hear me – *nothing*! I am a whore. And you? What are you, peacocking about so fine, I should like to know – speaking to no one?'

'What am I?' inquired Jonathan, his voice steady, his face taut. 'Go on.'

'A . . . a . . . Thames street gallant, sir. You look a courtier only in shadows.'

'Thank you.'

'Well, I'm sure you asked for it, sir. I shall make my own life – I am no longer a child.' She looked determined. 'I can sell oranges by day, and something else by night, and I doubt not I'll be rich on't in a year or more, as plenty are.'

Jonathan's face worked uncontrollably, as if in pain. 'I won't have it!' he broke out fiercely, seizing her in a cruel grip. 'I tell you I forbid it!'

She twisted herself free. 'You – can't stop me,' she panted and broke away from him, tears running down her face, as she pressed back into the throng.

The Duke of Buckingham, having consumed a large quantity of liquor, was feeling in indulgent mood. At the moment, with a girl hovering at one elbow and another just before him displaying an ample expanse of breast, he felt life was worth living just at that particular time.

Henry Jermyn broke his reflections by leaning forward to offer some snuff.

' 'Tis a new sort,' he remarked, 'which York gave me. Of French mix and said to be popular with Monsieur.'

'Let's hope 'tis not as tainted as he is, then,' responded Sedley.

'Faugh! If half the tales be true, he leads his wife a miserable dance. His Majesty loves his sister well, if he loves no other – and he hates Monsieur as cordially as you hate the Chancellor,

George.' Buckingham declined to be provoked into another dissertation on Clarendon's shortcomings.

'His time will come,' he said easily. 'Make no mistake; his enemies number even the rats in Whitehall garrets now – his fall is as certain as tomorrow's dawn.'

'And if night prevails, you, like Helios the Sun God, will burn up our esteemed Chancellor in your rays of intrigue. Am I not right?' asked Jermyn softly, flexing long bony fingers.

'Just so.' Buckingham smiled, and sipped his brandy reflectively. For him, scandal was an intoxicant; intrigue was the stuff of life itself. 'Where's George?' murmured his Grace indolently.

'Overdone,' responded Sedley promptly. 'Went out on the town last night with young Killigrew and was overtaken, or so I believe. He's not as young as he was – poor George. Could have told him m'self, but you know George. 'Struth, no man alive could give him advice. But weren't you there as well, Charles?' He turned to his neighbour.

Lord Buckhurst inclined his head. 'Last time I saw Etheredge he was being carried back down Ludgate Hill in a chair – *carried* I mean in the full sense of the word. We went to that den of whisperers in Bride's Lane, but it was all too much for George, as it always is. He'll have a head as thick as a carrier's today and he'll never learn different.' He shrugged.

'Etheredge is a fool,' remarked Sedley conversationally.

Buckingham stretched like an indolent bear. 'God's death, Sedley, the world is made up, for the most part, of fools and knaves. The only difference is that the latter remain undetected and the former do not. Did you never realize it? An example, I pray you, let me give. Our master, His gracious – lecherous – Majesty, we may count as knave. His incredibly saintly spouse – or should I say the nation's mistress, but that in His Majesty's case it has unfortunate connexions – is a fool. His Majesty, we must all agree, enjoys himself the more. The Queen has her confessor, the King has his whores.

'Very different ways of life. His Majesty has, however, one redeeming feature – he is subtle even in lust. The Queen . . .

she is delightfully fresh and *au naturelle*, is she not – in a sallow sort of way?' His voice was sarcastic and mocking.

Sedley looked around in vague disquiet. He disliked Buckingham's airing his views quite so freely, which was the main reason for Buckingham's doing it.

'She has the mind of a *bourgeoise*,' continued the Duke. He flicked a speck of dust from his sleeve. 'Conjugal fidelity is such a middle-class virtue, after all,' he complained.

His voice was of a carrying quality and could easily be heard above the hubbub of the tavern.

'That,' whispered Mit to Nell, 'is his Grace the Duke of Buckingham, no less. 'Tis said he and my lady Castlemaine rule the King.'

'The more fool 'is Majesty, then,' retorted Nell. 'And I don't believe it.' She remembered the tall, dark, figure, riding by on his horse through the streets, waving carelessly to the crowds. Surely no one could rule him? She looked across at the lounging figure of Buckingham.

'Fair fancies himself, don't 'e?' giggled Mit.

'I hate him, great fat toad,' Nell answered coldly.

Then, looking round, she found herself being regarded by two pairs of eyes; one pair cold, staring, and intense, the other low-lidded, and faintly humorous. For a second she looked from one to another, but Jonathan's steely gaze unnerved her – it seemed to reach into the very soul of her being and drag from her all that she would keep hidden from the world. Thankfully, she turned to the lazy but challenging glance bestowed upon her by Lord Buckhurst, a tall, dark, stormy, nobleman who wore his own curled hair long, one strand lying fretfully across a high brow. One eyebrow was raised as his glance strayed over Nell's small figure – and his opinion appeared to be favourable.

Deciding that a whore she was and would so remain, she smiled gaily at him and walked slowly forward until she stood by his chair.

'Was there something you were wanting, sir?' she enquired.

Lord Buckhurst's eyes glinted. 'Aye, sweeting,' he drawled, 'but perhaps you're not selling what I have a mind to buy.'

She ran her finger up and down the table top slowly and thoughtfully. 'Every man has his price, sir – or so I'm told. I make no doubt but that women have too.'

He grinned at her, surprised. As she put out her hand to stroke his cheek, he pulled her roughly down on to his lap and kissed her on the mouth. Nell leant back against his shoulder as he released her.

'What price range would you place me in, sir? The run is from the bitch of the Fleet Ditch to those at Court. 'Tis all a matter of the size of your pocket.'

Sedley and Buckhurst laughed heartily. 'You are pert, mistress.'

'Nay,' she retorted. 'I but have my wits about me.'

'Aye,' said Buckhurst, 'my pocket varies according to what I buy. Are you worth your price?'

She looked at him with chin upraised. 'As no man has bought me yet, sir, I cannot tell you. 'Tis for you to decide.'

'No man –.'

'None, sir, I assure you.'

He breathed out slowly.

Sedley whistled. 'Take her, Charles. 'Tis worth a King's ransom, is it not, sweetheart, and even then 'twould be to case a Paternoster Row purchase into shadows.'

Nell felt her heart beginning to hammer, but she made no effort to be free. This is my life, she told herself; this is what I was made for; this is what I must get used to.

'I really believe I will,' murmured Buckhurst, slipping an arm around her waist. 'You are the white meat in this butcher's yard, my dear, and if you have to be blooded, I would be the one to do it.'

Another arm came about Nell's waist, pulling her away from Buckhurst and lifting her as casually as a down pillow. A pair of grey eyes looked pleadingly into hers with a depth of yearning she could not believe she saw. An expression lingered in them, alone, which she had never imagined could be meant for her. Their thread of love was woven.

He placed an arm about her, and together, before the startled gaze of Buckhurst, they walked out into the street without a glance behind them.

He took her to a small, cramped, inn at Cripplegate, near London Wall, away, as he told her, from prying eyes. A winking landlord let them in and locked the door behind them, and they passed through the taproom and up a flight of steps to a set of rooms which Jonathan told her was his own. She asked him mischievously what name he held the chambers under, and he smiled at that.

'Under no name, or any name. People who lodge here have no name, as long as they pay their shot – they live here for one thing only.'

'What is that, pray?'

'The Brampton Road,' he answered shortly, ushering her into a large dark bedchamber panelled in black oak and richly furnished.

Nell expressed her admiration at the hangings and the furnishings. 'An apartment fit for a Thames Street gallant?' he quizzed her.

She laughed, but immediately looked troubled. 'Jonathan, when I said all those things I . . . 'faith, when I get angry I. . . .'

He laid a pair of fingers across her lips and silenced her, drawing her over to the window. Throwing open the casement they both breathed in the night air.

Before them lay the winking lights of the city; there was no sound apart from the far off rumble of wheels passing over cobbles, and the odd snatch of song wafting up from the taproom below. Far away above the pattern of the roof tops the moon shone on the black ribbon of the Thames, curling past Tower Wharf down to Wapping, the lights catching on the distant water.

'The air smells of columbine,' she sighed, stretching out a hand to touch the curling tendrils that hung over the sill.

He did not answer. She leant far out of the window, sniffing the perfume. Her voice was steady but her face was flushed as she spoke.

'When I said I should have to go to the theatre, I was thinking of something different – some*one* different. 'Tis said that many a donkey needs a push. I swear that my curs'd temper was not meant to wound, but to push someone – someone unwilling – to claim a girl he still thought of as a child. A girl who is now a woman and has no fine notions of herself. A woman who craves no money, nor the respectable life of a goody-nothing, but only the love of someone who is worth more than he lets himself think.'

She stared out over the water.

'Some men never dare to open a treasure chest, in case they do not find the treasure that they want; some because they cannot think the treasure is for them. Which is a pity. For then, the treasure is never enjoyed till a pirate comes along and rifles it –.'

She looked around to see Jonathan watching her with a curious gaze, half-yearning, half-uncertain. He came towards her, watching the night breeze ruffle her hair, while the moonlight picked out the whiteness of her brow and the shape of her body against the window ledge, her cloak drifting back. His hand touched her, caressing her face.

'Are you sure?' he asked.

She nodded dumbly. The need for words was past.

'Nell – oh Nell!' he sighed, drawing her close.

CHAPTER VIII

Rich the treasure,
Sweet the pleasure;
Sweet is pleasure after pain. . . .
                John Dryden

He undressed her with his own hands until she stood before
him in her shift; a small figure with auburn hair in a mass
down her back, long and unbraided. This was how she came
to him, simple and clear as the night air which came softly
through the open window, so that his body trembled with
desire for her. Like a child, she held out her arms to him and
he lifted her, placing her down on the bed gently, yet feeling
as he did so the movement of the smooth breasts that roused
him, and the texture of the linen-fine skin palely glowing in
the shadows. For both of them, as he ran his hands slowly
and wonderingly down her supple form, there was longing
and pleasure that coursed and ran from little moments of joy
towards eternity.

They never left the chamber until the lights on the Thames
had sparkled under the moon six more times. Their arms
clasped about each other to feel one naked flesh touch another.
And Jonathan would take the heavy weight of her long tumbled
hair in his hand, to smell the scent of her and feel her fineness.

Nell smiled as she felt his gaze upon her, and he suddenly
thought that she looked wise as well as beautiful. He marvelled
as he saw her – this small girl sitting hugging her knees,
placidly enjoying the night air on her cheeks; to her, this other
part of him, he owed something that he could not explain and
still less understand. She leant back against him with a sigh.

'I know not your name, Jonathan, nor perhaps ever shall. Yet
to me you will only ever have but one name. Jonathan,
Jonathan . . . my love, oh my love. . . . !'

He covered her throat with kisses, devouring the softness,
the yielding touch of woman. Then as he rolled away, he felt

her hand clasped tightly – he could feel her long nails grip his wrist as she held him fast. They looked at one another, her eyes a luminous hazel showing love and nothing more.

The sight was almost too much. He groaned. 'I had no right,' he muttered. 'What have I to offer you? Wealth? Children? No! No! Nothing at all but long nights waiting for me to return with the shadow of the gallows at Tyburn hanging over us both. I can give you nothing but that. You must understand. . . .'

He cast an anguished glance at her. She put an impulsive hand over his lips.

'Stay, my love,' she murmured. 'You give me yourself. I am not a duchess and I bring you no dowry. We but have each other and 'tis enough. Would that many a woman could have as much. 'Tis a bond which holds us close.'

He took her hand and kissed it.

'Until death,' he swore.

For Nell it was a time of regeneration. She felt as if her spirit were walking with the dew that came every morning and sparkled clearly against the leaded panes of the window. With each new day it came, filling her heart with a love which took nothing but gave everything.

He lay beside her in the great bed as the sound of viols or the whispered strumming of the lute wafted up from the taproom below. Shut away from people, it was as though their world contained only themselves, and their love was the only purpose in their living. It was a play that was acted out by two people, naked in shadow, who became as one when the thick damask bed-curtains closed on their fulfilment. Time ceased to have any meaning, but if the future was hazy Nell still had a curiosity about their past.

She lay one evening, curled up, studying him. The candles in their sconces shed a golden light around them in the bed but Nell was lying on the pillows, eating from a bowl of preserved fruit which was cushioned between them. She bit thoughtfully into a piece of ginger.

'Jonathan. Could you introduce yourself?'

He looked amusedly at his own naked state and laughed heartily. 'Is it not a little late for introductions, dear heart?' She choked on a candied cherry, and then, unsteadily, got from the pillows and stood up on the coverlet.

'My pleasure, sir. I am called Mistress Nelly Gwynne – late of Lewkenor's Lane. Your servant, I am sure.' She attempted a curtsey but overbalanced and landed on top of him laughing loudly, her hair tumbled over her shoulders. He gasped for breath and coughed.

'The pleasure is mine. Or should I say *has* been. . . .'

She pulled the pillow from behind him and placed it firmly over his face.

'Enough, sir, until you can be more courteous. . . .'

'I'll be damned if I'll get from this bed to make a bow to you – hussy.'

'Apologize, sir, for such familiarity.'

'I have many names, Mistress Nelly Gwynne – some of 'em are worse than others; my abode varies and I am *votre serviteur*.' He pushed her from him, still laughing. She returned to sit beside him, cradling her arms on his knees.

' 'Odsfish, sir, you are vastly wanting in manners. If you've lifted me petticoat, you could at least tell me your damned name.'

'Lord John Dawlish – your servant, as I have said.'

'Jonathan –.'

'My real name is shorter, m'dear, that is all.' The voice was amused and unperturbed.

'But what – ?'

'Why? How? Where, and when . . . ?' he finished teasingly. '*That* is a very long story.'

'Tell me.'

'It is tedious –.'

'Tell me.'

He drew her to him, putting his arm around her, and she lay back against his shoulder with one arm loosely about his neck, content.

'Shall we take "what" as the first question?' he asked lightly. 'It is as good a starting place as any. *What* am I doing in the back alleys of London? I wonder?' He took a deep breath and began. 'My father was Baron Dawlish of Hentsham. The family were granted the title for happening to change its support to York at the right time during the Wars of the Roses. When York usurped the Lancastrian king, the Dawlish family were carried on the surge of that wave to power. When Oliver Cromwell usurped his sovereign, a Stuart King, the process was reversed. My father was buried on the field at Naseby.'

Nell nestled closer to him and said nothing. After a pause he continued. 'I fancy that answers the question "what" happened to the Dawlish family, but not quite. My brother, my elder brother, died quite early on in the war. How I wished to avenge Harry's death, I remember. I used to pretend I was fighting Roundhead troopers in my fencing lesson. My one wish was that His Majesty should not obtain his inevitable victory until I could swing my sword for him. That would, of course, have made victory certain. How I used to dream in those days!'

Nell sighed, trying to imagine him as he must have been. Jonathan's eyes grew melancholy.

'We never thought of defeat. It was not so much that we trusted the King, but the thought that the Dawlish family could lose a war was impossible to conceive!'

'But it happened, Jonathan.'

He nodded. 'Yes – it happened. The King lost the war, my father died, my mother died also. Her heart was broken, you see.'

Nell's understanding was mute. Jonathan's hand stroked her hair.

'We must pass on to the question "why",' he murmured. 'Why – am I here at all, in London? I suppose because I followed the tradition my father left me. I still looked for victory for the King; I lacked the shrewdness of my ancestors and I certainly lacked the subtlety. In short, for me, the war had not ended.

'They came to take our estates away a year after my mother's death. *My* estates –.'

'But how could – ?'

'Confiscated.' He ruffled her hair with his hand. 'It came as a complete surprise, I remember. A troop of horses rode up to the Hall and swaggered in, with swords at the ready. *My* hall. A coxcomb of a trooper introduced himself as a Colonel Montagu, Colonel Edward Montagu. Then, if you please, he unrolled a trumpery piece of parchment and informed me as cool as you like that it was a deed of confiscation, signed by some unknown fellow styling himself the Lord General Cromwell.

'There was no answer, nor appeal. There was a new authority now; one which regarded people like myself as "malignants", to be stamped out as certainly as they intended to kill their King but three months later. They demanded that I pack and leave – as if I had only been staying there, as if that great pile of a house had not been ours – *mine* – for three hundred years! But the final straw came when I had the temerity to ask what would become of it.

'That damned Colonel pulled out another trumpery parchment, called, as he phrased it, a "Deed of Gift". This piece of *paper* gave Hentsham Hall and the lands apertaining thereto, which had belonged to us, to this unknown trooper, this coxcomb who called himself Montagu, Edward Montagu. He had the impudence to come and take possession of my house himself; to turf me out so that he could insert himself. And there was nothing I could do – nothing!'

Nell kissed him gently. 'Calm yourself, love. 'Tis all a long time ago.'

'Calm myself! But that I could hardly do that day. I – lost control, I fear. One of those clanking troopers pushed past me and went to the chimney-breast in the great hall, where our coat of arms was carved over the mantel, and started hacking at it with his sword, saying new owners had come to stay. It was too much.

'I drew my sword and lunged straight at the throat of

Montagu.' He paused. 'I meant to kill him, but rage guides a poor hand. I pinked him only, and then I was pinioned by as many troopers as could be crammed in the hall. I can remember the shouting and the infernal clanking of that tin armour they wore and the voice of Montagu screaming at me – "Treason! Murder! Malignant!" I believe he was somewhat unnerved.'

'Don't sneer, Jonathan. It makes me feel cold when your mouth goes thin like that.'

His face relaxed. 'They arrested me for attempted murder of one of the Lord General's esteemed colonels. But I escaped during the night, thanks to one of the family servants – it is a wearisome tale, of no interest. I fled to France.'

'To join the King in exile?'

'That was my intention. But when I arrived, I found the Dowager Queen could not even afford to heat her own apartments in the Louvre, while the King was too poor to pay his tailor. He could hardly aid me – there were too many like me and I did not want to follow him around Europe like a half-starved rat. I developed other lucrative methods of employment.'

'In the Palais Royal,' Nell supplied.

He looked surprised.

'When I last drove you into exile, you mentioned it,' she reminded him.

'Oh . . . I see.'

'What did you do?'

He turned around to face her. 'I relieved elderly ladies with much money and little sense of some of their riches. I charmed them – then I robbed them.'

'What a good idea!' Nell enthused. 'It must have raked in the cash, I warrant.'

'I was a pimp, Nelly!' he said aghast.

'A rich pimp, Jonathan,' she corrected. 'And beggars can't be choosey.'

'I did other things.'

'What things?' she asked, interested, leaning forward and resting her chin on his shoulder.

'I joined a company known as "Les Inconnus"; we robbed people.'

'You were not a highwayman!'

'I was. There were five of us for a time, then just two. Myself and Jacques.'

'Jacques? Who was he, your partner? Tell me please!'

'There are so many things I could tell you of that man. He was of a bravery they called *formidable*; I believe there was nothing he would not attempt. Jacques Le Pied, he was called, for he had the largest feet for his size that ever I have seen – *ce pauvre* Jacques. Nothing daunted him. I could tell you of the time he held up the Mayor of Paris in his own coach, the time we stacked our loot overnight in Notre Dame, behind the High Altar and Mère Voisin – she was to Paris what Madam Ross is to London. There is too much to tell, save that I did survive until I returned to London.'

'And Jacques?'

'We parted on the best of terms. He was determined to leave the road to marry a marquise or something – I do not know. Suffice it to say, there was nothing he could not accomplish if he wished. I have not seen him now for nigh on ten years. Paris had not seen him when last you – as you call it – drove me into exile. Somewhere, I have no doubt, he flourishes.'

'And you?'

'I have not flourished. But I have survived. I have carried on the same trade in London. I have lost my title, my name, my wealth. I have become a solitary person; people have felt uneasy to be with me. They have even given me a name: White Jonathan. I returned to London for revenge and obtained it. Many a fat merchant and Puritan squire I stopped past the Shoreditch turnpike and relieved of his ill-gotten gains. Once I caught one of Cromwell's pay messengers bound for Scotland, and got winged for my pains.'

'But Jon,' Nell burst out, 'when the King came back, why did you not regain your name, your title and your estates? Why did you not petition at Whitehall to His Majesty, like so many others? Lord knows, there were plenty who did.'

'Because, my dear child, I should perhaps have been arrested for attempted murder. Does the name Edward Montagu mean anything to you?'

'The Colonel?'

'The Colonel no longer. He is now my lord the Earl of Sandwich. It was due largely to his intrigues that Charles Stuart regained his throne. He and Monk engineered the whole thing when Montagu ruled the Navy and Monk ruled the Army. Monk is now his Grace the Duke of Albemarle. Montagu received an earldom for his pains. Could his Majesty either pardon me or return the estates now owned by his most loyal supporter? An embarrassing situation, to say the least. Montagu has chosen the winning side twice, my dear; he has successfully run with both hare and hounds and gained his rewards accordingly. His future is set fair.'

'And you, Jonathan?'

'My future is still set on the Shoreditch turnpike of a full moon, my dear, and there is no escape from that. Your lover is not "lord" anyone but White Jonathan the highwayman. I look not for a dukedom, but for Tyburn hill.'

'Don't, Jonathan! Don't say that! Please!'

He pulled her to him, murmuring endearments. 'Nelly, don't cry, dear heart, but we must face reality and look it in the eye. We must not look to a future, for there may not be one. We must look at the present.'

Tears stood in her eyes but she spoke clearly.

'I shall love you till I die.'

To be a highwayman, Nell learnt, was not a glamorous or romantic thing but a desperate, lonely, battle against the permanent spectre of sudden death – and even if that spectre were beaten off, the toll taken in shredded nerves, and hollow-ringed eyes, and weariness, was high.

Yet it was worse to sit alone and not be a highwayman, to sit through the still dead hours of night helplessly unable to turn aside the unseen shaft of a cruel fate that could come at any time. When he came home unharmed, she would lie in the great bed with him, her hair tossed back and her fine skin glistening with a faint, perfumed beading of the sweat of passion; her arms would wind about him fiercely with a pride of total possession.

She grew to hate the night, the coming of dark with its spreading shadow. But she determined he would never know, and it was a smiling figure he always remembered as he rode away into the night, and the same figure of quiet reassuring love that greeted him with the coming of dawn, and the touch of cool lips on his.

One morning late, as she lay drowsily in the bed, she realized suddenly that he was not beside her. Alarmed, she sat up just as he reappeared in the bedchamber with a small packet in one hand, wrapped around in a delicate lace kerchief. She opened it and took from its delicate wrappings the glittering magnificence of a fine string of diamonds, gathered in the centre in a roundel of wrought gold set in a cipher formed of tiny gems.

'Put it on, thou gawper,' said Jonathan, amused at her expression.

She traced the legend on the roundel and looked up in sudden amazement. 'Where did you get this, Jonathan?'

He smiled. 'Aye, I wondered if you might pause at that,' he remarked. 'You had ever a bright eye – like your sister, I doubt not.'

He lifted the necklace so that it dangled brightly through his long fingers as he traced out the legend it bore on its pendant.

'C.R. Charles *Rex*, if I'm not mistook. Methought the lady's face familiar as she leant from the coach, though her features were whiter under the moon than even she could have wished, for beauty. She looked well enough – well enough to identify as my lady the Countess of Castlemaine. I thought this' – he handed the necklace back – 'would look better about your neck than hers.'

'Did this really belong to *her*?'

'One could hardly mistake that face – or that body, despite

he cloak she wore. The face she showed me fitted the stories all London hears of her shrewish temper.'

'Then this necklace was given her –.'

'By the King,' he agreed, 'exactly so. It was a present, and as I told her la'ship, 'tis better to give than to receive. Especially when some receive so much. She did not agree. I swear I have not heard worse language from the Wapping boatmen. I wonder if Whitehall Palace has heard the words she used by the Brampton highroad.'

Nell ran the stones through her fingers as a thought came to her mind. 'How much is this worth, Jonathan?'

'A kiss at least, my sweet. . . .' He leant over towards her. She kissed him but repeated the question.

He frowned. 'That is the sort of question Rose would ask, Nelly. I don't know exactly. Some five hundred guineas on the open market, some two hundred on the market I am forced to use. Why?'

'Do you know someone who could take it for you, Jonathan?' she asked. 'Perhaps even our old friend Madam Ross –.'

'What do you know of her dealings?'

' 'Odsfish, she hardly enjoyed employing me, did she? And she was never really swooning for love of you, either. I can still recall you telling her sweetly that she would change her mind and take me back, last Christmastide. And she did! Am I right in saying you know something of Ma Ross?'

'I know what old Ross keeps in that damp old cellar underneath her bawdy-house, where the river's not the only thing that comes in o' nights.'

'What is she?'

'She is the scavenger of London's gutters, my love. She has never been too worried where her hands delved provided they came back clinking with gold. She is fence to the best part of the nubbing cheats and pretty-sliders London has spawned. I was once one of them till I found out what she was like. But I still know enough secrets about the old harridan to make it dangerous for her to openly make an enemy of me. She has never quite dared to do that.'

Nell sat up on the bed, swinging the necklace before his eyes. 'If you sell this, Jonathan, you could leave that damned high road for six months at least.'

He shrugged. ' 'Tis a gift.'

'I had rather have you in the bed beside me as a gift than ten o' these tawdries. And *that* I doubt Rose would say. . . .' She threw herself at him and begged him.

'Please sell it, Jonathan, and leave the road for a while. Please, an' you love me!'

He took the necklace from her and smiled a twisted smile. 'There is no answer to that.'

'Thank God!' she murmured, burying her face in his shirt. 'Promise you will not go back till midsummer comes! Please!'

'I promise, if you wish it.' He wrapped the necklace back in its kerchief. 'Though it will be difficult to dispose of. It came from the neck of a countess – His Majesty's whore.'

The words touched a forgotten chord in her memory. She could see Rose again, peacocking in front of a cracked mirror in the bedchamber of the tiny house in the Coal Yard, and hear her smug retort, 'it came from off the back of a countess.'

'Jonathan,' she said impulsively, 'tell me why you hated Jack Cassells.'

'What makes you suddenly remember him, dear heart?' he demanded, coming back and sitting on the bed.

'He once brought Rose a gown he swore he took from off the back of a countess.'

Jonathan snorted. 'Did he!'

'Was he a highwayman? Did you – ever work with him?'

'I? Work with Tyburn Jack? 'Oons, Nelly, what do ye take me for – a moon-crazed lunatic?'

'Was – *is* he a highwayman?'

'No,' answered Jonathan shortly. 'Nor is ever like to be, unless his spine be a good deal stiffer than 'twas of late. When you were a child, Nelly, did you never hear of the Sealed Knot?'

'Wasn't it a society which plotted secretly for the King's return?'

' 'Oons! I misdoubt whether it ever plotted secretly.

Secretary Thurloe had more spies in that nest of ill intrigues than ever spawned an honest plotter. 'Twas said he knew of every plot weeks before they were born. Thurloe took many men to serve him. One of them was Jack Cassells.'

'Jack always told Rose his family estates had been lost in the wars.'

'Jack Cassells never had any estates. Aye, he fought for the King – once – as a soldier of fortune. But when His Majesty ran out of cash and had to take to melting down his plate to mint wages for his troops, Jack Cassells' loyalty died a quick death. He gave his parole to the Parliament that he would not bear arms against them, and came to London in search of pickings.

'He passed himself off as a distressed gentleman. Some believed him. Some who should have known better babbled in their cups of plans to restore the Crown, and the gentlemen involved, and that is how I came to know Jack Cassells. I knew him for a rogue the instant I clapped eyes on him. But the others trusted him and I had no real cause to dislike the man.'

Nell's eyes fixed steadily on Jonathan's face.

'We had plans, I and others, to raise London and the West Country together. 'Twas Oxford's idea. We had written to the King and he promised to send Buckingham with a list of loyal men who would concert their rising in the west with ours. We all forgathered one dark night down in Paternoster Row. I remember it was to await Buckingham's coming. Only one man was absent that night.

'We heard footsteps coming down the street outside. Someone said " 'tis Cassells", then we heard more steps, and more. Then the door broke open under the thud of a pike butt, and in streamed the soldiers. I wrenched open the window and escaped into the dark. Some followed, but all were not so lucky. I heard them capture Oxford as he sat athwart the sill, just as I turned the corner of Paternoster Row. And then, under the shadows of the eaves, at the corner of the street, I saw him.'

'Cassells ?'

'Aye. He didn't see me. He was just standing, watching while the men who had trusted him were taken off to prison, Tyburn and the gibbet.'

'Why didn't you kill him, Jonathan?' she asked coolly.

''Odsfish, Nelly, I don't know. I had no proof you see. Cassells wasn't *with* the soldiers, he was just watching the proceedings. He could have come late and seen it all, and hid himself. I couldn't kill a man on that evidence – I would have been no better than our enemies. But he certainly made no move to help. He just slid off into the shadows. Haply he merely escaped, as I did. But I think not. In my heart I have always known him for what he is. Judas!'

Nell looked puzzled. 'Then what did he –?'

The neighing of a horse below the window, accompanied by the crash of breaking glass, interrupted her. A loud, deep voice bellowed up in rage.

'*Holà!* 'Old this bag of bones, this animal that calls itself an 'orse! *Parbleu!* Must I get down and 'old it myself? *Imbècil!* Fool!'

A surly voice declined the task audibly.

'*Ma foi!* You English, you are all as *maladroit* as ever. You expect your masters to be your servants, because you cut off the 'ead of your King, *n'est-ce pas?*

'Down on your knees!' the voice continued magnificently, changing its demands in a second. 'To Monseigneur le Marquis de Santé-Carlleroi, and be thankful my whip does not fall across your shouldairs.'

Jonathan and Nell went to the window, and saw the mauve plume of a fashionably tilted hat and the glimpse of a black periwig. The ostler gaped at him. A white glove pointed down imperatively.

'You are of a stupidness I find *incroyable*, my frien', but if you 'old this 'orse I will give you – *peste*, what do you call the coin? Ah, a groat. Yes, I will give you a groat.'

The ostler sniffed. 'T'ain't much.'

'*Comment?*' enquired the stranger icily. 'What is it zat you say?'

Jonathan suddenly leant forward, putting his hands on the

window sill. 'God's bones!' he swore softly and, running from the room, clattered down the stairs.

Nell looked after him in surprise and ran to the window in time to see Jonathan appear in the courtyard, picking his way over pieces of broken glass from the remains of several bottles, which, by the presence of a smashed tray, it seemed had been in the process of delivery to a customer. Dark puddles of wine mingled with the glass over a wide area.

Nell watched Jonathan as he executed an exaggerated bow and caught a flash of his blue eyes as he declaimed: '*Donnez-le-moi, Monseigneur, s'il vous plaît, et depêchez vous!*'

The stranger stiffened, the magnificent hat was swept from the equally magnificent periwig, and a voice replied, '*Est-ce possible? Mon ami, Monsieur le Baron?* I 'ad 'eard of this inn from La Voisin but nevair did I think to find – *mon ami*, it is you! *Vraiment!*'

Clambering from his showy chestnut mare, the stranger ran over to Jonathan and kissed him on the cheeks, bubbling with words of amazement. The ostler looked on in disgust.

'Foreigners!' he said, and spat on the cobbles.

Nell noticed how much smaller the stranger was as he stood by Jonathan. After a word – obviously concerning herself – he looked up at the window and then bowed, placing his hand over his heart.

'Your evair devoted, Madame.'

Nell stifled a desire to laugh and waved awkwardly from the window sill.

The ostler interrupted these pleasantries by pointing expressively at the broken glass by their feet. The gentleman dismissed him with one word, which, if the ostler did not precisely understand it, spoke sufficiently to convey its speaker's strongest feelings. Jonathan and he turned back into the inn.

Nell curtseyed shyly as they came into the chamber, though the stranger was talking so fast he had little attention for her. He was a stocky man – small, with an abundance of black frizzy hair from below which his nose protruded, large and pointed. Nell found herself fixed with a look from a pair of dark, beady, eyes which darted this way and that. All in all, Nell decided, he put her in mind of a blackbird or crow in his looks, despite his magnificent dress.

The stranger flourished his hat with a courtly gesture. 'Jacques La Touche, Madame – your evair obedient.'

Nell bobbed. 'Sir, yours.'

She glanced questioningly at Jonathan, who smiled. 'Nelly, I will not attempt to introduce this rogue from the past. Look you instead at his feet.'

'At his *feet*?'

Jacques shrugged eloquently. 'Alas, Madame, they 'ave always been my undoing. Always, on an 'orse or not, they 'ave given me away for who I am. *Eh bien*, they make me notorious.' He proffered a riding boot for Nell's inspection. The leg was short, but the foot at the end of the boot was large and out of all proportion to his size. 'People 'ave remembered me by these too often. It is they who 'ave made it necessary to leave France for a while.'

'Jacques Le Pied?' asked Nell slowly.

He nodded mournfully.

'That has been my name in the past, *certainement*, Madame; but I 'ope 'twill be so no longer. For such as I, it was a poor title. Me, I desire better.'

'What do you call yourself now, Jacques, my friend?' asked Jonathan.

'I am Monseigneur le Marquis de Santé-Carlleroi. My wife, who was honoured by my company for close on a year, could hardly refuse me her name, since she refused most else.'

'Was she the Marquise?'

'Assuredly she was the Marquise; of a family ancient and noble in France. It was one of my greatest coups that I should bind her with the marriage knot . . . *Bien sûr*, she could give a title of merit to her poor Jacques. I am, after all, of a brilliance seldom seen among men. The path to the rope and halter at the Pont Neuf is not for such as I. The thought revolts, it rebels –.'

'And so you came here,' interpolated Jonathan dryly, interrupting his expansive gestures. Jacques stopped.

'You see me,' he declared simply. 'She drove me from her; she was of a stupidity too much to be borne. She failed to see my greatness, lamentably she failed to see it. And, she picked her teeth in bed. *Peste!*' He paused. 'It has been a long time, my frien'; I did not know whether you were still alive. Fate, or the Devil, has brought us together again. Assuredly it has been a long time. It is good to see you in such health of spirits. Is it *l'amour*?' He looked at them both.

Jonathan's eyes rested on Nell. 'It is.'

Jacques took Nell's hand and brushed it with his lips. 'Madame, I felicitate you,' he said gravely.

Her eyes danced. 'I felicitate myself, sir.'

Jonathan turned to ask after several people Nell did not know, who obviously came from his days in Paris. Jacques shrugged, grimaced, swore, and gradually imparted most of the information Jonathan wished. In particular he expressed interest in Mère Voisin, whom, Nell remembered, he had called the Ma Ross of Paris. Jacques sighed heavily.

'*Alors, la mère*, she 'as become changed, my frien'. Her heart grew bitter since her little boy, Petit-Jean, was hanged for picking pockets in the Rue de Bouillabaisse. It has frozen the warmth in her blood and turned her spirit to the shadow. She has stopped selling potions and now brews things more deadly. *Eh bien!* it has raised her *clientèle*; you would be surprised how many masked ladies step from shrouded coaches to see *la belle mère* and buy from her the means to remove an aged husband or a rival to their lover. And *la mère*: she now conducts those rituals of which it is better not to speak. One lady in particular calls to indulge in that certain *rite de diable*. Perhaps one day the world may know of a lady called Athenaïs de Mortemart.'

'Why so?'

'My dear frien', she aims to win the heart of the King 'imself. She is a – friend – of Louise de la Vallière who becomes daily more pious, so I'm told, and sleeps less and less in the King's bed.'

'A friend?'

Jacques shrugged. 'What does the word mean at Court?

But nothing – *rien du tout !* And even less if La Voisin has her way. I had to leave – such a path is doomed, if not by the flames for sorcery, then by *la mort d'esprit*.'

He smiled suddenly. 'But now life begins again. I feel the strength rise in me. England shall see my powers now I 'ave arrived in your so dismal country of fogs and cold. Fate has willed it in our meeting. It is *incroyable* the world remains so insensible of my gifts. I am a great man, oh, but vairy great!'

Jacques stayed with them, and Nell came to love the droll little man with his large feet, and illusions of grandeur far outweighing his small stature. He would lead Nell in a pavane across the floor of the bedchamber, while Jonathan watched amusedly, humming frantically all the orchestral parts of a French court dance and waving one hand to the beat of the music.

'You are become a fop, Jacques!' Jonathan told him.

He drew himself up. '*Impossible*, Monsieur! Courtiers are made for flattery. Me, I am made to be flattered, *bien sûr*. Madame' – he made a leg to Nell – 'if it were not that this insulting *vaut-rien* were your 'usband I would spit him *comme la poule rôtie*.'

Nell protested. 'But he is not, Monsieur.'

Jacques' look of embarrassment and surprise was so palpably obvious that Jonathan and Nell both burst out laughing. Jacques recovered himself and sniffed to Nell.

'*Tiens !* I 'ad no idea that Monsieur was become so – so *French* in his habits since he returned home.'

'We are all become French,' Jonathan told him. ' 'Tis the fashion. Do not forget, Jacques, our King and most of his Court were exiles, as I was. The preachers cry out of a Sunday against our debauchery. London has its delights to offer, like Paris.'

'And its challenges –' added Jacques, his eyes gleaming wickedly like a jackdaw's. 'Per'aps I might find the old sport on the Brampton Road of which you used to tell me, an agreeable substitute for the Rouen highway.'

Nell opened the lid of the chest at the foot of the bed and

rummaged under a pile of linen until she found what she was looking for. Drawing out the package, she picked the necklace from its wrapping and showed it to Jacques. He handled it reverently.

'*Nom d'un nom!* This is of beauty quite exquisite,' he breathed, watching it as it caught the light and winked brightly, revolving slowly in a string of cold, liquid, fire.

'It belonged to the King's mistress,' Nell informed him.

Jacques nodded understandingly as he examined it and found the pendant with its inscription. 'It must be a fine thing to be the mistress of such a King. For all his magnificence, our own golden monarch bestows his riches less generously.'

He gave the necklace back to Nell. 'So this is what can be found on the road at nights, my frien'?'

'Not always, Jacques; I own I was surprised to find such a prize encounter. As was the lady, of course.'

'I begin to see,' mused Jacques, 'that this England 'as its own possibilities.'

Nell saw him look speculatively at Jonathan, and she felt suddenly, unaccountably, afraid.

She was standing in the courtyard in front of the inn, watching as a cumbersome stage waggon disgorged its shabby occupants, when Jonathan brought her the news she had been dreading.

'Jacques has found that a baggage train is take route for the Great North Road, tonight, love; 'tis said – so Jacques tells me – that there is close on five thousand pounds in gold. It is payment for Lauderdale's soldiers in Scotland. A rare prize.'

Tears stung her eyes as she said quietly: 'I thought you would not return to the road for a month or two. The necklace –.'

'Stolen goods are not sold so easily, dear heart, and 'twould be but a short rest. This is a rare undertaking and would bring enough to keep me from the highway for years.'

'It might well have rare guarding, then. Pray God it does not keep you from the road for ever. This is Jacques' doing!' she said in sudden passion.

Jonathan took her hands and carried them to his lips. 'This

200

is my life, Nelly; this is how I must live. How else can I exist –
idleness would make me but a distempered pauper soon enough,
I'll warrant. There can be no leaving the road. I have no other
future, I never had the right to stop you from being a whore
an' you wished; as you told me, it was written in the gutter
where you were born. My future was written in the mud of the
fields of Marston Moor and Naseby. I told you I had no other
life. But keep me to my promise and I'll not go.'

She longed to tell him; with all her heart she wanted to prevent him from going, even as she heard her own voice say
quietly, 'Go, Jonathan, go. I'll not keep you. I have no right.
'Tis but a poor woman who wishes to chain her lover to her
side.'

The shadows seemed to gather about them. Jonathan drew
her to him and kissed her hungrily on the mouth. Then,
abruptly, he turned as Jacques came out into the courtyard,
pulling on his gloves.

'Ah,' he said, breathing deeply, 'the night is fine.' When he
saw her face he shook his head. 'Oh, you women! Always you
wish to keep us tied to your skirts. It is *ridicule*; you chain us
fast with your tears and we obey.'

'I did not try to – stop him. It is just that I did not think that
he would go, not for some time. I –.'

Jacques patted her hand. 'Do not worry. I will bring him
back safe before dawn. And richer by five thousand pounds
in gold. Enough to keep him from the road for a long
while.'

She nodded silently. He walked away to get the horses just as
Jonathan came out of the inn. She looked up and smiled shyly,
slipping her arm around him.

'After tonight, Nelly, there'll be no need to wait on the full
moon for many a month. 'Tis gold, my dear. I see no difficulty
in ridding ourselves of that.'

She watched as he buttoned his coat at his throat and tucked
in the tell-tale glimpse of the white cravat, till he stood dressed
in the severity of black from head to toe, so that his face looked
pale and thin and his eyes over-bright as he turned to her.

She felt the icy touch of the air on her face. Was it her imagination? She could not tell, as he pulled her to him and dropped a kiss on her forehead. Then, with a hug, he left her, and walked across the courtyard to the stables, his riding-boots crunching against the cobble stones. As the dark figure strode away to where Jacques was holding the horses, she was seized with a wild, terrible, feeling of dread that would not be ignored. Tripping over her skirts, she ran to him and caught him to her, clutching him, running her hands down his back to feel the living warmth, and lifting her face so he could cover it with the silent, strong, kisses of the lover. They looked deep into each other's eyes, Nell's large and scared, Jonathan's blank and careworn.

'Get me – some earrings to match the necklace,' she said, smiling tremulously.

He nodded. Jacques brought the horses over and Jonathan mounted his black mare.

'Adieu, Madame Nelly,' called Jacques boisterously. '*A bientôt.*'

She stayed in the courtyard, silent tears coursing down her cheeks, after the sound of the hooves were long gone.

The bedchamber seemed stuffy as she closed the door and leant on it, sniffing the sweet smell of the pine logs burning on the wide hearth. Dragging the counterpane from the bed, she draped it around her shoulders and trailed over to the wide seat that stood in the window, which was open. From outside in the trees, she could hear the muffled calls of an owl as it began its nightly hunt for food. She lay back against the dark oak of the seat, cushioning her cheek with her hand, and despite herself, in the stuffiness of the room, her eyelids began to close.

As the candles burned to their sockets, the shadows began to encompass her and the fire became a dull-red bed of coals. The atmosphere was oppressive as the shadows came about her and drifted over her, dragging at her senses. The air from beyond the window, that breathed the fragrance of the columbine, could no longer reach her or rustle across her brow.

The darkness came in at her, closer and nearer, engulfing her.

And though she fought it in growing panic, she felt herself sinking into the deep pit of hopelessness from which there was no escape. Jonathan was near her, she felt his presence coming towards her, she could see the whiteness of his face and feel the searing breath of the spent horse careering onward, its nostrils flaring in fright. She could smell its sweat and hear the drumming of the hoof beats. The sound was breaking around like the waves of the sea. And then she heard the noise ring out from somewhere behind. Everything slowed down as the light descended into her brain, pulsing with its message of doom. Nell could see Jonathan's face with a look of utter surprise on it; then his mouth opened – for an instant they gazed at one another, grey eyes looking into brown across the traverse of the thread of life. He mouthed the one word, then he slid from the saddle and fell heavily to the ground. Nell saw the hand, with the solitaire ruby ring on one white finger, jerk and then be still. The thread had snapped.

Hoof beats thundered towards her and over her, towards the body lying crumpled in the dark. Nell screamed; an animal scream of pure horror. With a start she woke up still screaming, the sweat pouring off her, though there was nothing but the stuffy night air behind the curtains in the bedchamber, and the steady tick of the clock. But Nell sat numb staring blankly forward. In the room there was no sound. A shaft of pale light, showing through the curtains, touched her immobile features which were set like one dead. And this was the position Jacques found her in, when he staggered into the chamber, holding his hand to a wound in the shoulder seeping blood, before the light was more than a hint of greyness on the court-yard outside.

She did not see when he took his hand away and the red sticky ooze of blood soaked through the cloth. She did not hear when he described the guard around the coach, the headlong flight in the dark, the chaos of terror as sudden death came from behind. She did not hear that they brought back no gold and left Jonathan's body in the ditch by the highway.

He shook his head sadly and went away to bathe his wounds

while she still sat silently, watching the thin ray of stagnant light which came through the curtain heralding a new day, but no renewal of life.

Later that day, Thomas Killigrew, with his colleagues Michael Mohun and Edward Kynaston, together with the great Charles Hart, glumly faced each other across mugs of sack in the Crown Tavern behind the Exchange. Killigrew was holding forth on what was swiftly becoming a favourite topic: namely the decline of the theatre, and the fortunes of the Theatre Royal in particular.

'I tell you, Charles, I can't bear it any longer. The place is become little better than a bawdy-house, full of trumpery girls selling oranges and a good deal more, and a crowd of coxcombs who come to look up the skirts of the leading lady sooner than watch any acting.'

'You didn't say that a few weeks ago,' Charles Hart reminded him.

'No, well,' Killigrew temporized, 'I had less reason then. Drury Lane's not doing so well as it did. Since that little baggage Moll Davis appeared at the Duke's Theatre our trade has been suffering. God knows Beck Marshall is no answer to the dancing of little Mrs Davis – I wouldn't answer for the stage if she started, she grows fatter daily, I swear. The King does not honour us with his presence as he did. Since relations with my Lady Castlemaine have cooled we have seen him much less.'

'They say Madam Stuart does not approve of the theatre,' agreed Kynaston. 'She thinks it lewd.'

'Lewd!' said Killigrew outraged. 'She, the latest of the King's *belles amies*, dares to call my theatre lewd!' His tone was incredulous.

'The Queen also does not approve of the theatre,' said Kynaston.

'It has never stopped His Majesty from attending before,' protested Killigrew. 'No, gentlemen all. We need to find a new attraction – new blood. How about you, my dear –,' he said suddenly, leaning back to deliver a sharp slap to a fat serving wench's bottom.

She whipped round, red-faced. 'You can keep your filthy ideas to yourself, Tom Killigrew! Me? Dressed up in nothing, prancing across those 'eathen boards for all to see? I'd rather stay as I am, with no money and an honest living. His amorous Majesty can whistle for the likes o' me to warm 'is bed.' She pulled her skirts down around her ample thighs as if she expected them to be lifted any minute.

'Hoighty-toighty,' chided Charles Hart. 'Though, 'odsfish, the legend is swift becoming true – that Davis wench has the slimmest legs this lecherous city has seen for a long while. I'd fancy her myself, did not my sovereign lord have her close as a flea in his chamber.'

'It's not enough,' remarked Killigrew thoughtfully. 'You know as well as I do the girl's a peagoose; no more brain than a damned monkey. She'll last no more than a month or two, until His Majesty spies yet another pair of legs or another pair of fine upstandings. To keep him, a woman would need the looks of Castlemaine, the temper of the Queen, the elusiveness of *La Belle* Stuart – and the wit of His Majesty himself, to boot.'

'A paragon!' declared Michael Mohun.

'Impossible,' scoffed Hart.

'Aye, I wonder if she could ever exist,' sighed Killigrew. 'If I knew her, she'd be on the boards of the Theatre Royal within the hour.'

'She doesn't exist,' said Edward Kynaston with a note of finality. 'Have some sack, Tom, and stop chasing pipe dreams.'

Jacques looked glum as he passed the closed door of the chamber where he knew Nell was hiding herself. It was not healthy, he mused to himself – two days had gone by, and he had hardly seen her. She had locked herself in her room, refusing any food and not answering if the door were tried. Two days, but he had never heard any sounds of weeping. The one time she had let him in, the day before, he had found her still sitting by the window as if, even now, waiting for him to return. Her face was white and corpse-like. It was almost as if she were trying to join him, for she did not belong to the world or seem to know of its existence.

Parbleu! Jacques swore, it was not natural!

The sound of a door opening made him look up in surprise. Slowly, down the stairs, still wearing the clothes he had seen her in two days earlier, Nell approached, carrying a riding-coat rolled up in a bundle. She did not greet him, or seem to notice him, until he asked her where she was going. Then she paused, and looked up as if surprised at the question.

'I am going to take him his coat,' she said in a curious mechanical voice. 'It is cold out there on the road – I know – he has often told me. He will be cold without his coat; I have mended the tear in the sleeve and –.'

'Nelly! Stop it!' said Jacques clearly. *'Cherie, tais-toi!'* He shook her by the shoulders. 'You can't bring him back. He is dead, do you understand! Dead!'

She looked down at the coat and her hand stroked it slowly. She made a small, choked, noise.

'He is dead, Nelly. He is gone for ever.' It cut him to the heart as he repeated the words. Her eyes were blank and uncomprehending, like a child's.

'Dead?' she murmured, and the expression in the eyes became troubled, and the tears welled to the surface. The coat dropped heedless from her hand and she stood there, her face torn as if in pain, racked by sobs and a passion of weeping that made Jacques fear for her mind. She turned, oblivious of his presence, and stumbled back to her room. How long she lay on the bed weeping she was not sure, but when she woke from a sleep of exhaustion it was beginning to get dark.

As if in a daze, she got from the bed and began to pack her few belongings, and then looked round at the room which had held their laughter and the bed which had held their love. A sword in a plain leather sheath stood in the corner against the wall, next to a pair of riding-boots. She left them where they were, but fingered for a second the stones of the necklace that she had put beneath her gown. She felt she would leave life behind when she left the chamber. She had no future, for she did not wish to go on living. But one thought bound her will, through the mists of grief.

She was *not* going back to Lewkenor's Lane. The fat, loathsome image of Ma Ross came to mind and her words that fell like sickly honey on her ears, 'Master Killigrew wants you, my dear – you could be one of the first at the Theatre Royal . . .'

Through the tears, Nell snorted. One of the first laid, more like, she told herself. There was no point in thinking of the future, the only future her life had held lay in a ditch, huddled and cold, by the roadside at Houndsditch turnpike. She might as well die. She went over to the mirror and looked at the blotched, woebegone, face which stared back at her. For all the grief, it was the reflection of a young girl, only just ripening to maturity, with the open look of one at the threshold of life. The hair flowed in copper waves down her back; the skin was pink, flushed and fine, the eyes bright with tears.

Life was over, life had finished, and life must still go on. The next day, she decided, she would go to the theatre.

CHAPTER IX

Anyone could guess she was once an
orange girl from her swearing . . .
            The Duchess of Portsmouth

Sir William Batten looked worriedly at his friend Sam Pepys, as he and Sir William Penn settled back in a hackney outside the Dolphin in Tower Street. Sam, he decided, was getting too damned serious in his attitude to life. Here they were, after a goodly repast – a brace of stewed carp, a jowle of salmon, and a dish of neats' tongues washed down with canary – and what must the man do but talk interminably of problems of trade and the danger of a Dutch war! Portly Sir William Batten blew out his cheeks in aggrieved protest. There was a limit surely to devotion to duty. Samuel Pepys was getting ambitious and it showed.

Indeed, relations between him and Sir William Penn could hardly be described as anything but frosty these days. A state of ill-disguised rivalry existed between them. Now Sir William Penn gazed haughtily out of the window of the coach, pretending not to notice his companion. As Sam leant forward to speak, Sir William Batten wriggled uncomfortably and wondered whether this tedious subject would continue all the way to the play he had persuaded a reluctant Pepys into seeing, as an afternoon's enjoyment away from his office.

' 'Tis all very well for His Majesty to be pleased with the launching of the *Royal Catherine*. No one is more glad than I to see the Navy revive. But this activity is not enough to prepare us for war with the Dutch. When I was leaving the launching ceremony with Elizabeth, and my man Hewer, I heard that fool Cartaret gabbling on to the King about how her Grace of Buckingham had been took poorly coming by water in her barge! This at a time when all our Channel ports lie under the threat of invasion and our Navy is all unread!'

'Parliament has voted two and a half million for the war,'

protested Sir William Batten soothingly.

'Aye, and how long will it be until the money can buy the timber, build the ships, stock the guns and ammunition and impress sufficient men? Let alone the money that will stick to various fingers as the process goes on.' He glanced at Penn. 'I warrant the Dutch will not wait so long.'

Sir William Penn snorted. 'I would that His Highness of York were here to listen, Pepys. I dare swear he might resign his post as Admiral were he to hear how you have all the solutions to our problems at the Navy Office.'

'I tell you, Penn, rumour has it the Dutch are cruising off Folkestone with twenty-two sail and nothing done to prevent it. Yet when I was down at the Hope, past Tilbury, last sennight, the men were still fixing the mainmast on the *Royal Charles* – the second one, mark you, for the first was discovered rotten on delivery!'

'Coventry tells me that His Highness wishes to see me upon this very subject,' drawled Penn insolently. 'Of course, as a seaman *I* can tell him the sort of problems he needs to have explained. There is no substitute for actual experience.' He looked at Sam, who, as he knew, had never been to sea. 'Indeed, I am told by some words Mr Coventry hath been kind enough to lay in my ear that both he and I are like to be included in His Highness's inspection voyage next week.'

Sam's face reddened in anger. 'Yes, Coventry told me that, since my lord of Sandwich – my *cousin* of Sandwich I should say – is to be gone to Tangier as governor, 'twere better I stayed at the Navy Office since the main responsibility for running affairs will rest upon me, while the staff are away....'

'Staff – ?' barked Penn. 'What d'ye – ?'

'I hope that the play will be better than that last one we saw at the Duke's, Penn . . .', interjected Sir William Batten hastily to stem the barbs in the coach. 'I swear the last production of theirs – *A Love's Cheat* or some such nonsense – was too farcical to take belief. The veriest coxcomb of a play.'

Both men looked at him for a second and grunted. 'Tom

Killigrew tells me that Lizzie Weaver is worth a viewing,' volunteered Pepys.

'Aye, so indeed Sir John Minnes said,' agreed Sir William Penn. The tension gradually relaxed. Sir William Batten sighed in relief as the hackney turned into Drury Lane.

Orange Moll looked over her orange girls critically as they stood in a ragged row in front of the apron stage, with the large shallow baskets hanging loosely from crooked arms, whilst she berated them soundly. 'Hold that basket lower, girl, or you'll find their 'ands pluck at more than the oranges.' She stooped to replace a couple of the tawny fruit that had rolled from one girl's load. 'And remember, 'tis sixpence each to gentlemen and no argufyin'. You get any trouble and you just call on me. That'll settle 'em.' The girls looked at the brawny woman standing, arms akimbo.

'Sixpence each, Madam Moll?' queried one.

'Less you can *persuade* them to take more, sweet'eart. But there's one thing' – Moll's eyes flashed a warning –'Don't you go tellin 'em they owe you for a dozen they never 'ad. You might recall what 'appened when a prick'louse slut, no longer with us, tried it last week. The place looked like the Papists 'ad invaded. I'm still payin' for the damage the greedy bitch caused, so try it and you'll be *out* – with a black eye for remembrance like the last one.

'You dallies for a sale, and not for your own entertainment – see.'

' 'Ere, Moll . . . come and give us 'and will you?' A scene shifter, buckled under the weight of a pile of long ladders, took her attention. Nothing loth she strode off to give her aid.

Eyes gleaming, one of the girls watched her go. 'I swear to God she's feared more 'n the plague. Who'd argue with her? As well eat cherries at Deptford!'

It was at three o'clock in the afternoon that the doors were finally opened and the crowds began to stream into the theatre. The sun was still high in the sky and the sunlight picked out the deep colours of huge feathers curling round hat brims, the glimmer of satin, and the bright glow of green or red homespun, as people of all classes pushed and jostled each other to gain entrance. The crowd was a belligerent, impatient, happy one, which spread out in a mixture of patterns until the pit was filled and burst with the throng of people in eager anticipation.

Standing in the upper gallery, looking down at the bustle below, was the tall, handsome figure of John Lacy, dramatist and actor of the King's House. As he watched the crowds stream into the theatre, his expression was thoughtful, and his voice was so soft as he spoke that his fair companion, small as she was, had to stand on tiptoe to catch his words.

'Be not soothed by yonder crowds, Knipp. They come only as 'tis first showing, for the novelty, drawn as children are to new toys. And, like children, once seen they'll quickly tire of it.'

The lady nodded. 'The King does not come to grace first showing as once he was wont to do. Haply 'tis because Hart takes the lead. His Majesty makes no secret that you are his favourite actor. Does not your own portrait hang in the King's closet ?'

Lacy shook his head violently. 'God's wrath, gel! 'Tis not the lack of a *male* lead that bores His Majesty. 'Tis rather that the King's House no longer lures with the promise of beauty as once it did.'

'Indeed ?' questioned the lady with a sparkle in her eye.

'Don't be foolish, Bab. You have no need of my flattery. Men's opinions of you show themselves daily outside the women's shift in a tedious stream of flowers and tawdries. But for all that, I fear you lack the fascination of Mrs Davis. Davenant has taken all London to Portugal Street with her in his company.' He took a small snuff-box from his pocket and inhaled lustily. 'Where the King goes, the Court goes also, and shows the frailty of the mode. Luck has a peevish will. Look you, Knipp – the pit knows only the vulgar, and the pit is full. Above the pit, what ? The middle gallery ? The upper gallery ? A sprinkling of gentlemen like the frosting on marchpane.'

Bab Knipp pulled a fair curl thoughtfully round one finger. 'I doubt those here will be roused by Lizzie Weaver. Since His Majesty sent her his compliments two months back, she's trod the path of that lapwing Anne Marshall. I left her, if you please, lying on cushions with that little black boy of hers presenting her with a cup of jocolatte. Without it, she says, she cannot and will not go on. 'Tis not as if she is captivating when she *is* on, either. She grows fatter by the day, and her looks do not promise cheerfully. Master Killigrew grows testy withal, but God knows the remedy.'

'Unless Mrs Marshall or Mrs Weaver can prune themselves, I fear Master Killigrew's vexed humour must endure. Or till fate can usurp them both.'

'I may be playing immortal Zeus, but not even I could bodily take Lizzie Weaver from our midst –.' Grimacing comically, Michael Mohun minced up to them, the elegant heels of his filigree-buckled shoes tapping on the boards as he walked. 'You realize, of course, that the beauty of Helen of Troy was one of the wonders of the ancient world.'

Bab Knipp giggled. ' 'Twill be paint and whalebone corseting at Drury Lane.'

Major Mohun looked down at the Royal Box. 'I fear me the lady will not take the town by storm. More is the pity.' He nodded downwards. 'I see that Killigrew's brought a friend with him.' Two figures took their places in the box just above the stage.

' 'Tis Robert Duncan,' said Lacy heavily. 'He's a city merchant and Killigrew has hopes of gleaning some moneys from him, invested in the theatre. I swear he's a hard task there; the man's the dourest Scot and he'll not part with a penny groat unless he sees the chance of a guinea return.'

'It's getting to be low tide with the King's House,' fretted Mohun. 'Aye de me! I must be off – they expect me safe positioned in the wings by now. The voice of immortal Zeus must be ready to sound the clarion that begins the fatal war of Troy. I must say I don't see myself as the voice of Zeus; it's not me at all.' Shaking his head he strolled back down to the stage.

In the cradle of the pit, the crowd pressed up against the stage which projected far out into the audience. Some people indeed took their seats upon the stage in a row of seats at the side. Up towards them in solitary splendour, rose an indescribable cacophony of noise from the people below. They smoked, quaffed ale, spat, shouted, laughed, and ate oranges. Standing with their backs to the stage stood a row of orange girls, young and seductive, some winking at the audience, shouting, 'Oranges, will you have any oranges?' To which call they received a variety of replies.

'They're packed tight as quartern loaves in an oven,' bawled one beauty to her neighbour above the hubbub as the crowd settled. 'If 'twere not for the tobacco I think the stench of 'em would knock me over. 'Tis as if the slums of Seven Dials had come to Drury Lane this day.'

'Come wash me down then, sweetheart,' called a voice and the girl tossed her head in reply. 'Do you take the gangway on the left, Nelly, and I'll take the right. 'Odso, you cheesecurd, keep your filthy hands to yourself or I'll break this basket across your skull!' She turned and wove through the lounging crowd while behind her a slim girl with a rose stuck jauntily in her hair swung her hips around the apron and pushed into the throng calling 'O – ranges. Sixpence!'

As she reached the end of one gangway, she was stopped by another of the orange girls, who pulled at her sleeve as she passed. 'Psstt, Nelly!' Her companion jerked her head over her shoulder. 'Have a care to your fruit, Nelly, a' God's name! Jem Curd's returned with 'is mob o' 'prentice friends from Cock Lane. Last time 'e took me basket from me and cast the lot on to the stage. Master Killigrew was not best pleased, and neither more was Orange Moll.'

Nell shrugged. 'That pocket tipstave? He's as gawky as a crane and weak as water. A clout round the face would settle his sauce.'

'Aye, but 'e's brought a mob of drapers' 'prentices with 'im s'afternoon. I should keep away from them if you've a mind to sell.'

Nell smiled, and was about to reply when the blast of a trumpet from the stage made her pause. The play was about to begin.

The orange girls wandered up and down, in between the rows, while the people sat gazing open-mouthed at the stage above. Nell sold a few of her oranges and then passed to the side of the gallery, to lean back against the rails watching the play. Her attention seemed devoted to the figures of Charles Hart and Beck Marshall on the stage, but her mind was on other things.

In the depths of her eyes there still lurked a shadow unnoticed by all, a sign that some part of her, if not dead, was at least numb, though outwardly she had regained all her old vigour and native wit. It was impossible to remain stricken in the bright and noisy world of the theatre; impossible to brood on past grief in the midst of the living, bawling, crowd around her. A part of her remained separate, but day by day the hands of death which had gripped her were releasing their hold. Gradually she was reviving. The scar would remain for ever, but the pain was fading into memory. Nell's eyes wandered over the audience sitting in the pit and down to her basket of oranges.

She plied a trade that was reserved for dalliance of a sort. There were, as she knew, degrees of whoring. She could become a 'guinea love-bird', employed to sit in the head-dressers' shops in her best finery to entice in the customers. She could rent chambers on a less grand scale at Bankside or Southwark, or rely on the fairs – the May Fair or the Horn Fair – where she could take a barge from London bridge and go to find a gallant at Cuckold's Point. Or she could hire herself out on a more permanent basis if she promenaded in St James's Park, though she would get little but her meals and the odd glass of brandy for it.

Instead she had chosen to parade at the King's House. She felt as if she had been in the Lane for years, part of the entertainment of the city to match with the tavern over the street and the cockpit next door. She had sold her oranges and she had exchanged many a coarse jest with her customers of an afternoon. Not as yet had a feeling again moved her heart as once it had been moved, nor until it did would she allow a hand to touch her as once she had been touched.

Yet the day was sunny, the crowd willing to buy; and, as she looked up, she saw a familiar figure sitting opposite in the middle gallery, leaning forward, regarding the stage. A smile transformed her face. It was Mr Pepys. Hurrying forward, she pressed through the crowd in his direction. Indeed so intent was she on reaching him that she did not notice the lounging, carousing bunch of young men that sprawled across her path, talking to each other and paying scant attention to the play. One, a tall, thin, youth with prominent ears and spots, grinned delightedly as he suddenly saw the fair figure weaving her way towards them.

'Stir up, lads,' he said over his shoulder. 'I warrant here's sport!'

'Alack the day that Paris saw my charms! I would plunge this dagger deep into my bosom rather than any should die for me!' declaimed Mrs Weaver, standing in the centre of the stage, festooned in draperies of an unlikely violet shade. The audience seemed singularly unimpressed.

'I shouldn't try it, girl, for you'd never get it out again!' called a voice from the pit.

Helen of Troy cast him a look of positive hatred and then launched into a monologue regarding her undying love for her husband Menelaus. The crowd sighed.

Up in the box, Killigrew's companion sat bolt upright nursing a cane between his knees and looking down at the stage under a pair of beetling grey brows. 'Why does she keep dabbing at her face wi' that kerchief, Tom?'

'She betrays her sorrow at the slaughter her beauty has caused.'

'Oh aye?'

A moment later Duncan stirred again. 'Why does she wave her arms about like that? Has she the colic or something?'

'No,' explained Killigrew patiently. ' 'Tis a dramatic pose.'

'Oh – humm. How long d'ye say this war of Troy lasted, Tom?'

'Ten years, Rob.'

'Och, mannie! I canna wait that long. I feel as if I've been here a clear year a'ready.'

Killigrew coughed and regarded the ample form of Mrs Weaver dispassionately. It was not surprising, he thought, that the crowd were restless. The woman had run to fat amazingly in the last few weeks.

'And d'ye say that two armies fought over her a' this time?' murmured Duncan incredulously. Killigrew nodded. 'Och, man! She'd not interest a bullock in a cow byre.'

The play was not going well. The crowd had not seemed either devastated when cowardly Paris stole Helen from her husband, or even interested when Achilles fought a duel to the death with Ajax. The griefstricken outpourings of King Priam of Troy left them unmoved. In fact they were obviously bored. They listened attentively when the imposing figure of Charles Hart took the stage as Menelaus and coaxed their imaginations to life, but when he left interest slumped. It seemed an afternoon for disasters. First the sacrificial fires had refused to light, and when Agamemnon had sacrificed his daughter to the flames, all that showed was a wisp of smoke that curled around the recumbent form of Beck Marshall, cast in the role of Iphigenia, and then drifted into nothing, to the huge delight of the audience. Next, when the horse of Troy was introduced, it had stuck on its castors and taken a full five minutes to drag on stage, revealing, at its rear, portions of Mrs Weaver as she lent her weight in the wings to push it on. Those moments, thought Killigrew gloomily, were the only ones in which the audience had livened up at all.

Now Mrs Weaver drew to the end of her monologue, describing the fall of the city of Troy, the carnage below as her warrior husband fought his way to her through the Trojans. 'Behold him come, my Menelaus! Clad in the armour of Aphrodite, girt with the sword of Poseidon! Through the blood of Troy to me!'

She swept a magnificent gesture with one arm, but it was a little too dramatic. Her hand caught one of the stage columns of light wood which promptly fell over to reveal Michael Mohun standing thoughtfully, with a pale blue hair-bow on one side and brocade waistcoat to match, regarding his face in a small hand-mirror. He blinked up at the aghast Mrs Weaver.

The audience took one look at them and howled. Cheers swept the pit and Michael Mohun giggled feebly. Above him, Killigrew buried his head in his hands while his companion wheezed uncontrollably at his side.

But the afternoon waxed hot, Mrs Weaver continued her mono-logues, and the audience drifted into a state of drowsy inertia. Charles Hart eventually came on stage to claim his long lost bride. He paused and then stretched out his arms to her. 'Lady, the gods, who allowed our parting, look down with tears on our joy.'

An orange flew through the air and bounced between his feet. Hart, an experienced actor, kicked it behind him and continued his speech with a weather eye open for any other missiles which might suddenly arrive. They moved into an embrace. 'Begone dark shadows that have fed upon this lady's injured virtue . . .,' said Hart. Another two oranges hit the boards. Killigrew stirred in his seat and peered into the pit to trace the cause of disturbance. He saw a thin figure holding an orange basket aloft just out of reach of a panting, swearing, orange girl who strained in vain to reach it. The tall figure ignored the girl's curses and began to toss her oranges one by one to the ground. Occasionally he tossed one on to the stage, while around him a group of louts jeered and hooted as the fruit rolled all around. Killigrew frowned, but though he looked everywhere, Orange Moll was nowhere in sight.

The girl's imprecations began to rival Mrs Weaver's in volume. 'May high Olympus favour us for our love,' intoned Mrs Weaver.

'Whoreson knave! Give me back that damn basket or I'll kick the guts out of you!'

217

'May we, our swords stained with the blood of war, claim love our guide and love our sweet endeavour . . .,' declaimed Hart, striding forward on to the apron stage. A yell greeted him. Killigrew looked down and saw the thin figure dancing with pain holding his knee and the girl in possession of her basket gathering up her oranges lying all around. The thin figure went for her with an oath. She dropped the basket to vent her wrath, attacking him with her nails. 'You stinking toad!' she screamed. 'God help me if I don't take both your pox-ridden eyes out!' Her clawing hands scored two red furrows down each cheek.

Insensibly, the audience's attention, like Killigrew's, drifted from the play and bestowed itself upon the two struggling figures in the pit. The cheers and boos of those around added to the noise. Lizzie Weaver opened her mouth to reply to Hart, saw no one was listening, shrugged, and gave up.

'Knock the jelly out of 'im, sweet'eart!' advised a waterman from the row in front. But Nell did not hear him. Jem Curd made a grab for her and her dress ripped away at the shoulder. As his foolish, guffawing, face came near to her, she acted.

Taking hold of his nose between finger and thumb, she twisted violently. He yelled and tried to free himself. But however hard he tried, the grip remained fixed. 'Try and ruin me, would you, you poltroon?' shouted Nell, shaking his nose from side to side. 'Thought you'd make me a laughing stock?' With each word she lambasted his shins with hearty kicks. Jem Curd knocked her arm down at last from his throbbing orifice with an oath and snarled at her.

'We'll teach you to meddle with us! We'll rip those clothes off you and pass you around, you filthy little whore! And when we've done we'll –.'

But Jem Curd's threats never finished. Breaking free of his grip, Nell directed a final kick at his groin. Jem screamed, and as his mouth opened she rammed an orange in it, and in the same movement gave him a hefty push. Goggling, with eyes bulging, Jem Curd fell backwards and toppled right over the form behind him to hit the ground with a sickening thud, with his legs waving in the air. A screaming fury followed him.

'Rip my clothes off would you, you sack ferret? "We'll pass you around . . .", "we'll teach you . . .". I note you said "*we*" not "*I*", you snivelling little rat! 'Odsbud! Take *that* for your sauce and *that* for your threats and *that* for your knock-kneed, whoreson carcase.' Oranges flew at him, bombarded him. Feebly he raised an arm to protect his face, while all around him his companions doubled in mirth to see his struggles. As the final orange bounced from his head, Nell advanced threateningly.

'And since you've taken all me fruit, I might as well shut up shop –.' She broke the wicker basket with a swipe right across his head. A terrified Jem Curd slumped to the ground moaning, struggling backwards to escape her.

'Mistress Gwynne . . .,' came a sweetly polite voice from above, 'may we watch the play now?'

Surprised, she looked up to see Killigrew's clear eyes bent upon her. Behind his eyes she saw a suspicion of a twinkle. 'I lack aught more to throw at him, sir, so please continue an' you will.'

'I am so glad,' said Killigrew politely. ' 'Tis very kind of you. I swear the gods of Olympus will be eternally in your debt that the war of Troy may – at last – end.' He turned back to the stage, and Charles Hart loudly spoke the closing lines to a fuming Mrs Weaver.

At the end of the production, clapping filled the pit. Robert Duncan leant towards Killigrew. 'It's not that besom they're applauding, but yon lassie with the spirit in her and the kick of a mule.'

Killigrew nodded. 'But don't you dare tell her so – saucy hussy.' Duncan grinned. 'If I were you, Tom, I gi' the oranges to the Weaver and I'd put the little lassie on the stage of Drury Lane. She's got more life in her than a score o' Mrs Weavers. In fact if you'll take my advice, I warrant I'll find a bit to help ye on your way.'

Amazed, Killigrew turned to him. 'You mean it, Rob? After this afternoon? After all the –.'

'Man,' interrupted Duncan, 'that wee lass down there will

fill your house to bursting if ye can once train her to the boards. Look at her! She's no afraid o' man nor beast. Did ye hear her language? I never heard the like.'

Amused, Killigrew recalled Nell's disruptions. 'Aye, maybe you're right. I'll see what Lucy and Mohun can make of her. Haply I'll take her in charge myself.'

Down below, the pit was almost empty. Jem Curd had been helped, limping, from the playhouse by his friends. Duncan peered across at the overturned forms and the orange peel littering the ground. He looked up at the stage, bare except for the props and scenery, which jutted out into the empty theatre. 'What's the lassie's name, Tom?' he asked without turning his head.

'Gwynne, Nelly Gwynne,' said Killigrew briskly. 'Will you broach a vessel of tent with me before you go, Rob?'

PART 3
LONDON SPRING 1665

CHAPTER I

Strangers are taken for dainties, wives as physic . . .
                    Samuel Pepys's father

'Monsieur de Courtin, a moment, I beg of you!' The immaculate figure of the French ambassador stopped on the threshold of the Queen's apartments and looked up to see the King beckoning him over to where he, the Queen, Frances Stuart, James, Duke of York, and his Grace of Buckingham, were sitting round a table playing at Basset. Charles' eyes were alight with mirth and he waved his hand even more urgently. 'Over here, my friend. We need your advice.'

Courtin strolled over to the table. 'Madam Stuart here confesses to a strange dream, Monsieur *l'ambassadeur*, which might interest you,' began Charles. Courtin looked across at a charmingly confused Frances, who dimpled and looked down at her cards.

Charles rumbled good-naturedly. 'She confesses to a dream last night in which she found she was in bed with all three of the French ambassadors we have received at Court. Methinks your master would be glad to know he has such a devoted servant at my side.'

'Oh, but your Majesty, I told you I lay on the side of Monsieur de Verneuil who is a bishop, and at least seventy summers besides.' Frances blushed. 'Excuses, excuses . . .,' chided the King. ' 'Twas only that he could give absolution after all was over, I warrant. Your conscience inserted him betwixt you and Monsieur de Courtin here.'

'Monsieur, I appeal to you!' protested Frances.

Courtin smiled. 'I fear me your protests will be ignored, Madame.'

'Even her damn dreams are virginal,' muttered Buckingham.

'A sensible dream and a necessary barrier,' nodded Charles ignoring him. 'Monsieur de Courtin and I have both agreed already that we share a common interest in the frailer sex.

Nobody loves them more than we two. But, d'you know, I think my brother loves them more, eh, James?'

The Duke of York smiled. 'A poor strategy, Charles! In love, as in war, only the vulnerable attempt attack as their defence.' Courtin bowed and backed away politely.

'Lord, York, don't place the two together or we'll be driven to find what resemblance each lady of our acquaintance has to a battle,' protested Buckingham. Opposite him the Queen's eyes opened wide.

'Sur-r-ely, Duke, it is rather what weapon each woman resembles, I t'ink.'

''Odsfish! I know a woman *has* weapons. Eyes, nails, and tongue – oh, especially tongue.' Charles shook his head. 'No woman is as harmless as she looks, Buckingham. Even the smallest, demurest, lady can sometimes show the most amazing deadly temper when she wishes to fight for her own.' He looked across at the Queen, and when their eyes met she smiled back at him. 'Quite deadly,' repeated the King. He placed a card down on the walnut table top. 'Mine I think, James.' A sizeable pile of guineas slid to one side of the table. In the candlelight, James pulled a face while Buckingham gave a disgusted snort. 'You have all the luck tonight, Sire,' he congratulated the King gloomily. 'That's a cool thousand you've lifted from me.'

'Go to, and join a coffee house, if you have no taste for gaming,' remarked a voice behind him. 'No wonder. Dr Stillingfleete sermonizes at us and writes us all off as licentious.' Buckingham turned and looked over his shoulder. Thomas Killigrew's lazy blue eyes gazed directly back at him. 'And with the country in a state of war with the butterboxes, too,' reproved Killigrew.

He bowed very low to the Queen. 'Your Majesty, I am honoured to accept your invitation this evening.' Catherine nodded back, pleased.

'A pleasure to see you, Master Killigrew. Indeed, I might echo those sentiments; the Dutch threaten to eat us up and yet to see the gaming here in Whitehall! *Madre de Dois!* You would t'ink there was no such thing as war at all. The country must needs fight on credit.'

'That paltry sum Parliament voted isn't enough to run a peacetime navy, let alone to equip the fleet for war,' complained the Duke of York. 'And yet they expect instant victory, and the bells of London to cry out over captured Dutch ships in the Thames any day. I fear they may wait in vain.'

'Damned merchants!' said Buckingham contemptuously. 'They'll not help to pay the nation's bills. No wonder the country's bankrupt! And there are other causes . . .'. He looked over the rim of his wineglass at Catherine. 'It's not only the merchants who do not pay their bills. Princes can be as parsimonious as other men when they pay their servants, equip their armies. Or dower their daughters!'

There came a little gasp from Frances Stuart. It was well known at Court that the Queen's dowry, only ever part paid, had never been discharged by her brother the King of Portugal, despite repeated English requests. Buckingham's remark was close to open insult. James's face flushed deep red and his hand strayed to his sword hilt. Catherine was very white. Charles' hand lay negligently toying with his wineglass. 'I really believe, George, that this London fog does not agree with you. You have taken a corpse colour of late – sadly drawn. Yes, I really do think Whitehall must deprive itself of your admirable wit and famed charm for a while. Shall we say for at least three months ?' His dark eyes looked up at Buckingham, while Catherine agitatedly glanced from one to the other. Suddenly there was a tiny crack – the King's wineglass had broken at the stem.

'Your Maj –.' began Buckingham.

'Goodnight, my lord.'

Getting up from his chair and bowing low, Buckingham backed away, and then turned with an angry swish of his coat-skirts to retire in a fury.

'I believe 'tis your turn to deal, my dear,' Charles smiled at Frances. 'Come, Killigrew –,' he indicated the seat vacated by Buckingham, – 'join us, an' you will,' Killigrew sat down.

15

'How goes the King's House, Master Killigrew?' inquired Catherine to break the tension still lurking in the atmosphere. 'I declare, 'tis an age since I last saw a play.'

Killigrew looked gratified at her interest. 'We hope soon to produce something that will give the company at Your Royal Highness's theatre' – he inclined his head to the Duke of York – 'something of a surprise.'

'Oh,' murmured Charles, 'what is that, pray?'

'We have commissioned a new work from Dryden, Your Majesty, of which I have the highest opinion. I believe it is the greatest composition he has ever writ.'

Charles looked interested. 'A lure, Tom! You know well I ever esteemed Mr Dryden above all other playwrights. Do you seek thus to recall your errant patron back to the Theatre Royal?'

Killigrew smiled. 'In truth, Sire, I but speak the truth. 'Tis a new play about the Spanish conquest of Mexico, called the *Indian Emperor*. 'Twill take London by storm, I doubt not, especially' – he paused – 'if Your Majesty should lead the world to Drury Lane.'

'Master Killigrew! This I know, *absolutemente*! You came to us this evening just to obtain this favour. Confess it!' accused Catherine, with mock severity, her eyes alight with mischief. 'And I was per-r-suaded you had come to my card party for amusement and nothing more!' She turned to her husband. 'Charles, how can you keep Master Killigrew hanging in doubt? Promise to attend the new play.'

'I have another surprise for Your Majesty,' broke in Killigrew.

'What is it, Tom?'

Suddenly remembering Catherine, Killigrew stopped in confusion and mumbled lamely. 'You must come to the King's House to see it, Sire.' Catherine looked puzzled and then suddenly she burst out laughing. 'For shame, Master Killigrew! To come to my card party to arrange an assignation for my husband.' She glanced wickedly at the King who was pulling at his lip in amusement as he regarded Killigrew.

'*Mi esposa*. I t'ink bot' of us go to the theatre to see this play, and to see this – surprise.' She cut the cards with a now expert hand. 'You must deal, Frances!'

CHAPTER II

Then enter Nelly on the public stage
Harlot of harlots, Laïs of the age.
           Satire of my lord of Rochester

You need only *think*,' said Charles Hart seriously, 'that is all., Think and remember. You can be a fine lady one moment and an old man the next. Watch them as they come in the pit: how they talk, how they laugh, as they sit down, as they eat their oranges. One grabs and sucks the flesh greedily – he has no teeth, you note. The lady delicately peels – oh, so carefully – she is at all times so very precise in her movements, 'tis as if she does not ever wish to eat the thing till she pops it, segment by neat segment, into her round little mouth. Watch them as they walk –.'

To Nell's astonishment, Hart minced towards her, pulling his kerchief from his pocket and waving it disconsolately, as he placed his other hand on his hip. 'Marry and amen, I dare swear 'tis too hot to breathe at all! And me with the misfortune to leave my pomander at home . . . .' His whole face changed its character, his lips pursed, his eyelashes fluttered as he dabbed at his nose. 'I fear I shall take the megrim this close weather –.'

Nell began to giggle, but was stopped by the whine of a bent figure with hollow cheeks and drooping eyes, who leered up at her with his head on one side, sucking in his teeth. 'Don't despise a poor old man, mistress; spare a groat for an old soldier. This summer will be my last, I'll warrant – the Thames mist will cough my last breath away come November.' A rackling cough bent him even lower and his legs bowed outward.

Immediately, Hart straightened and addressed the dismayed Nell with a twinkle, not dissatisfied with her obvious awe. 'That, Nelly Gwynne,' he said grandly, in his normal deep musical voice,' is the sort of thing I mean.'

It seemed to Nell that she had never worked so hard in her life. Every morning, before the company arrived, she was tutored carefully and patiently by Charles Hart, Michael Mohun or Killigrew himself. Every evening, after everyone had gone, she would stand alone on the stage in the empty theatre, lit fitfully by tallow rehearsal candles, and dance breathlessly to Lacy's terse command. 'God's wrath!' he would bawl at her. 'You look like a cow on stilts fed on Venice treacle. Are those feet, or pudding bags?'

If she was surprised at Charles Hart's virtuosity, she was even more amazed to see the bulk of John Lacy capering across the stage, curtseying to right and left, and shouting, 'Follow me, gel! Pick your feet up! 'Tis a bransle – light and quick – not the kicks of a curs'd carthorse at the market fair! God's wrath, pick up your damned feet!'

The days were spent murmuring lines ready to come under the scrutiny of her tutors, either that or being twisted and turned around by Beck Marshall in the women's shift behind the stage, fitting costumes on her and teaching her how to apply her paint ready to tread the boards. Between them all, the company of the King's House coaxed out of her the latent wit and humour that lay unpolished beneath the Cockney ribaldry and badinage. Killigrew taught Nell the arts of the lady – the languishing ways of the Court and the seductive tricks of the courtesan – and brought her to a fine pitch of sophistication. Rose, now a grass widow, but happily entangled with a burly captain in the King's Guard, would chaff Nell about the day of her *début* when she returned home to the Coal Yard at night, exhausted after her exertions under Master Lacy's eye. But then Rose moved to a set of elegant lodgings in Goldsmith's Row, under her captain's protection, and Nell saw her but little. She could not be sure of answering Rose's question at all. She was, she knew, being carefully observed, and each criticism made it seem as though she could never be an actress. The unending days of watching, copying, and repeating, seemed to go on for ever.

So for weeks, until one day Thomas Killigrew called her into the tiny office and put two guineas into her hand and said 'Welcome to the King's House, Nelly Gwynne.'

Lewkenor's Lane looked much as it always did in the early morning. The various stools used the night before lay on their sides under the board tables. Pools of stale ale gave a sour odour to the tavern despite the door and windows flung open for the spring air to cleanse the atmosphere. Scarcely anyone was up yet. Madam Ross never showed herself before noon unless there was business to deal with, and the chambers were still occupied.

Only the small figure of Mit, the skivvy, was evident, bent double in the fireplace, trying to coax a fire of obstinately dead coals to life. Her face was covered in smuts from the soot which her ineffectual blowing had disturbed and her mob-cap was pushed to one side as she crouched to redouble her efforts, picking hopefully at the cold hearth. So engrossed was she that she did not hear the light footfall behind her until a soft voice whispered, 'Hello, Mit!'

She looked over her shoulder and uttered a faint squeak of joy, dropping the poker. 'Nelly!'

Nell laid a finger to her lips and cocked a significant eyebrow upwards. 'Sssh, Mit! Is the old cow abroad yet?'

'Nah, Nelly. She did ask for a glass o' lambswool when I come down but she ain't 'ad it yet 'cos o' this curs'd fire.' Her sharp freckled countenance looked puzzled and she rubbed her nose on her sleeve. 'Why are *you* 'ere, Nelly? Surely you ain't come to ask for a job again? I thought you was on the orange lay at the Lane.'

'No,' came back the whisper. 'I've got a new job, Mit. I'm a member of the company of the King's House! I'm an actress with the Theatre Royal!'

Mit's mouth formed an 'o' as she gazed at Nell. 'Well, slit my guts!' she whistled. 'A King's Servant, Nelly?'

'I don't know about that, Mit. Haply 'tis better not to be a servant of His Majesty, for all the world knows he can't pay the servants he's got a 'ready. But Mit, I'm not on the Love Lane level now. I've just got lodgings in the Lane – nothing grand, just a couple of rooms at the Cock and Pye tavern near Maypole Alley. It's an old place, but 'tis a bloody palace compared to

Ma's flea-pit. I've got enough to buy clothes, Mit, and enough to live well, if I'm careful. How would you like to come and share it, Mit?'

'Share it, Nelly?'

'I thought perhaps I could do with someone to look after things a bit, darn my gowns, sew my costumes, and that. Would you like to come, Mit? I can't pay much at all. 'Oons, there won't be much to spare I know, but it's a start, Mit, for me and for you.'

From above them came a shrill scream. Mit hurried to the door behind the bar counter and answered the scream with an equally indistinct yell. She turned back to Nell. 'She wants 'er drop o' ruin.'

Deliberately she straightened her mob-cap in front of the mirror and then walked to the threshold of the bawdy-house at Lewkenor's Lane, turning with a mulish expression. 'She can bleedin' get it 'erself,' she said. Nell burst out giggling.

'What about your things, haven't you – ?'

'Nothing worth 'aving, Nelly, and that's God's truth. I'll come just as I am, if it's all the same to you, and *she* can scream till she's sick, for I'll not have to look on 'er poxy blinkers agin.' A broad gap-toothed grin lit up her smutty face. 'Oh, Nelly, it's the grandest idea I ever 'eard!'

With Mit ensconced at the Cock and Pye, Nell sallied forth one morning to a meeting of the company that had been called by Killigrew to announce news of a new production. The slight figure of Killigrew awaited them all on the stage, and the actors of the King's House ranged themselves in front of him to hear his words. Mrs Weaver pushed past Beck Marshall and Nell with a whispered oath –. 'Out of me way you little gutter cats!' – and sat regally down on one of the seats at the side. Bab Knipp's lips twitched slightly but the rest remained standing while Killigrew cleared his throat and began. 'Ladies and Gentlemen all! I have called this meeting to announce the name of our new production – one which I hope may restore our declined fortunes somewhat. I have bought the rights to a new drama by Mr Dryden whose *Rival Ladies* was so deservedly popular last August. Indeed, I might say I have high hopes of this work, high hopes.'

Mrs Weaver sniffed audibly.

'The name of the play is *The Indian Emperor*. It concerns the Spanish invasion of Mexico and it is a passionate love story. Enough of details; they will be filled in soon enough. Here are the parts I have apportioned.' He read down the paper in his hand. 'Montezuma, Emperor of Mexico, I have given to Major Mohun.' Michael Mohun bowed. 'For the prime role of Cortez, the Spanish general, I have chosen you, Charles. Bab, will you grace us this once and be our general female understudy?'

Mrs Knipp nodded and smiled. 'I'll poison them all in turn, Master Killigrew, an' they fall not ill on their own accord.'

Killigrew's eyes twinkled. 'The main female role is that of Cydaria, the princess of Mexico who falls in love with Cortez. It is perhaps the most important role in the play.' Mrs Weaver rose majestically from her seat. Killigrew looked up from his sheet and carried on firmly. 'I have therefore given it to Mrs Nelly Gwynne.'

Mrs Weaver's mouth dropped open, and so did Nell's.

'Mrs Weaver, will you take the role of Alibech, sister to the Indian Queen?'

Mrs Weaver nodded feebly. Killigrew turned to Nell. 'I have great hopes of you, my child. So, too, have we all, including Master Lacy, despite what I think you called his "Fleet ditch howls".' Nell curtseyed shyly, and Lacy boomed with mirth.

'I have two particular pieces of information that might cheer you,' Killigrew continued to the company in general. 'The work is dedicated to the Duchess of Monmouth, and both she and the Duke have promised to grace the first showing. And I have garnered another favour. Upon the promise of Her Majesty the Queen, both she and His Majesty will grace the Theatre Royal with their presence and that of the Court.'

A burst of cheering greeted him so he paused, well pleased.

'You have indeed been busy, Tom,' congratulated Lacy.

Killigrew bowed. 'Nearly as busy, I dare swear, as Mrs Nelly Gwynne these last few weeks.' The company laughed loudly. 'And now, ladies and gentlemen all! To work!'

Rehearsals began immediately, and Nell was soon as exhausted as she had been before. Yet it was obvious that Killigrew staked a great deal on the new production. It was apparent that Robert Duncan's money was being put to use in the purchase of new props and scenery, new hangings for the stage, and new costumes, which were gradually gathered together for the play. Killigrew allowed the actresses to choose and design their costumes under his supervision, and Nell – bright-eyed – designed a long, slender, skirt of shimmering green net that curved tightly around her hips into a tossed train at the back.

Mit sat up late at the Cock and Pye to finish it in time and Nell made sure that some particular alterations unknown to Killigrew were included by Mit in the pattern. One March night, Nell tottered back to the Cock and Pye and found Mit in her chamber holding up the dress in front of her. She greeted Nell excitedly. 'Look 'ere, Nelly. 'Tis finished and I've put the feathers together an' all!' Nell picked up the dress and held it against her.

'I'm terrified, Mit, and I don't mind admitting it, marry and I don't! It's tomorrow, and I'm that frazzled I'd as lief take ship for the Americas as face 'em all, I promise you!'

Mit grinned and brought out the headdress she had spent all day fashioning. Stitched to a thin circlet, a huge cluster of green ostrich feathers curled back and outward in a hazy array of plumes. She placed it on Nell's head and turned her so that she could see her reflection in the cracked mirror on the wall. The green admirably set off Nell's pale complexion and the warm tawny colour of her hair. Her eyes were large and bright as she regarded her reflection and noted how the dress showed her delicate colouring and fine-knit figure to perfection.

'Nelly, sweet'eart! They'll be swooning in the aisles. I'll look for your failin' tomorrow like I'd look for Ma Ross in a convent!'

'Lord, Nelly!' ejaculated Bab Knipp hurrying into the low ceilinged women's shift the next day, when Nell was nervously applying her paint. 'Nelly, I've never seen aught like it. There's my lord Buckhurst and Sir Charles Sedley sitting in the pit!'

' 'Oons, perhaps they have a taste for low company or an eye for the vizard pretties.'

'No, Nelly, you silly slut! They're in the pit because there's no room elsewhere. The Duke and Duchess have arrived with a score of hangers-on and the upper gallery's filled to bursting!'

Nell carefully applied her eye kohl. 'I only hope their humour's good, a' God's name. Or 'twill be a fond diddly for Master Killigrew after the money he's spent.'

Bab Knipp continued excitedly. 'Aye, and Nelly, there's someone else in the pit. Guess who – Robert Duncan, Master Killigrew's friend you know.'

Nell smiled slightly and touched a small brooch of brilliants tacking her cloak to her shoulders. 'I know, Bab, he sent me this for good fortune. I must seek him out to thank when the performance ends.'

'I warrant he has thanks enough in mind a'ready, sweetheart.'

'Pooh!' said Nell. 'He's not of that kind. He's a praying Presbyter!'

Outside by the entrance to the theatre, with a couple of lackeys and Orange Moll hovering behind him, Thomas Killigrew awaited his most important guest of the afternoon. Nervously he paced up and down, tapping his walking cane as he walked. Indeed three o'clock lacked only five minutes when two running footmen, each armed with a slender trumpet, ran down Drury Lane and round to the theatre's grand entrance in Little Russell Street.

There they stopped, raised aloft their gleaming trumpets, and blew a long, sustained clarion call. Sweeping up behind them came four coaches, the first of which Killigrew noted with satisfaction bore a gilded crown at its apex and the Royal Arms blazoned on its panels. It was followed by three other magnificent equipages. The first coach stopped in front of Killigrew's low-bowing figure.

Descending easily from the carriage came King Charles the Second. He was gorgeously dressed in a coat of silver tissue. Across his chest lay the blue of the Garter sash pinned with the George edged with diamonds. His dark, curled, wig brushed in ringlets across magnificent embroidered shoulders. He nodded greeting to Killigrew and then turned back to hand out the Queen, clad simply in burgundy velvet, Lady Suffolk, and Frances Stuart.

'I have brought my own company of lovelies with me, Tom,' he announced. 'So your play had best keep my interest if we're to avoid a scandal!' He clapped Killigrew familiarly on the shoulder and walked him under the entrance way, with the Queen hanging shyly on his arm. The other coaches disgorged their occupants and a bejewelled thread of people followed the King and Queen up the narrow stairs and into the Royal Box. As he entered, the people in the pit looked up, and one or two cheered. A large character by the stage stood up and raised his tankard to the King. ' 'Ere's to the Black Boy' he bawled above the din. Charles nodded his head and smiled. 'And to you, my fine friend,' he called back and threw down a coin. 'Drink my health again.'

There was a bustle at the rear of the crowded box and then there burst into Charles' presence the beautiful tempestuous figure of my lady Castlemaine. 'Sire . . . .' She curtseyed low and then looked up at Charles demurely. 'I was in the next box and heard Your Majesty arrive. I vow I was never more took aback, 'tis the veriest coincidence!'

Catherine held herself stiffly and looked coolly at her husband's mistress.

'I find your *surprise* ver-r-ry surprising, Madame. I thought all the Court had known that His Majesty intended to attend the play on this day for a month past. And yet your booking of the box is, as you say, the veriest coincidence.'

Barbara's eyes flashed but she said nothing. There came an audible whisper from my lady Suffolk to Frances. 'The harpy seeks to show the world she is not yet out of favour – she has the impudence to thrust herself forward so.'

If Charles heard the whisper, he gave no sign. As he watched Barbara's face exasperatedly, he saw the fear lurking at the back of those flashing eyes. He could accept her insolence or he could publicly disgrace her in front of the Court. There was the tiniest pause. ' 'Pon m'soul Barbara, rise an' you will and join us. Though where you're to sit I know not. Haply' – he glanced wickedly at Lady Suffolk – 'you could sit on my Lady Suffolk's lap.'

As the Court settled around them, the King's eyes swept the stage. At the signal from Killigrew the herald strode into the centre of the apron and swept the flag on his trumpet for silence. The play began.

Nell stood in the wings and watched while Charles Hart took the stage. As his powerful voice filled the theatre, the audience sank into silence and gave their full attention to his narrative of the primitive customs of the Indians. 'For all their Customs are by Nature wrought . . .', declared Hart.

' 'Tis much like Whitehall then,' murmured Michael Mohun to Nell and she giggled nervously. Lizzie Weaver turned and frowned. ' 'Tis our cue now, Major, if I mistake not!'

Assuming a sudden dignity and regality that even now astonished Nell, Michael Mohun drew his cloak about him and walked with measured steps out on to the stage – Montezuma, Emperor of Mexico – drawing behind a train of feather-clad courtiers amongst whom was Nell Gwynne.

She found she hardly dared look up at all. She could see the Royal Box out of the corner of her left eye but she did not dare to raise her eyes. So she listened to Mohun's voice rising and falling until suddenly he turned, and she realized her moment had come. 'Cydaria,' said Mohun, 'your new lover's Garland take . . . .'

It was her cue. Frantically she tried to remember her line, desperately she tried to recall Killigrew's advice on stance and Hart's on voice projection. Somehow she found herself on the apron stage and heard a voice she realized with amazement must be her own declaim the words clearly in faultless order, 'Can I love him, already loving you?'

As she looked down into the pit at last, she saw to her surprise two friendly faces. Rose waved at her sister, laughing, and her captain raised his tankard in jocular salute. Schooling her features into impassivity, she turned to walk back to Mohun. Down at the corner she caught a glimpse of Robert Duncan leaning forward on his cane, and then she was back and Mohun had led her off the stage. Gradually she realized she had trod the boards and survived. A new confidence surged through her. All her fear dropped away. Eagerly she awaited her next entrance, to meet Hart as her lover Cortez, her mouth slightly open, her breathing quick and excited.

Once back on the stage, she found her excitement mounted as the play progressed. She could feel the presence of all the people in the theatre, all around her, feel their attention rivet on her as in the silence she and she alone took their thoughts and gave them new direction. As she and Charles Hart looked into each other's eyes, she declared her love in a passionate voice and felt the sigh of response in the audience as it almost visibly reached back to her. As she turned away from him she saw Duncan, his chin resting on the knob of his cane, looking intently back at her, a light smile on his lips.

Sometimes it seemed as if the play were the reality and the other life but a dream. When Hart told her, ' 'Tis true I lov'd, but she is Dead, she's Dead . . .,' Nell thought of the hunched figure lying in the ditch by Houndsditch turnpike, and she wondered strangely for an instant what had become of Jacques Le Pied. Then her mind jumped back, as she gazed at Hart, to the low beamed squalor of the bawdy-house at Lewkenor's Lane, the smell of stale ale, and the fat, terrifying figure of Ma Ross. In a way it was as though she could truly live her part as she spoke.

'Poor heart he pities and bewails her death!' As the audience saw the tears in her eyes, she found her hands clasped in those of Charles Hart and looked up to see with a shock an expression in his eyes that she remembered from someone else some months before. There was hardly a sound in the theatre – no sound of quarrel or laughter. The audience was bent forward, rapt in attention. As she clung to one of the columns at the side, she saw a pair of stormy eyes looking back at her, and she remembered a night at Lewkenor's Lane and a voice which had told her, 'You are the white meat in this butcher's yard, my dear . . .'. The intense eyes of Lord Buckhurst passed before her, as if in a dream, as she told the audience in a voice trembling with a real passion, 'If as a Prisoner I were here, you might have then insisted on a Conqueror's right, and stay'd me here; but now my Love would be the effect of force and I would give it free. . . .'

It was as though time ceased to have meaning and she had been taken out of the Theatre Royal to another world where only the low tones and gentle grip of Charles Hart could remind her of the world of the living. So, until she took the stage for the last time, and Cortez, to the audience's obvious delight, took Cydaria in his arms and planted a kiss upon Nell's mouth which appeared to her to speak of more than dramatic passion.

Then both she and Hart walked slowly forward hand in hand to take their bows. Nell stopped in the centre of the stage, and turning deliberately towards the Royal Box, she took her dress in her hands and gave it a brisk pull. It fell into two halves, exactly as she had designed that it should and as Mit had deliberately stitched it. The slit up the side of the green net revealed her long, slender, leg up to the thigh as she sank into a long curtsey to the dark figure above her. And as she raised her eyes, she realized something with a shock. Charles the King leant forward, his mouth twisted slightly, and his eyes looked deep into hers as though they shared a secret no one else could know. He eyed her legs extended for his view beneath the dress hanging loose. 'You are clever with your hands, Mistress,' said the King interestedly.

'And so, your Majesty, are you if what the ladies tell me be true.'

The Royal Box choked with repressed mirth, the Queen smiled slightly, and Charles gave vent to the deep laugh so

238

often heard in the córridors of Whitehall. 'A veritable rogue,' murmured the King, 'and one of much wicked spirit withal.' He took a last glance at Nell's legs before she retreated to the back of the stage and tripped off at the side.

Nell's mind was in a turmoil. Suddenly she had seen the same expression in the eyes of the King that she had seen in the eyes of Hart and those of Lord Buckhurst. She recalled the words of Jonathan, 'Rank does not stop a man from noticing a pretty face my dear, or a well-turned ankle. . . .' Nell knew with surprise that a King – a King surrounded by the glories of his position and adorned with the sweep of his bejewelled Court, like a peacock with its tail spread out, could feel the same as other men. This god-like figure was but a man, with at least a man's failings, if not more.

Bab Knipp met her in the wings and hugged her. 'Nelly! Nelly! You were beyond anything this day – listen to them clap, listen, sweetheart!' Through the mists of her brain Nelly heard a thundrous roar of approval, a stamping of feet on the boards in the pit, and a wave of clapping across the confines of the King's House. Bab Knipp squeezed her hands.

'I've already had an inquiry from the Royal Box, my dear. That whoremonger Jermyn was down to discover your name and direction, and convey his Majesty's compliments. Nothing can stop you now, sweetheart! Lord! Listen to them cheer!'

Late that night Mr Samuel Pepys made his way wearily down Seething Lane. He took his key from his pocket and quietly let himself in without disturbing his wife or the servants. Carefully, he lit a candle and carried it into his book-lined study.

With a sigh he sank into a chair and poured himself a glass of reviving claret. The fire was still alight and he warmed himself at the coals which gave an eerie glow to the room as the flames cast weird reflections on the walls. Mr Pepys tossed off his wine and then unlocked the drawer of his desk and brought forth his diary. His eyes were tired as he sharpened his quill. He had been at the Navy Office until late. Damn this Dutch war! he thought. Men hard to find, ships even harder, no money! Samuel shook his head as he dipped the pen in the inkwell. And now he was appointed Treasurer of the Tangier Commission – a fine honour, but more work still. Problems seemed to lie all around him. And today he had found another shock.

He began to inscribe the date and then wrote underneath: 'Great fears of the sickness here in the City, it being said that two or three houses are already shut up. God preserve us all!'

He remembered the houses he had passed in Drury Lane that day, with the red cross daubed on the door and the pathetic entreaty, 'Lord have mercy upon us.' Samuel Pepys shook his head. When the plague came, it respected neither rank nor person, and cut down the young with the old. He sprinkled sand over the page and then replaced the heavy volume in the drawer. Shading his candle, Mr Pepys stood up to go to bed. ' 'Ods my life,' he murmured. 'Whatever does the future hold, I wonder.'